DARK DAYS

SEMESTER 1

A PARANORMAL ROMANCE BY

Liz Meldon

DARK DAYS: SEMESTER 1

**A vampire desperate to escape his past. A wolf shifter
determined to protect her future.
A killer on the loose.**

One year ago, wolf shifter Emma accepted her dream job teaching PE at a Norwegian international school, finally freeing herself from her mother's incessant matchmaking. As the alpha's heir, walking away from her pack, from her obligations—potentially even her fated mate—weighed heavy on her heart. But deep down, she knew it was the right decision.

Unfortunately, her sacrifice may have been for nothing —because the new history teacher has fangs.

With a reputation for kidnapping and selling shifters to research labs, a vampire is the *last* thing Emma needs in her life, but she refuses to be intimidated. This is her territory and she's not going anywhere, so that grumpy, gorgeous vampire can *suck it*.

Forced together at a prestigious boarding school, two supernatural enemies are torn between ripping each other's clothes off...
And ripping each other apart.

Eager for a fresh start, vampire Calder accepts an invitation to teach history at a private school above the Arctic Circle. Its remote location appeals to his sensibilities, and years of practice have taught him how to charm his human colleagues, but a certain gym teacher is seriously trying his last nerve.

All Calder wants to do is teach, so if the strikingly beautiful shifter refuses to see him as anything *but* the big bad vampire, perhaps he ought to lean into the part and really give her a show.

As summer turns to winter, humans disappear from nearby villages, gone without a trace and presumed missing—or worse.
Only one thing is certain: there are dark days ahead.
Even for creatures of the night.

Dark Days is a standalone enemies-to-lovers paranormal romance duet. While Book 1 has a cliffhanger, all will be resolved with a supernatural happily-ever-after in Book 2.

CONTENTS

Acknowledgments	ix
Paranormal by Liz	xi
August	xiii
1. Emma	1
2. Emma	19
3. Calder	34
September	47
4. Emma	48
5. Calder	63
6. Emma	71
October	83
7. Emma	84
8. Calder	100
9. Calder	110
10. Emma	125
November	143
11. Emma	144
12. Emma	152
13. Calder	163
December	177
14. Calder	178
15. Emma	187
16. Calder	196
17. Emma	205
18. Calder	215
January	229
19. Emma	230
Thank you for reading!	239
About the Author	241

ACKNOWLEDGMENTS

*Much love to Amanda, the first to squee about
Calder and Emma.*
*Thank you Sandra, for catching all my little
mistakes along the way.*
*Gorgeous cover art courtesy of Daqri @ Covers
by Combs.*
*A million thank yous to my ceaselessly supportive
friends, family, and readers.*

*And to my Sun and Stars: I couldn't do any of it
without you.*

PARANORMAL BY LIZ

The Hunt – a Demon Romance

Predator (#1)

Prey (#2)

Stalker (#3)

Killer (#4)

Never miss out again! Sign up for Liz Meldon's **newsletter** to stay up to date on book news and claim an exclusive freebie!

AUGUST

1

EMMA

Hi Bean,

Just checking in! As I recall, your welcome-back assembly was supposed to be sometime around now. I hope you have a good batch of students this year! I'm not sure how you put up with the smell of sweaty preteen humans all day, but I suppose you manage.

You know I don't approve of you teaching so far away, but I'll still support you. Dad is just being Dad. He'll come around eventually. You know that he loves you.

The pack has decided on Cancún for our winter break this year. Your brother is taking care of all our tickets—I guess he knows a special way to get a group discount? He's started dating that flight attendant, the fox shifter. Some of the old-timers still don't approve, but I just say give them time.

Now, on a more serious note: I read in the online newspaper that another person has gone missing—a woman this time, right? That's six this summer from the towns around Solskinn. I really wish you would have considered taking that job here in Maine. Did you get the posting I sent you? I would just feel a lot better if you weren't living so close to the problem areas. I

*thought being north of the Arctic Circle would be quiet. Please
tell me you're being safe, at the very least.*

*And write back properly this time. You owe your mother,
the woman who spent forty hours in labor with you, that much.*

Lots of love!

Mom

Yeesh. Nobody knew how to lay on the guilt thicker than my
mom. How many times had I heard the labor story? Too
many to count. Sometimes it was forty hours, other times
seventy. She really ought to get her numbers straight.

Still, she wasn't wrong: yesterday's reported
disappearance of an elderly woman from Heggelia brought
the number of people who had vanished from our little
county in northern Norway up to six, all in the span of about
three months. We might have been in the middle of
nowhere, but this was bound to make national news. Thus
far, police hadn't reported the disappearances as suspect; it
wasn't unusual for folks to come and go from the smaller
rural communities in the Troms region. Some came up for
summer work; others went south for the winter.

But then again, most of those who had been reported
missing were younger—in their twenties, thirties, the kind
of population who *would* drop everything and leave the
northern wilds for work, university, or a relationship. The
older woman—that was a break in pattern. I'd caught up on
her story in Solskinn's local paper online, perusing the news
on my phone during the flight from Oslo to Bardufoss
yesterday. Last I'd read, police were checking with relatives
across the country, working under the assumption that Inga
Hansen had merely taken an impromptu trip without
telling her neighbors.

With a sigh, I scrolled through Mom's email again to

make sure I hadn't missed anything the first time around that required an immediate response. Nope. Just the standard stuff, albeit with slightly less pack gossip. Usually I got a full rundown on who was doing what with whom, but that was the way with shifter clans. Everybody knew everybody. We were all in each other's business. Gossip ran like wildfire and mutated weekly.

She claimed I'd relocated above the Arctic Circle because it was quiet, and she wasn't wrong. I *had* chosen Solskinn, practically in the middle of nowhere, because of its remoteness, its wildness, and, of course, for the highly reputable international academy that was actually interested in hiring me.

Most of all, I had chosen it to escape pack drama.

To escape my alpha dad's plan to marry me off to some other alpha's son before my twenty-fifth birthday, which, coincidentally had come and gone last year—and not a peep from the old wolf in the meantime.

Dad is just being Dad. He'll come around eventually. You know that he loves you.

Right. My eyes narrowed at that particular line, cheeks warming, heart thrumming just a touch harder. Dad was just being Dad when he had told me that if I took this job at Solskinn International Academy, if I finally got a passport and fled Maine like I'd always wanted, I may as well go and not come back. Sure, those were the words of a father who loved his eldest daughter. As of this email, Mom was either still in the dark as to what Dad had growled at me before I left, or she was being willfully obtuse. Neither made me feel any better.

Just as I was about to hit the Reply button, my phone's timer shrieked from the bedside table, its piercing cry sharp enough to make me jump. A half-hour to go before the

Welcome Back assembly started in the auditorium; as always, Mom had a mind for dates. August 25th marked the start of term, but given it was a Saturday this year, classes wouldn't commence until Monday.

Students had arrived yesterday by the truckload, some one hundred and forty teens from across the continent shipped in by parents hemorrhaging money. I had arrived amongst them but opted to walk back from Solskinn proper rather than climb aboard one of the academy's transport buses jam-packed full of rambunctious teenagers.

Since then, I'd been hiding in my room, taking the time to recover from my summer vacation, half dreading the start of a new term, half chomping at the bit to get back to it. The rest of the teaching staff would have arrived over the course of the last week, but given I had no classroom to set up, no books to order, just a gymnasium to inspect and equipment to take stock of, I was probably the last to return.

A quick glance at the clock in the corner of my laptop's screen told me I needed to get my ass in gear. While I had wrangled my thick dirty-blonde mane into a braid crown about an hour ago, that was all I'd managed before plopping on the bed to go through my emails. Most of the administrative ones could wait until after the assembly, but Mom had flagged hers as important—classic Mom move.

So, instead of getting ready for the assembly, I'd focused on that, worried something had happened to my brothers, to my pack, only to discover it was the same old news. *Come home. Be safe. Dad loves you. You're too far away.* Thankfully, there hadn't been any *the pack needs you*, or *the Brownstone pack's new alpha grew up soooo handsome—look at the photos I attached* this time. Maybe Mom had clued in to the fact I didn't respond to those emails and finally decided to take a subtler approach as our pack's resident busybody and matchmaker.

And I'd reply to that much subtler approach sometime tonight, when I wasn't running late. After marking her email as unread, I closed my laptop, turned off my phone alarm, and rolled off my cozy double.

While we were welcome to furnish our suites in the staff lodgings as we saw fit, the furniture provided by the academy had suited me just fine, as had the studio-sized apartment. Tradition dictated that the newest staff members lived in the smallest space; once you had a year under your belt, you could upgrade to the larger suites provided one of the more seasoned faculty had left SIA. Last year, the senior-level IB history teacher, Remus Ivanic, had taken a job in Sri Lanka, which meant his roomy two-bedroom apartment on the second floor was vacant come term's end.

I had opted to stay put. I had everything I needed. The double bed. The six-foot dresser. The desk overflowing with lovingly worn-in paperbacks and spools of wool. The bay window overlooking the ivy-laden stone wall surrounding campus, my trio of plants soaking up all the sunshine they could before winter hit within the next month or two. The ensuite bathroom with a shower *just* big enough for one.

Sure, the living quarters were a tight fit, but I spent all my time elsewhere—at the gym, in the teachers' lounge, the dining hall, the dog kennels, the greenhouses, and the great outdoors beyond the academy's walls. I didn't *need* a mammoth suite; it was just little ol' me living here, and that wasn't about to change anytime soon.

What I could have done with more of, however, were clothes appropriate for this type of assembly. Most of the time I was in uniform: collared tee with the Solskinn International Academy emblem on the breast pocket, then a pair of black track pants and well-used sneakers. Today, I had to actually put on makeup. Do my hair. Rock a pair of stockings beneath the pine-green A-line dress, my one of two that I usually dusted off for special occasions. Stuff myself into a crisp black blazer—and *heels*.

Ugh. Faculty had to look somewhat "professional" today; after the assembly was over, we would be lined up to pose for a photo headed straight to the upcoming parent newsletter.

Mercifully, I managed not to snag my tights when I yanked them up my legs. Little blonde hairs stubbornly poked through the nylon, and I frowned; probably should have shaved this morning. Well, no time now. Next came the dress, just a touch too snug around the nipped-in waist, followed by the blazer, which was missing a button.

"For fuck's sake," I muttered, glaring down at it, then to my teeny, tiny closet. How the hell had that happened? Gnomes? No time to fix that, either, so I left the blazer unbuttoned and scampered off to the bathroom. My braid had managed to hold, the flyaways minimal, and I quickly slapped on the makeup basics: foundation, mascara, blush, and a nude lipstick. There. I smoothed my hands down my sides, nodding at my reflection. Somewhat presentable. Could I have done something with eyeshadow to make my brown eyes pop? Sure. Did I care enough to do so? Nope.

My bedside table clock told me I had twenty minutes to get there—no way was I slinking onto the stage late. So, I shoved my feet into my lone pair of three-inch black heels, shoes that had unquestionably seen better days, grabbed my keys, and, already a little sweaty, cracked a window before I left.

Shifters ran hot, and since I'd been out of my living quarters for the better part of three months, the place was stuffy—but give it a day and the tepid late-summer breeze would freshen it right up. One of the other reasons I had chosen a job at a private school in Norway over, say, Dubai, a city where I'd also been invited to interview, was because of the climate. Sure, the winter was miserable and wet and freezing, but the wolf in me *loved* it. While nearly everyone else used the underground tunnel system between the buildings from October to May, I preferred to brave the elements, rain or shine.

My heels clacked noisily down the vacant hallway, and I picked up the pace when I heard voices around the corner. The staff lodgings were nearly identical to the student dorms nearby, albeit with larger suites. Girls and boys were separated into a pair of four-storey buildings beside ours, which made night patrols easier, but you always had to make sure your curtains were firmly closed to avoid some of the nosier kids catching you in a compromising position. Unsurprisingly, the married couples were all upstairs, while most of us single folk had the first floor all to ourselves.

Glossy dark wood floors ran throughout all three buildings, the walls a neutral taupe with the odd landscape of Norway and black-and-white photos of the school here and there. The main doors of all three had an enormous bulletin board posted nearby as well, and while the student bulletins would have things like board game tournaments and movie nights and club listings, ours had the night patrol schedule, among other tedious administrative info. Occasionally, someone would find a flyer for a theme night at one of the pubs in Solskinn, the Norwegian scratched out and translated into English for us expats.

I bypassed our board completely, knowing I'd have to give it a proper look sometime before Monday, when I spotted my two favorites headed out the front doors.

"Lord and Lady Howard!" I grinned and waved when Robert whirled around, utterly bewildered. Honestly, who else would go yelling something like that at them? He motioned for his wife Phyllis to wait, and soon enough I was wrapped up in two enormous bearhugs that squeezed the breath out of my shifter lungs.

Robert and Phyllis Howard had been at SIA longer than anyone on staff—nine years this month—and were two of the loveliest, warmest people I'd ever met. Both taught the ninth and tenth grades, like me; Phyllis managed the chaos of the art room five days a week, while Robert waxed on about symbolism and similes in English class.

In their late forties, the Canadian couple pushed well over six feet, towering over my statuesque five six, and were built like linebackers. I'd only heard Robert raise his voice once last year, but the guy could bellow like a foghorn. They had been navigating the international school scene all their married lives; no kids, they bounced around the world, teaching wherever the wind blew them, until they finally settled at Solskinn.

As much as I adored them, I envied them too: I wished I could say that I had lived on every continent. The first time I'd ever boarded a plane was the one I took from Maine to Norway just last year—but better late than never.

"When did you get back?" Phyllis asked when she finally released me, smoothing a hand over her thin, wispy brunette curls. She had wrangled them back into a little ponytail today, and rather than the usual flowy beige linens, the woman sported a fitted navy pantsuit, the trouser hem a tad too short. I shrugged, unable to stop smiling.

"Oh, you know—yesterday," I admitted, then, at the sight of a pair of identical frowns, cleared my throat and hastily added, "but I was just sleeping and unpacking, honestly."

Usually we three had dinners together. The Howards had taken me under their wing when I'd started last year, and while I insisted that I didn't want to third wheel with them *every* night, they wouldn't have it any other way. This year, however, I intended to stand on my own two feet.

"Well, you had a busy summer," Robert said, his sandy-blond locks a little greyer around the sideburns than the last time I'd seen him. Phyllis gave an approving nod.

"So much travelling. We loved getting your postcards!"

I had wanted to tell *someone* about my travels through Scandinavia, but if I sent a postcard to my mom, I'd have to send one to everyone in the pack as well to avoid hurt feelings. And not everyone was thrilled with the fact that the alpha's heir had skipped town to teach at some human boarding school in Norway, so Phyllis and Robert had received all my updates.

Slightly edited updates, mind you. They were under the impression that I had done all my camping, hiking, swimming, and sightseeing with friends. I'd told the small lie to avoid Phyllis fussing over me, or, worse, offering to meet me in Stockholm so I wouldn't be alone.

While I hated to personify the lone-wolf stereotype, I was currently a wolf without a pack. Why not stick to it? Do it right? *Be* alone? If it was just me and Mother Nature, there was no personal drama to contend with. No gossip. No matchmaking. No elders trying to scout the rest of my life *for* me while I waited on the sidelines for them to figure it out. Sure, I had friends in the SIA staff. I liked, or at the very least tolerated, all my coworkers here.

But no one had been allowed to get too close.

Because if I wanted to live my own damn life *finally*, to

move through this world with me at the center of it and not the pack, that was the way it would have to be.

We left the staff lodgings together as Phyllis and Robert filled me in on their summer. While they had gone back to Canada to visit relatives for about a month, the rest of the time had been spent here, which meant someone had been around to water my plants, thankfully. As long as you were okay with cooking your own meals and cleaning your own suite—and signing a waiver that absolved the academy of any responsibility in case of an accident—staff were permitted to remain on campus over any of the holidays. The towering pair had spent a lot of time plodding away in the greenhouses and travelling around to the surrounding villages.

Beneath a rare cloudless blue sky, we weren't the only ones headed to the auditorium. Familiar faces greeted us from every direction, with students wrapped up in their crisp black-and-grey uniforms—and a few pushing the no makeup and nail polish dress code already.

"Hi, Miss Kingsley!"

"Mr. Howard—loving the sideburns."

"Mrs. Howard, did my pottery project get thrown out? I forgot it!"

It was an assault from all sides—and I realized I had *missed* it over the summer. In all that solitude, I had missed the sound of a dozen questions being hurled at me at once. I had known I'd wanted to teach since I was in elementary school, and being able to do it full-time somewhere this beautiful was a dream.

As I smiled and waved and greeted those who addressed me by name, I couldn't help but breathe in deep, gorgeous lungfuls of the balmy late-August breeze. It rustled through the surrounding forest on the other side of the six-foot stone perimeter, an interwoven tapestry of pines, spruces, alders, and birches. In the distance, grey-capped mountains loomed, along with one of the many northern rivers that sliced through the landscape—a river I sampled in wolf form every time I went for a run beneath the midnight sun, deep into the forest, far from curious human eyes.

The interior of the Solskinn International Academy landscape was no less stunning. When I had first walked through the main gates last year, the best I could manage was some unattractive open-mouthed gawking—because the pictures didn't do the place justice.

Beyond the wrought iron gate and the two security huts was a stunning roundabout drive with a landscaped center, flowers in bloom for such a short part of the year. The campus itself consisted of ten buildings, plus the garage: three greenhouses, where biology students had hands-on experience and the cooks could grow their own herbs; three dormitories—staff, boys, and girls; the auditorium and dining hall combo; the main building, shaped in a wide V, that held all the classrooms, the library, the infirmary, the staff offices, save mine, and featured an outdoor atrium; the rescue dog kennels, which I had spearheaded last year; and finally, the gymnasium.

Grey stonework tied all the buildings together, the conical rooftops questing skyward. The exterior aesthetic harkened back to the enormous Gothic iron gate that greeted visitors when they first arrived. Groundskeepers kept the foliage fresh and green for as long as possible, before the oppressive winter hit, and a janitorial squad consisting of Solskinn locals kept the buildings' interiors clean and updated. While the campus may have looked dated, like some old European settlement, the academy boasted modern conveniences and top-tier education for their students. Parents paid a fortune to ship their teens here; we had to deliver—or shut our doors. It was that simple.

And I loved it—all of it. The challenge of living up to those high expectations. Teaching kids who had lived all over the world, who hailed from military or political families, some already with huge trust funds to their names. The wilds around us. The beauty within the campus's four stone walls. The staff. The maintenance crew. The thrill of being—not in Maine, under my alpha's thumb.

I fell more and more in love with Solskinn each passing day, and as we approached the auditorium situated behind the main building, just beyond the outdoor atrium, excitement bubbled through me—made my smile hurt. Anticipation. This year had a thousand possibilities awaiting, and as the school came alive around us, I couldn't wait to dive in.

I'd been fortunate enough to start teaching straight out of college, and it was the same every year. The lead-up to the first day back was fraught with emotion—anxiety, dread, fear, and just a dab of excitement too. Once I was there, however, surrounded by students, breathing in the atmosphere, *smelling* the gymnasium I'd call home for the next year, eagerness trumped everything else.

We followed the herd to the auditorium, climbing the wide-set stone steps with a mass of chattering students. Phyllis and Robert managed to worm their way through the glass doors ahead of me, while I was stuck holding them open, smiling and nodding at those who greeted me, just waiting for the tide to ebb so I could slip in too. As soon as there was a dip in the rush, I darted in—and was smacked *right* in the face with the scent of teenager.

Mom was right; working with humans who had such a

distinct smell at this age could be trying on my heightened shifter senses. As I stood in the foyer, pummeled on every side, I took a moment to collect myself. Body odor and a liberal usage of various perfumes gave me an instant headache, as did the amplified, echoey clamor of chattering students.

Off to my left, through two sets of double doors, was the dining hall. As soon as one set opened, the scent of freshly baked brownies and cakes intermingled with the less pleasant smells. My inner wolf retreated deep inside me, in no mood for this mess.

Dead ahead were the auditorium doors, another pair of twin sets, made of metal this time rather than wood with stained glass windows, as if that would contain the noise of band practice and terrible musical theatre performances.

Rubbing my temple, I flashed a quick smile when Phyllis waved me through, most of the students *just* reaching her shoulder as they peeled around her and into the auditorium. My next deep breath was easier to stomach, my nose better adjusted to the cornucopia of smells a high school wrought. The noise was something I never fully adjusted to, but I could accept it for what it was.

What I couldn't accept were the hairs on the back of my neck suddenly standing straight up. A shiver shot down my spine, wolf senses on high alert, and my somewhat strained smile dropped completely as I scanned the foyer for the source. Solskinn, in general, was a harmless community. Low crime rates. Pleasant people. Given many of our students hailed from influential families, we had private security on campus for added safety.

I hadn't once felt threatened since I moved in, and the summer's supposed disappearances hadn't rankled my feathers either.

Yet now...

Familiar faces hurried by me, along with many I had never seen before, but that was the way with international schools. These kids bounced around, year to year, the nature of their mom or dad's job dictating they never settled for long. Brows furrowed, I studied each unknown as they shuffled by, maybe a little too intensely given the way a few scrambled into the auditorium to get away from me. It wasn't them. They weren't the threat. My inner wolf resurfaced, her snarl catching in my throat, dragging up goosebumps under my fitted jacket.

What the hell is making me—

"Miss Kingsley," Phyllis called. I shook my head, forced the smile back up, and did another sweep of the steadily emptying foyer. The clock over the dining hall's doors told me we were two minutes out from go time; most of the school would be finding their seats by now.

"Sorry, yeah, I'm coming." I crossed the space, the clicks of my heels echoing with each step. Scratching at the back of my prickling neck, I paused in the doorway, giving the room one last once-over. Maybe it had just been a reaction to the sudden onslaught of teenager. My frown deepened. No. I could handle teenager. This... was something different.

Unfortunately, as the lights flickered on and off inside the auditorium, there was no time to investigate properly. For now, whatever had ruffled my hackles would have to wait.

Given the academy's max capacity for two hundred students at a time, I was surprised to find about a quarter of the cushy black auditorium seats empty. Maybe this summer's local disappearances had had more of an effect on student enrolment than the administration anticipated.

As I made my way down one of the two paths on either

side of the audience seating, I scanned the sea of black-and-grey uniforms for something *off*, something that might still be triggering my internal alarm bells, but the sections of ninth, tenth, eleventh, and twelfth graders looked much the same as they did last year. Black uniform pants and skirts. Dark grey sweaters and collared tees. Laughter. Conversation. My arms crossed as I darted around students still making their way into the aisles, then scampered along when the lights flickered again, calling for everyone's attention.

Unfortunately, I wouldn't be allowed to just stand off to the side, hiding along the walls built to amplify sound for concert and choir performances. As much as I wanted to hang back in the dark, dreading the spotlights, there was a seat waiting for me up on the stage. Red velvet curtains, pulled open and tied back with gold tassels, framed the seated faculty—IB senior-level staff members on the left side of the stage, then the junior-level staff on the right, all of us subjected to tiered seating so each student could see our faces no matter where they sat. It had been a fucking nightmare last year, and I suspected it wouldn't be any less awkward today.

While I didn't mind barking orders at a gym full of sweaty, panting, exhausted kids, standing up in my Sunday best and introducing myself to a hundred and forty of them wasn't exactly my idea of fun.

Downstage, dead center, stood Principal Foster, a thirty-year-old teaching prodigy from the US who made it very clear the first time we met that he had a severe hard-on for the academy.

Making it great was his mission, and while I loved my job, my students, my home, James Foster took that love to the next level. His entire life revolved around SIA; it wouldn't have surprised me to learn that like Phyllis and Robert, he had spent his summer here, making schedules and drafting memos, preparing for another year of micromanaging.

He shot me a slightly exasperated look as I jogged up the stairs at the side of the stage, wobbling just slightly in my heels as I crossed to my seating area. Phyllis and Robert had saved me a spot between them, and I offered an apologetic smile as I climbed through the row of already seated staff members, then plopped unceremoniously into my chair.

Ugh—one of the band room chairs, same as last year. Decidedly *not* cushy.

"You all right?" Phyllis whispered as Foster started tapping his microphone. I nodded, rubbing at my neck again, wishing my body's alarm bells would just shut up.

"Totally fine. Just thought I saw somebody smoking outside."

Her eyebrows shot up, and I shook my head.

"I didn't. It's fine. Nothing to panic about—"

"Maybe I should have someone check," Phyllis whispered as the lights over the audience descended fully, and seconds later the hot stage lights lifted, shining a beacon straight onto all of us. We both squinted, and before I could tell her not to bother, Robert hushed us, a finger to his quirked mouth.

Foster started his welcome-back speech with the same material as last year—with the same nasally, nitpicky voice that had haunted my dreams. For the most part, I tuned him out, trying to look beyond the intense stage lights to the sea of faces, but even with my heightened vision, I couldn't make out much detail.

Something was still triggering me. Something was off. My

heart, ordinarily a steady, efficient, slow-pumping machine, drummed harder against its cage, and I fidgeted with my dress, my hair, as I continued to search out the problem. All I knew for certain was that my internal alarms didn't sound over nothing—and I was starting to sweat under these damn lights.

Definitely should have ditched the jacket.

I rolled my eyes and fiddled with my cuffs, uncomfortable, suspicious—and trying my best not to show it, especially to an auditorium full of teenagers who could smell weakness a mile away.

Honestly, they were worse than wolves sometimes.

We'd had two student teachers cry last year.

Foster's speech lasted a record forty minutes, a good fifteen longer than last year's, and by the time he handed the microphone off to Andreas Gunner, the higher-level German-language teacher seated in the first row of the IB staff, everyone around me looked 100 percent zoned out. Cool. At least I wasn't the only one not paying attention.

One by one, the senior-level staff introduced themselves to the student body. The whole lot of them were accredited to teach the two-year long International Baccalaureate diploma program, something I still wasn't qualified for but should really get on top of at some point.

Because the IB physical education instructor, Walter Otterman, was a fitness freak from Colorado who had a *thing* for weight training and shouting at underperforming students. We rarely saw eye to eye on the curriculum, and I really could do his job better. Foster had been encouraging me to get certified since we met, and I was eager to see it through someday.

Unlike this feeling, which needed to stop *now*. It refused to budge, my heart still pounding, my hackles still raised, my inner wolf grumbling deep inside, and I couldn't find its source.

And, honestly, *that* was more frustrating than the actual feeling.

"Oh! Emma, look." Phyllis nudged me a few moments later. "I've been meaning to ask—have you seen the new senior history guy? Positively *scrumptious.*"

She said the last bit with a horrendous fake British accent, which startled me out of my slow scope of the still-too-dark student body. "What?"

"Really, Mrs. Howard," Robert whispered across me, slowly shaking his head at his wife, "you're a married woman."

"Hush, you." She waved him off, then swatted at my leg. "Just *look.*"

Oh my god. Clearing my throat, I glanced at the other side of the stage to appease her—only for my blood to run cold the second this new "history guy" stood with a microphone in hand, the last of the second row.

Deathly pale skin.

Haunting blue eyes.

A mess of thick, finger-combed black waves and a tailored three-piece suit, complete with a pine-green tweed blazer and leather elbow patches that only *this* man could make look so damn good.

To quote Phyllis: scrumptious.

But beneath the gorgeous veneer, I saw him.

I saw him for exactly what he was.

No wonder my inner wolf had been on high alert from the second I walked into this building...

The new history teacher was a fucking *vampire.*

2

EMMA

"Hello, my name is Calder Holloway—standard and higher-level history."

"That *voice*," Phyllis whispered giddily, like she'd never seen a tall, dark, and conventionally handsome guy waxing away in an English accent before. "Isn't he breathtaking?"

"That's one way to put it," I managed. Each word clawed up my tight throat. My inner wolf snarled to life, immediately on the defensive as I stared down a real-life *vampire*—of all the places in all the world, here, at SIA. I gulped as the students clapped politely, the vampire nodding along with a serene smile.

I'd never seen a vampire before.

Not in person, anyway, but I'd heard enough to never want to.

"I enjoy travelling," he continued, schmoozing everyone in a one-mile radius with that English charm, that deceptively handsome smile. Predatory. That was the better word for it. Calder Holloway was a predator—a danger to everyone in this auditorium. He offered a disarming one-shouldered shrug, as if fumbling adorably for something else to share about himself. "And this is my first year teaching at Solskinn International Academy. I've taught primarily in Britain, but I look forward to getting to know each and every one of you."

I bit my cheeks, swallowing the snort-growl that threatened to slip out. Get to know each and every one of us —take a *bite* out of each and every one of us, more like.

And "travelling". My eyes narrowed as he passed the microphone back to Principal Foster, who then headed toward my side of the stage. *Travelling.* Did he consider it inappropriate to include kidnapping and black-market shifter trading as some of his hobbies?

Over the last thirty years or so, vampires had earned themselves a dangerous name in the still-super-secret shifter and supernatural community. An apex predator in a sea of fellow predators, they had taken it upon themselves to expose some of us to government departments, crime lords, weapons manufacturers, biological testing agencies—the list went on. Even as a pup, I'd heard rumors of what roving gangs of vampires did to shifters, to faeries, to witches. The rumor mill had been churning out horror stories for decades.

Vampires were, without a doubt, the world's most dangerous creature—the most viable threat, even to those of us who far surpassed human strength and abilities.

No wonder my alarm bells had been screaming. My inner wolf had sensed Calder fucking Holloway long before I laid eyes on him.

Another snarl crept up my sandpapery throat, but I disguised it as a muffled cough. What the hell was this vampire even *doing* here? Calder Holloway, with his stupid gorgeous accent and three-piece suit and beautiful smile and piercing eyes and—

No. Focus. I blinked hard. My dad had once told me most vampires came in pretty packaging—and that I shouldn't let it distract me. The attractive exterior was just another tool that made them efficient killers. Hunters. Trappers. Rogues. Alluring, sharp-toothed *fucks* who thought they had dominion over every creature that walked the earth.

Positively bristling, my gaze slid back to him—and my heart skipped a beat when our eyes met. Time seemed to slow around us, the assembly, the drone of my coworkers, the faint buzz of the stage lights all fading to the background. My whole body tensed, and I death-gripped the rigid brim of my chair, nails threatening to chip the metal. Most of the time, I could look at someone and get a decent read on them. It worked best on humans, but I had grown more adept at reading shifters too; my mom insisted it was my alpha blood, whereas I'd always thought I had a knack for body language.

Calder was unreadable.

Until he smirked.

And then the guy read loud and clear.

Challenge issued. Game on, vampire.

I glowered back. If this asshole thought he could infiltrate SIA, my *home*, and kidnap the wolf shifter PE teacher, then sell her to some deep underground government lab—well, he had another thing coming.

Chin lifted, I refused to cower. I held his stare, made sure the vampire knew that I *saw* him. Beyond the handsome exterior, the sinful smirk, I saw the hunter, the predator, the killer. Hackles up, I only hoped he realized I wasn't some mousey herbivore shifter, that in *my* eyes, he saw a predator too. Let him see the wolf, the warrior, the alpha's daughter.

Let him know—

"Emma?" Phyllis nudged my arm, and I flinched, startling out of my thought spiral.

"What?" The word echoed through the auditorium, the damn microphone close enough to my mouth to catch it as Phyllis stared at me expectantly. Titters erupted from the students, and, red-faced, frazzled, I grabbed the mic and stood. Light-headedness clung to me, this wolf, this warrior, this alpha's daughter, a touch sweaty and disoriented beneath the glare of the stage lights—and the glare of the vampire. Clearing my throat, I forced a smile, knowing that it wouldn't look the least bit authentic. "Uh, hi. My name is Emma Kingsley, and I teach ninth and tenth grade physical education and health. I also run the rescue dog program, so congratulations to all the seniors selected. Uhm." Lips pressed together, I swallowed hard again, throat raw, mouth too dry. My stomach looped. "I enjoy hiking and swimming and camping, and, uhm, I've been here for, uhm, this is my... second year of teaching in Solskinn. I'm originally from Maine."

Holyfuckingshitgoddamnitughhhhh.

I handed the microphone off to Robert in the painful silence that followed, then sank down onto my chair, mortified.

Robert chuckled, his grin warm. "Well, see, we're all still a little sleepy from the summer, eh?"

More laughter from the kids. I shot him a look that said I was somehow in on the joke, my stomach in knots, all the while resisting the urge to slowly drag my jacket over my head.

Across the stage, Calder Holloway's stunning vampiric smile stretched so wide it threatened to crack his gaunt, porcelain cheeks. He flicked his eyebrows up when our gazes collided once more, and a growl rumbled deep within my chest.

Right. I could ignore that horrific case of word vomit, pretend it had never happened, that I had been eloquent and succinct and hadn't said a single uhm—but I couldn't ignore *him*.

Calder fucking Holloway.

A vampire who, if I had my way, would be out of here by sunset.

Humanity's pop culture mythology of vampires was full of shit. Not only did Calder cast a reflection in every window he passed, he only winced *slightly* when he stepped into the late-afternoon sunshine after the assembly.

Honestly, I'd been a bit disappointed when he didn't burst into flame, screaming and howling for all of five seconds before crumbling to ash on the front steps of the building. Hollywood had gotten my hopes up for nothing.

Still, the mythos about the bloodsucking creeps got at least one thing right: vampires required a wide berth. As I tracked him back to the main building, I noticed many of the students kept their distance, allowing him to pass unchecked.

Mind you, after my embarrassing performance during introductions, no one bothered with me either, but the same couldn't be said for the Howards. The couple were popular amongst all four years; their swarm of admirers in the foyer had given me the opportunity to slip away unnoticed, my sights set on the back of Calder Holloway's stupid head.

I'd hoped he might retreat to the staff lodgings, as there

was an even slimmer chance of what was about to happen being seen by any students. However, as we skirted the outdoor atrium and headed for one of the side entrances to SIA's V-shaped education wing, I decided this could work in my favor too. Sure, the support staff might be in their offices, janitorial making their rounds. But for the most part, the classrooms would be empty. We were only a half-hour out from dinner; the majority of the campus inhabitants would be meandering into the dining hall—an enormous room with vaulted ceilings, a trio of Victorian chandeliers, and four long tables for each grade, plus a smaller staff table at the helm.

And our kitchen staff was *phenomenal*. I gained ten, maybe fifteen pounds my first year here because the food was just so delicious. I knew now to pace myself, how to properly feed this shifter body of mine, but the smells wafting out of the hall were a siren call difficult to resist.

Well, not for the school's newest faculty member, I bet. As Calder disappeared through the side door, I couldn't help but wonder how he managed surrounded by so many racing pulses. Then again, that was probably the point; a place like SIA, in the middle of nowhere, teeming with humans, was a vampire's all-you-can-eat buffet. I scowled as I paused at the same door, waited a few beats, and then slipped inside. His footsteps echoed on the stairwell to my right, and I stepped out of my heels, following on stockinged feet.

While my heart threatened to beat out of my chest, I kept myself composed. *Focused*. A wolf on the prowl, her quarry in sight. Even my inner wolf had stilled, the pair of us thinking, breathing, in perfect unison as I climbed the spiral staircase up to the second floor, then waited at the door, peering through the double-pane glass window. As I'd suspected, Calder had been given his predecessor's office: dead-center of the V, overlooking the roundabout in front of the building just beyond the main gates. Hotly contested real estate among the senior staffers, or so the rumors went.

I didn't care about any of the rooms in here; as far as I was concerned, *I* had the best office on campus—because the entire gymnasium was basically my office, and when I had a free period, she was all mine.

Well, mine and Walter's, but he had a penchant for the weight room and the office he'd forced Foster to give him in here, next to the first-floor teachers' lounge.

Adrenaline coursed through my veins, my shifter side desperate to break free—to charge my enemy and pound him into the ground. While some of the mythos about shifters was also incredibly inaccurate, we were, in general, hot-tempered and impulsive, harkening back to our wildest selves.

But hunting a vampire required patience. His senses would be exceptional, perhaps even surpassing mine. So, I waited. I breathed deep and even, settling my pounding heart, until he had unlocked his office door and stepped inside. With the hallway empty, the building asleep, I crept through the stairwell door, closing it gently behind me, and padded down the corridor. I set my heels next to his classroom some ten feet from his office, hoping I wouldn't need them to, you know, gouge his eyes out—or something equally gruesome.

While Calder had let the door swing shut behind him, it hadn't clicked into place, caught on the stubborn latch bolt. Nibbling my lower lip, I risked a quick peek inside through the small oval window. Boxes, most unopened, stacked high on either side of the small square room, his desk in the middle, a chair tucked behind it. I frowned. Why wouldn't he take advantage of that gorgeous bay window? Why face away from it?

Probably so he could watch the door for intruders. Smart.

For now, however, the vampire had his back to me, tweed blazer folded and set on his desk.

Okay, Emma—what's the plan here?

Barge in demanding answers?

I retreated when he started to look over his shoulder, pressing flat against the wall, breath even. No, I needed the element of surprise. I needed to get him *out* of here.

Sneak in and somehow render him unconscious? Then, what, transport his body off campus? Stuff it in the luggage compartment on a bus to Oslo? I pursed my lips. Kind of a wild-card strategy, but there *had* to be something in there weighted enough to knock even a dead man out if my shifter strength wasn't up to par.

This is so stupid.

I shook my head. *No. This is proactive.* Get him before he got me.

Sure, let's go with that. If my inner wolf was game, then so was I—and so far, she hadn't made a single *you moron* huff that she liked to do whenever my head and my heart clashed.

My fingers skimmed along the smooth dark wood of the doorway, its hue a perfect match to the floor, and the door bounced a little when I nudged at it. Another quick check through the window showed Calder with his back to me again, fiddling with something at his desk. Silently, I eased the door open further, praying all the hinges had been oiled recently, then tiptoed inside.

I moved like a ghost, not a sound whispered with each step. Carefully, I let the door ease back into place, pausing when the vampire sighed heavily. Once I was in, I hesitated, estimating about five steps to reach him, six to be right on top of him. If I could slam his head hard enough against the desk, I could at least get him in a daze.

Right. Plan in motion.

My steps were slow, precise—soundless. I kept myself out of the bay window's reflection, hiding behind Calder's taller, far more muscular frame. At step four, I paused, the air still between us, and reached out for him. One more step and my hands would be at his shoulders, then I'd thrust down with all my might.

Okay, here we go. On three. One—

Calder whirled around on two, snapped up my outstretched arm at the elbow, and *flung* me onto his desk in the time it took me to blink. I yelped, my back and shoulders slamming hard against the tabletop—the completely *empty* tabletop; apparently he had been fiddling with nothing. My hands lashed out instinctively, teeth bared, but Calder was on top of me, pinning both arms, in about five seconds flat. With one muscular thigh thrust between both of mine, the vampire knelt over me, trapped me, caged me in.

Kneed me squarely in the—

My cheeks flamed as I struggled against him, and Calder cocked his head to the side, midnight-black locks tumbling over his eye, then grinned.

"Down, girl."

A flash of rage darted through me at the insinuation, and I fought harder—but shoving and flailing and kicking and snapping my teeth at Calder was like doing all that to a hunk of granite. Some looming, smirking, immovable statue.

What had I been thinking? Somewhere, a distant

memory surfaced of my dad giving his inner circle a rundown on a local vampire nest between our territory and our neighbor's. Seven-year-old me had perched at the top of the stairs, peering through the round wood bars, fascinated.

"They'll outmatch you in your human form, but you'll have the upper hand if you shift. Don't hesitate."

Here, pinned beneath some unyielding porcelain god, I hesitated. My shifted form wasn't exactly subtle; double the size of larger wild wolves, I would dwarf Calder. Eclipse him. And, if someone *did* happen to stroll by at just the right time, I could potentially out myself and my kind.

So, I snarled up at him but remained in human form— for now. The reminder, the knowledge that I *could* best him physically if I needed to, gave me confidence.

"Get *off* me," I growled, finally stilling beneath him, on the verge of panting—but I refused to give him any other "dog" metaphors to toy with. Calder snorted, those haunting blue eyes unreadable. They didn't match the twisted smirk on his lips, but rather appraised me coldly, calculation simmering beneath the ice.

"Oh, you just wanted to *talk*, right? How silly of me..."

Much to my surprise, he retreated. Slowly, his movements graceful, lyrical, like a highly trained dancer, he eased off the desk and stepped away. Glowering, I sat up, my hair flyaway city and my outfit rumpled. When those bright blues flickered to my thighs, I yanked my dress down, heart thundering, and slid off his desk to square off with the dead man properly.

Maybe attacking him from behind had been the dishonorable thing to do. Not that there was room for honor in survival, but as we stood facing each other, me about a head and a bit shorter, boiling with anger, while Calder stood tall, showing nothing, I felt we were on more even footing now.

We held our respective ground for an eternity, sizing each other up, the air thick with our auras—mine white-hot, wild, and quivering, and Calder's black and still, silent, overwhelming.

I tensed when he started to move, ready to shoot off from my back foot, launch myself at him, only to straighten, confused, when he detoured around his desk, pulled out the academy-provided chair, and settled in. Long fingers threaded together, the cuffs of his light-grey dress shirt held together by twin links that appeared to be a coat of arms, maybe a family crest.

Blinking the distraction away, I prowled closer and pressed my palms flat to the surface of his desk. A whiff of cologne emanated from his discarded blazer: heady, musky —the scent of a *man*, yet not the traditional shifter male. The scent implied refinery, a gentleman who could still roll up his sleeves and throw down when the situation called for it. Elegance. Luxury. Danger.

Three adjectives suited to the vampire peering up at me, his obsidian locks swept out of his eyes yet threatening to fall again, in need of a firmer hand.

I swallowed hard, forcing my gaze back to his face, and breathed shallowly for a few moments to adjust to his scent. Refusing to show he had any effect on me, I leaned forward, crossing the buffer between us.

"What—the *fuck*—are you doing here?"

Calder tsked up at me. "Manners, manners. Isn't there a swear jar in the staffroom, or is that just some delicious rumor?"

I bit the insides of my cheeks. There was, in fact, a swear jar in the teachers' lounge. While we were all adults, we still had to put a krone in the jar if we cursed to deter the habit on school grounds. I'd lost about five hundred krone last year; apparently I lacked restraint.

I said none of this to Calder, and instead glared down at him, my question still standing. The vampire waited a moment, then huffed, that infuriating smirk falling away.

"I'm here to *teach*. Same as you."

I scoffed. "Bullshit. I know how most vamps earn a living these days."

His jaw clenched, muscles flickering beneath the dark stubble, and to my surprise, the faintest pink flush illuminated his porcelain cheeks. I had struck a nerve. Good to know that was possible.

"Well, I'm afraid I'm not most *vamps*," he sneered as he settled back into his chair. "Are we done?"

"No." Not by a long shot. I moved in, my hips nudging the desk, practically bending over it if it meant invading his personal space. "What the fuck are you doing *here*? The academy is mine—"

"Oh, what"—Calder rolled his eyes—"did you pee in all the corners and now it's *yours*?"

"Fuck you, dead man."

"Oh, I believe that's *four* for the swear jar now." The impish look returned, splashed across his face as he waited for me to take the bait. It didn't take a genius to see he was goading me, hoping I'd snap, but I refused to get sucked into something so childish.

This was very real for me—the threat of vampires on the shifter community had been painfully real for years. Two from a neighboring wolf pack had been taken after that conversation between my dad and his inner circle. The shock wave that rippled through our tight-knit community —I'd never forget it. They weren't *our* packmates, but we understood the loss viscerally. The grief. The agony. Wolves lost their mates, their *fated* mates. Taken from them far too soon. This wasn't a game to me, and I wouldn't treat it as such, no matter what Calder said, no matter how he gazed up at me, mischief shimmering in his bright blues.

So, I waited, schooling my features and remaining steadfast, strong, glaring, until he let out another long sigh and the impishness fell away.

"Look," he muttered, surging forward so suddenly I flinched. He must have had to slow his movements considerably around humans; we all had to moderate ourselves outside of our communities. Calder, however, seemed not to bother around me, moving swiftly, surely, our faces suddenly a few precarious inches apart as he leaned over the desk. His scent intensified, his presence washing over me, but I refused to balk in our little game of chicken. Unfortunately, as he tipped his head to the side, that intense stare of his utterly unblinking, it seemed Calder wasn't about to either.

"I've been doing this, teaching history, for seven years now," he said softly, voice low and rumbly. "And I intend to do it here too. Not only do I enjoy the subject matter—"

"Because you lived through it all already?" It was meant to be a slight toward him, but really, it probably wasn't far from the truth. Calder pressed his lips into a thin line for a moment, then huffed again, a lukewarm rush of air dancing across my cheeks.

"I also happen to enjoy the fact that it gets *very* dark here for many months of the year," he continued, his words strained now, like he was trying to control himself—fighting the urge to shout. I bit the insides of my cheeks and swallowed a jab about sunlight; I could figure out just how sensitive these dead men were to the big orb in the sky on my own. At no point did I want, or need, Calder Holloway to *teach* me.

He eased in closer, cutting down the inches between us from five to two, and still I wouldn't yield. My fingers curled, nails digging into the varnish.

"So, get this through your thick skull, shifter," he whispered, eyes narrowed, each word oozing an unspoken threat. "I have no plans on leaving Solskinn anytime soon just because you've bared your teeth and growled. I *get* it—the academy is wolf territory. Fine. I'm not here to take it."

Bullshit. There had to be an ulterior motive. Sure, not everyone fit their species' stereotypes, but I wouldn't be doing my due diligence, for my own safety and that of the humans inside this campus, if I didn't approach him assuming, preparing for, the absolute worst.

Silence settled between us, thick with words unsaid. Somewhere inside one of his unpacked boxes, the *tick, tick, tick* of an old clock punctuated the moment, beating as swiftly as my racing heart.

Calder could have been feeding me lies. He could be waiting for me to turn my back on him—and then he'd make his move.

Or, he could just be here to teach.

I had no way of knowing, not when I struggled as much as I did to map his body language, the nuances of his expression.

"If you *touch* me," I whispered at long last, "I will rip out your cold, dead intestines and feed them to my dogs."

All the answers I'd hoped to find evaded me, and as we glowered at each other, a dozen more questions and uncertainties sprang to mind. For now, I would walk away, but had every intention of doing my own digging, with Foster, with the other staff who had spoken to Calder, maybe even in his personnel file, until I knew for certain we were all safe.

Or not.

And if not, then I would find a way to correct that. People might be disappearing in the surrounding villages, but there would be no blood spilled inside these four walls. I would make sure of that.

Calder glared at me a moment longer, then straightened with a chuckle and a smirk, the flush of color faded from his cheeks. "I'll consider myself warned, then, shall I?"

I pushed back too, fingertips catching the edge of his desk. "Yeah, you do that."

His grin sharpened. "Oh, I will."

"Good."

One thing was clear: I wouldn't be sleeping tonight. Instead, I planned to prowl campus after dark, beyond the reaches of all the security cameras, in the blind spots, the shadows, just in case a certain vampire decided to do the same.

After shooting him one last withering glare, I headed for the door.

"Goodbye, Emma Kingsley," Calder called from his desk, as if unable, unwilling, to let me have the last word, "a fan of hiking and swimming, and, *uhm*—"

I slammed his office door shut, the crash echoing through the empty corridor branching off in either direction. However, through the door, muffled, I still heard his voice.

"And camping!"

"*Ugh.*" I snatched up my shoes and marched the hell out of there as fast as my stockinged feet could carry me.

3

CALDER

I so loved ruffling a shifter's feathers—or, in this case, fur. Although she had left me in peace since yesterday's ridiculously laughable encounter in my office, I suspected it wouldn't be the last time Emma and I clashed. Vampires and shifters were, after all, natural enemies.

At the very least, my kind had gone about creating that rift over the last century or so. For her age, that would be all she knew: vampires were the enemy, a threat, True Evil.

In fact, I had already predicted several more bouts between us, all equally amusing, until a certain Emma Kingsley, wolf shifter, realized that I was, in fact, here to *teach*.

Honestly, the gall of that creature, the sheer ego, thinking I had trudged all the way to the ends of the earth just for her.

Maybe in an age gone by; she was an exquisite specimen, after all. Young, fiery, beautiful, strong—fertile, likely, just ripe for popping out a horde of pups anytime now. There would have been a bidding war over her, government agencies scrounging up what little funds they had to compete with the more insidious groups eager to exploit her. I'd seen it before. Emma would have been the belle of the ball at an auction. Derelict humans would crawl out of their holes from all corners of the earth to claim her, to add her to their creature collections of which the masses remained ignorant.

Yes, quite exquisite indeed.

Pretty little thing...

It surprised me to find her *here*, so far from a pack. Most shifters ran in clans, wolves especially, and she was the right age to breed. Strange. Imagine my shock when I first felt her in the auditorium, a lone wolf in the middle of nowhere, her energy, her vibration, her *aura* hot and explosive, positively pulsing, pluming, filling the room. Emma Kingsley, for all her bark, was certainly intriguing.

But, of course, also arrogant, foolhardy, and impulsive. If what had occurred in my office had been *planned*, well, I likely had nothing to worry about. But if it was meant to make me underestimate her, then perhaps I had a more worthy opponent than I'd initially thought.

Still, compared to the gargantuan task of establishing oneself at a new school, proving to all those rambunctious human children with their mobile phones and social media that I was a man deserving of their respect, and perhaps a touch of fear, Emma Kingsley was just a blip on my radar. I had come to Solskinn to teach and to put some distance between myself and what I'd left behind in England; some yappy blonde mutt wasn't about to change that.

I kept that in mind as I darted across the gorgeous campus grounds, the sun dipping below an amber horizon, headed for my first real staff meeting the night before classes resumed. The day had been spent adding the final touches to my classroom, which I'd taken the last week to prepare, and then finally unpacking my personal effects in my new office—which still stunk of shifter.

Not wet dog, mind you, but rather Emma's oddly aromatic scent, harkening my mind to Grecian fields of lavender. Either way, I'd left the windows open all day, hoping that would rid the space of her.

With my books finally unloaded, my trinkets in place, the academy had started to feel more like home. For home, to me, was wherever I had a bed, a blood bag, and my belongings. Ancient tomes with fractured spines. A creaky old yellowing globe that I had acquired in the 1950s. My prized pen collection, some of the older, more delicate feathery quills enclosed in their own special display case. Ships in bottles. Sanskrit tablets. Cuneiform limericks on fragile papyrus. Bits and bobs, glass, wood, metal, acrylic, that I'd collected over the centuries, all on display amidst dozens of books and journals.

All easily packable, shippable, deliverable.

All creature comforts.

All I needed in this world—these days, anyway.

Now that everything was in its proper place, my lesson plans for the entire year complete, I was actually looking forward to the term starting tomorrow. A bit on edge, as always when it came to a new institution, but the nerves would disappear after my first few classes. The me of twenty years ago would have balked at the fact that I taught; I'd never been a fan of children, not even as a human, but I had come to tolerate them. While the younger sort still drove me up the wall, the older teens with their odd little minds could be quite interesting. One or two usually impressed me each year, and I looked forward to meeting them this week.

In fact, I just looked forward to throwing myself into the work. Emma's accusations, while unsaid and thinly veiled, had dredged up the past—a past I had been working so damn hard to forget, and I could certainly do with the distraction.

A staff meeting ought to do the trick. While past experience suggested these sorts of gatherings could be rather dull, it would give me the opportunity to learn the social mores of Solskinn International Academy and to glean information about my coworkers. Tonight's meeting had been called by Principal Foster, a rather intense, spry, neurotic sort of man who appeared to have a hand in everything at this school. Thrice last week he had popped into my classroom with *suggestions* about how to arrange it, none of which I had taken seriously.

Evening descended across the grounds, long shadows blending together, wind rustling through the meticulous landscaping. Students would be attending dinner at this hour, sequestered in the dining hall and monitored by some of the support staff. Meanwhile, the rest of us faculty had a meal of our own waiting in the staffroom—none of which I intended to partake in, naturally, with my evening meal sitting inside the little fridge in my office.

As I neared the back doors to the main building, cutting across the outdoor amphitheater, I caught my reflection in the tinted windows cut into the grey stonework. Yesterday had been, perhaps, a touch too formal for Solskinn, my three-piece suit the only one of its kind amongst the male faculty. I would continue to wear them to teach, of course, for I was a man of class, accustomed to a certain style in a professional setting. For tonight, however, I'd kept it simple with just a crisp black button-down, a blue-and-silver checkered tie, and dark grey slacks.

My off-duty attire—consisting of a vintage leather jacket

worth thousands—would have been completely inappropriate.

After marching briskly through the otherwise silent, echoey corridors, I strode into the staffroom to discover that I was among the first to arrive. I forced a smile when three sets of eyes darted my way, then checked my watch. Given we were five minutes out from starting, I'd thought I was late. Apparently not.

"Ah, Calder!" Foster strolled over to shake my hand. "Hope you found the place all right."

I forced a chuckle, catching the man's slight wince when he clapped down on my shoulder and perhaps discovered it was akin to smacking a stone statue.

"Thank you, sir," I offered. "I've been looking forward to seeing how things are run here."

He insisted I dig into the platter of sandwiches and the steaming pot of soup situated in the middle of the enormous round table. I indulged him by pouring myself a cup of coffee instead, bringing it up to smell—for the smell of coffee would never go out of style, even among my kind— but refusing to take a sip. Food and drink that we vampires had once enjoyed now tasted like ash, and I had no intention of trudging through the charade tonight. There were plenty of other opportunities to choke down a bite or two of food, just to prove I did, in fact, eat.

As we waited for the rest of the lot to arrive, I chatted politely with my new colleagues. I knew my neighbors in the staff lodgings fairly well, and the rest I could tolerate professionally, though all their irksome little quirks still had time to surface over the next few weeks.

Once again, I was woefully overdressed. One by one, the academy's faculty waltzed into the staffroom in their casuals, jeans, cozy sweaters, and long-sleeved cardigans as far as the eye could see. They all went straight for the food, a pack of ravenous hounds, then perched on the depressed, aging sofas arranged around the outskirts of the room. Some of the younger staffers—a clique of men in their mid-twenties who all appeared to be very close—even cracked open a few bottles of local ale, something I graciously refused, citing I was still working through my coffee.

A few minutes after the hour struck, we all settled at the round table, and in scampered the last of us: my new favorite shifter. Her wild blonde mane sat in a dreadfully messy bun atop her head, and—my god, were those *pajama* pants? When our eyes met, I realized my jaw had dropped, but how could it not? The woman was wearing flannel pajama bottoms and moccasins, then some flimsy black tee like she had just rolled out of bed. While the rest of the human staff were bundled up in a layer or two, the summer nights nippy this far north, Emma Kingsley stood out in her T-shirt—for more reasons than one.

She ought to enjoy this climate, I thought as I pressed my lips together and curled both hands around my piping-hot coffee mug. Something stirred within me, something alien and unsettling, at the memory of her body's intense heat radiating through her clothes yesterday.

Had she been affected by my frost in turn? Cold enough to warrant the I Have Bad Circulation talk with anyone new, my skin must have burned like ice to her.

After snagging the only seat left, directly across the table from me, the shifter loaded up her plate amidst the soft chatter of our coworkers, then sunk down with a scowl. At first, the look was reserved for her overflowing plate of food, but soon enough it found me, her eyes narrowed, her cheeks flushed pink.

She needed an opponent—someone who warranted her anger, her suspicion, her instant dislike.

So, I grinned back and gave her a little nod. The color in her cheeks deepened. It was always so much more satisfying *not* to react in situations like this, to show that her glares, her snarls, her attitude had zero impact on me.

Scowl all you want, wolf. I lifted an eyebrow, wishing, just for a moment, that vampires and shifters were telepathically compatible. *I can take it—easily.*

Even without the mind connection, she seemed to read me loud and clear, pointedly avoiding my stare when she asked Robert Howard, if I remembered his name correctly, to fill her dark blue mug with ale as Foster called for our attention.

"Everybody, thank you," the man said, standing in place while the rest of us peered up at him. "First of all—welcome back for another fantastic year at SIA. I speak for the whole administration when I say that we're thrilled to have all of you on staff."

Grins erupted all around the table, a few of the faculty clinking knives against their mugs. I tapped my nail against the rim of mine as a show of unity, steam spiraling up from the scalding liquid inside.

"Second—the disappearances." The atmosphere turned grim as Foster nodded, hands slipping into his pocket, a notebook open with indecipherable scribbling across both pages on the table in front of him. "A representative from local law enforcement has insisted that the disappearances this summer are coincidental and not linked. If parents contact you directly regarding the situation, please reassure them that we take safety precautions here very seriously. Refer them to our security page on the website, and if that isn't enough, please direct further inquiries to the administration. It isn't your job to deal with this, er, unfortunate situation."

Unfortunate situation indeed. I had been monitoring the disappearances from the surrounding communities all summer while I was still living in Bath. It wasn't that I cared about a few missing humans; in my world, humans went missing every day. There were plenty of other nefarious supernaturals who fed on the bottom of the food chain, not just *my* kind. Unfortunately, people were paying attention to the disappearances now. There were enough to spark curiosity, interest, and public speculation.

All of which were the *last* things I needed. I'd chosen Solskinn not for its impressive reputation or prestige, but because the school had been quite literally plunked down in the middle of nowhere. Any additional attention was a risk to me—a risk that someone from my past could discover where I had run to this time.

Beyond that, I didn't need Emma getting any wild ideas that I had turned the communities dotted across the dense landscape into my new hunting grounds. I hadn't been hunting in years, nor did I intend to start now.

With the more gruesome bits of conversation out of the way, Foster fell into the administrative side of things, the sort that I'd expected from staff meetings. Owed paperwork. Upcoming events. The fall and spring theatre productions. Emma's rescue dog program. Each of us were required to spearhead a student club, and the signups would go up during Spirit Week at the end of September. Foster then went around the table, forcing us to announce what we planned to run.

Film Club. AV Club. Comic Book Club. Biology Club.

The pajama-wearing shifter across from me had a dodgeball league in the works, which was supposedly very popular last year. My offering of a debate club was met with lukewarm smiles by all but Foster, who insisted he had a number of ideas he wanted to run by me.

I nodded indulgently. Fantastic. Couldn't wait.

This year's homecoming theme was announced: a night in Paris. The student council had voted on it before they adjourned last year, and on the final Friday in September, the faculty were required to decorate the gymnasium for the dance the following evening. I'd honestly rather shove two-inch nails in my eyes, but everyone else seemed rather excited about it.

But then again, *homecoming* was a rather American tradition, wasn't it?

I'd taught in the IB program for several years now, but this was my first venture into an Americanized international school; I still had a lot to learn about the expected customs.

Perhaps I ought to do a bit more research into—

"Last item on the agenda," Foster boomed, startling the room out of the warm, sleepy fog that had started to gather after nearly an hour and a half of this never-ending meeting. "Night patrols in the dorms."

A collective groan erupted from around the table, and I sat back with a smirk. Given that I needed no more than an hour or two of sleep each day, I had no qualms about monitoring the student lodgings between the hours of eleven and three. However, I could understand the unwillingness from the others, particularly the humans greying around the ears.

"I know, I know, I know," Foster continued with a chuckle, settling the room with a wave of his hands. "No one likes it, but it's a necessary evil. It's only once a week, and at least you aren't doing it alone. Speaking of which, Calder..."

I sat up straighter, annoyed to be singled out. "Yes, sir?"

"As you're our newest staff member," he started, then paused, blinking rapidly, his hollow cheeks tinted pink. "Wait—has everyone *met* Calder?"

Oh, for fuck's sake.

Mercifully, everyone around the table nodded and smiled, sparing us all from what was bound to be a horrendous introduction speech or some absurd name game. Emma, meanwhile, stared me down from across the table and took a noisy slurp of her ale. I made sure my smile was extra barbed, just for her.

"Oh, good." Foster cleared his throat and took a quick sip from his enormous water bottle. "Anyway, since you're our newest addition to the SIA family, I've paired you up with Emma."

The little wolf choked on her most recent mouthful. I pressed my lips together to smother a snicker.

"She was in your shoes last year, so she'll show you the ropes. Right, Emma?" Foster shot her what could quite possibly be a flirtatious smile, and I noticed a few eye rolls around the table. Emma, on the other hand, appeared to have missed it as she schooled her shocked expression into something more situation appropriate.

"Of course," she said tightly, the corners of her mouth kicked up—but her eyes positively livid. "I'd be happy to."

Foster beamed. "*Excellent.* You're in good hands, Calder."

"Oh, I can hardly wait," I mused. While I had no interest in spending more time than necessary with the shifter who had threatened to disembowel me, her expression, her misery, made it all worthwhile.

Naturally, I might not be so amused come our first patrol together, but for now, I relished her discomfort, nursing it as one does a fine wine.

The evening reached its end when one of the apron-clad

workers from the kitchen, a local girl with near translucent skin and perfect teeth, knocked at the staffroom door bearing desserts. Miniature *tilsorte bondepikers*. A plum-topped *plommegrateng*. Fried *klenät* balls with raspberry dipping sauce. And a tin of crumbly butter cookies. Eyes widened around the table, and Foster, perhaps sensing that he had lost his people to the native delicacies, conceded that we would pick this up next weekend.

Next weekend?

Were we in store for one of these *every* weekend?

I looked to Emma to confirm or deny, but she was already happily loading up her practically licked clean plate with a mountain of fried dough. My eyes rolled skyward; I'd forgotten about a shifter's insatiable appetite until now. It almost made my stomach roil to consider just how much food the woman would pack away in a single meal.

Yet somehow still fit, trim, and toned despite consuming upwards of eight thousand calories a day—was there really a wonder labs around the world were so interested in studying them?

With the desserts delivered, and the sweet little kitchen wench insisting in broken English that she couldn't stay, the staff meeting devolved into a tipsy social hour, the ale flowing freer now to all present, save myself. Still, I could pretend. I could laugh and smile and joke. I could adapt to the shift in mood with ease; if there was one thing shifters and supernatural creatures alike excelled at, it was blending in.

Seizing the opportunity to get to know my new colleagues a little better, I made the rounds, forcing myself to ask thoughtful questions so I could better understand the cliques. While a few had filtered out over the hour since we had broken for dessert, most remained, showing in that moment what a tight-knit little family the SIA faculty considered themselves.

"Yes, yes, just a moment," I insisted, slipping out of a rather long-winded conversation with the Howards under the guise of switching to decaf. However, I hadn't made it more than two feet before I knocked into a certain wolf shifter, who also appeared to be escaping a huddle of her own. Her warm smile dropped the moment she realized who now blocked her path, and in an instant, she was back to glowering at me. I craned my head down to meet her eyeline, the fullness of the small room, all these humans, forcing our bodies closer than either of us wanted.

"Well, hello, *partner*." I flicked up a challenging brow. Surrounded by her colleagues, her work family, Emma was less likely to lash out physically, which gave me the advantage. "So looking forward to our weekly strolls through the long, lonely corridors of the student dormitories."

Her glare intensified, as did my grin.

"For the record, I didn't ask for this." At least I could prove to her that I didn't spend my nights sneaking into dark bedrooms to feed. Maybe I ought to show her my blood stash too, just to quash those thoughts.

Still, that venomous glare deserved to be knocked right off her face; not only was she being absolutely ridiculous, but she seemed to be under the delusion she could physically overpower me in her current form. Or, at the very least, she thought she stood a good chance.

Which was preposterous.

The sooner she got that through her dense shifter head, the better.

"Let's look at it as an *opportunity*, shall we?" I inched closer, her heat whispering across my skin. Her eyes were rather intriguing, like cognac, the outer ring a dark brown but the inner iris flecked with shades of gold and amber. I blinked hurriedly, shattering the allure, and focused on not breathing her in too deeply. Instead, I adopted a leer, the kind of look that always roused an unimpressed woman's hackles. "Now you and I have the chance to get to know one another better, more *intimately*. We can learn all each other's secrets, roaming the darkness together—"

Still scowling, Emma grabbed the end of my tie—and dunked it in my cold coffee. Heat flashed in my chest as I sputtered down at her. The wolf smirked, her arms crossed, her hands no longer in little trembling fists at her sides.

"Like you were going to drink it, anyway."

"This—is—*cashmere*," I hissed.

Emma stuck out her lower lip in a mock pout, then eased around me, eyes positively alight with mischief.

"Talk to you later, *partner*," I heard her coo behind me, her chuckle making the hairs on the back of my neck rise. Gnashing my teeth together, I stalked to the coffee bar at the far side of the room, then set my mug down more forcefully than I intended. Cold black liquid sloshed over the rim. Fuming, I carefully extracted my tie and squeezed the coffee remnants out.

And at the sound of Emma's laughter rising above the rest, I retreated to my private suite without a word.

Positively fuming.

SEPTEMBER

4

EMMA

All things considered, my first two weeks of the new term were a breeze. Not only did I enjoy pretty much all my students, but the seniors selected to participate in the rescue dog program were great, and our weekly class rotation meant I had at least one full day off on top of my weekends.

Sure, the off day was still spent in the office, working on things like my year-long dodgeball league, dog care, and upcoming lesson plans, but it was one extra blissful day where I wasn't drowning in the very distinct, very potent stench of thirteen- to sixteen-year-olds. Already there were a few who might need a tactful, subtle reminder that they were at an age where they could, and should, wear deodorant.

What I *wasn't* thrilled about, however, was wasting my Friday night with SIA's resident vampire. Since our run-in at the first staff meeting, I had done a halfway decent job of avoiding him—just as he seemed to have a knack for evading me. Of course, there was the occasional eye contact made at dinner, a charade I could barely stomach as Calder pushed food around his plate, pretended to take a bite, and tossed it all out fifteen minutes later citing he was "full". Then there were the Sunday-evening staff meetings where we glowered across the table for the first few minutes, then went back to pretending the other didn't exist.

Mercifully, our classes had nothing to do with each other—we weren't even in the same building, nor did we live on the same floor in the staff lodgings.

The academy's campus was large enough that if I tried, I could dodge him for the rest of the year and keep Calder fucking Holloway out of my mind permanently. So far, I was on track for that—excluding the digging I did on him in the first week. Foster had been all too eager to chat about his new hire one night, brimming with pride at the highly sought-after teacher he had poached from some elite private school in Bath. The vamp had a clean record according to our academy database, which I dipped into last Friday night while all the staff were off celebrating their first successful week of teaching.

Hell, I had even reached out to a friend in the States, another wolf who worked for a tech company that, among many other duties, tracked vampire coven movement across shifter territories. Nothing. The guy was squeaky clean— but that certainly didn't make him innocent.

For now, however, it meant I could get a good night's sleep at the very least, and while I still intended to keep an eye on him, I could ease up, just a little, and get back to my life here. To my knowledge, no student had been spotted with a set of fang marks, and a casual chat with one of our more ditzy nurses confirmed there hadn't been any sudden cases of anemia from anyone on campus.

Calder Holloway was still on my radar, mostly because he was a vampire, a predator, a threat, but also because the guy was kind of a pompous ass.

And come eleven o'clock, ten minutes from now, I would be spending the next four hours showing said pompous ass the very simple ropes of night patrol. When Foster had announced that we'd been paired together, my first instinct had been to pitch a snarling, howling fit—but I refused to give that smug, dead-eyed jerk the satisfaction. So, I would do my job tonight. I'd show him all the spots students liked to congregate after hours, the places they thought us staffers didn't know about. I'd be civil. I'd be professional.

I would *not* ruin another one of his ties.

My lips twitched at the memory.

Across the walkway, beyond the well-maintained hedges, the door to the staff residence slammed shut, and I pushed off the railing that sliced up the grey stone steps to the girls' dormitories, arms crossed.

Night in Solskinn, even this time of year, was so very *dark*, and if we didn't have all the scattered lampposts illuminating the grounds, it would be almost impossible for any humans to catch Calder strolling along the concrete path. Despite the bright white lighting, he seemed to naturally gravitate to the shadows, shrouded in darkness as he glided toward me in a pair of jeans and a thin black cardigan. A gust of cool wind rustled in the space between us, swirling the small clusters of fallen leaves, toying with my hair. I smoothed a hand over it, half my dirty-blonde locks in a braid, the rest spilling down my back.

The wind tussled Calder's obsidian waves too, and he speared a hand through them, looking more runway model than stuffy history teacher. I bit the insides of my cheeks when they started to warm; this outfit was a vast improvement from his never-ending array of three-piece suits.

Actually. I swallowed hard, forcing myself to fiddle with

my fingers. The three-piece suits didn't look terrible either —with a body like that, the guy could wear a garbage bag and make it look good.

But that didn't change the fact that he was a dick.

The hairs on the back of my neck stood as his footsteps grew louder, my inner wolf rumbling and my heart dancing just a touch faster when he stopped directly in front of me, a few inches too close, lips quirked.

"Partner."

I crossed my arms. "Partner."

Calder's bright blue gaze swept up and down my figure —nothing more than a quick once-over, but it had the unique ability of making me so incredibly aware of myself. Of the way my black leggings highlighted the curve of my calves, the muscular tone of my thighs—and the way my baggy beige sweater should have hidden the rest of my curves, but my crossed arms hoisted the knit over the swell of my hips *and* pushed my chest to center stage.

Like I was serving myself up for him.

Toes curling in my runners, I dropped my arms back to my sides and took a deep breath.

"So, go on then," Calder said, nodding toward the four-storey building beside us. "Show me the ropes."

Damn it. I'd wanted to be the one to kick-start things. Squaring my shoulders, I motioned for him to follow me up the steps, pausing at the pair of thick metal doors, my fingers coiled around the handle.

"Kids need to be in their assigned rooms by ten, lights out at eleven."

"Seems lenient," he muttered as he scanned the main entrance, eyebrows up. "You'd think nine would be more appropriate."

I rolled my eyes just as my phone alarm chirped; eleven o'clock, on the dot. Time to get to work.

"Come on." I held the door open, cheeks warming when he flashed a quick smile and slipped inside.

We started the night in the girls' dorm, making our way at a good clip through the four levels, one for each grade. Given we were halfway through the first month of the new year, most of them knew the drill by now. Yes, I had to shoo a cluster of chatting, giggling juniors out of the third-floor bathroom, and there'd been a senior still studying on a couch in the fourth-floor common room, her enormous headphones on, totally oblivious to time and space until Calder crouched in front of her and tapped his finger on the top of the textbook in her lap. Then, red-faced and apologetic, she had shuffled back to her room down the hall, door slamming, lock clicking, and neither of us heard a peep after. Besides those two instances, plus a handful of *lights out, ladies* and gentle knocks on the doors, the building was in good shape.

And I didn't snap at Calder once. I came close—the guy had a face made for snapping at—but I kept my cool and remained professional. We checked on all the dark, shadowy spots inside the building where the SIA girls liked to congregate after curfew. We ensured all the exterior doors were locked save for the main two. We even checked through the bushes out back, a notorious hangout last year for seniors who liked to smoke.

All in all, a job well done—on my part. Last year, I'd been left to fend for myself during my "training" for night patrols, which had consisted of the former history teacher bailing on me to call his girlfriend in Romania all night. While Calder sucked for a whole host of reasons, I refused to be *that* useless.

Calder, however, didn't seem the least bit impressed, or grateful, that I had taken the time to do this properly.

"Wow," he said, standing a few steps down from me at the top of the north stairwell. His condescending smirk made me white-knuckle the wooden handrail. "Telling children to turn off their lights and go to sleep... I'm not sure I'm ready for something quite this advanced. Perhaps I should have been taking notes."

My cheeks buzzed with color once more, only this time it wasn't because I thought Calder looked scrumptious in those jeans.

"Oh my god," I grumbled as I stomped down the first few steps. "Are you always this patronizing, or is it just with a species you consider inferior?"

I paused briefly, so that despite being on different stairs, we were at eye level, and watched as Calder blinked a few times, his smirk falling away.

"I... never said that," he insisted, sounding taken aback by my statement. I stared at him for a moment, then rolled my eyes.

"Whatever." I knew by reputation, from gossip, from war stories, that vampires considered themselves the apex creature of this planet, superior to all supernaturals, shifters, and humans. In fact, it was one of the reasons I had been so instantly suspicious of Calder; given their predilection for holding themselves above everyone else, it was rare to find a vampire in an everyday, normal job. The idea that Calder, in all his vampiric glory, *chose* to teach teenagers—*human* teenagers—was kind of insane to me, and I couldn't imagine a shifter out there who would disagree.

Biting the inside of my cheek, I stepped around Calder and marched a few steps down, slowing when he followed.

"So," he said as we neared the third floor, the staircase wide-set and winding, "how are your students this year?"

I stalked across the landing and started down the next staircase without breaking my stride. Did he think we were just going to carry on like nothing had happened? Make polite small talk until our shift ended?

His footsteps fell softly behind me, so much so that I had to strain to hear, but I didn't need to glance back to know he was there. The hairs on the back of my neck were up again, my inner wolf rumbling but not growling. In fact, the shrieking alarm bells from the first day we met had dissipated considerably over the last two weeks. No, my hackles were up—in response to his *voice*?

Palms clammy, I swallowed hard and skipped down a few steps.

"I'd say only about eighty percent of mine are idiots this year, which is honestly a bit shocking. I was expecting more," Calder continued, popping into my peripherals abruptly, suddenly at my side. I stopped on the second-floor landing, brows pinched, heart pounding—incredulity rising.

"*What*?"

Calder pushed his sleeves up to his elbows, unveiling a pair of forearms corded with muscle. "What?"

"Eighty percent..." Just like that, the allure of his silky voice, the appeal of those muscular forearms—*gone*, replaced with white-hot indignation. "How can you *say* that?"

The vampire shrugged, frowning at me. "Because it's fact. They can't all be winners, despite what it says on the academy's website—"

"We're barely into the first month," I snapped, instantly on the defensive, my innate protective instincts kicking into overdrive. "Don't judge a kid until they've had time to prove themselves to you."

There was that smirk again. "I do believe that would be the pot calling the kettle black, no?"

My eyebrows shot up. Was he suggesting that I had, what, judged him before I'd gotten to know him? Something tightened in my chest, and I turned stiffly and skipped down the rest of the steps to the ground level, hands in fists, Calder at my heels.

If I had just embraced a *vampire*, treated him like any other colleague, then I'd have been a moron—possibly a *dead* moron, or a moron locked deep inside some government lab by now. I pushed through the door out of the stairwell, then marched down the corridor toward the main entryway.

Calder might not be here to bag himself a wolf shifter, but my initial reaction to him, my *fear*, had been perfectly justified.

The sass he received in the days that followed came courtesy of his sparkling personality.

"I'm going to go check on the boys' dorm," I muttered when he strolled up to me, hands in his pockets, his expression annoyingly expectant. If he was waiting for a retort, or some segue into a *real* conversation about our shifter-vampire dynamic, then he'd be waiting a long time. "Stay here. Continue to make the rounds—sometimes they sneak out when they think we're done. Text me if something is wrong."

Not that I had willingly given a dead man my phone number; at our last staff meeting, we had all been instructed to put each other's numbers into our cellphones, an order straight from the administration to heighten security measures after all the local disappearances.

"But, Miss Kingsley, you're supposed to be showing me the ropes." Calder followed me through one of the front doors, but he lingered there, holding it open and leaning against the bar in the middle. "I think I require more *thorough* tutelage."

I glared from the bottom step when he grinned and sauntered back inside, the door falling shut heavily behind him.

"Ugh." Massaging my burning cheeks, I stalked down the cobblestone path to the boys' dorms, noting that many of the windows still had lights on long after eleven.

While both usually needed a reminder of lights-out times and curfew in general, the boys' building tended to be a little louder, a little smellier. The janitorial crew did an excellent job at keeping the dark hardwood floors spotless, the windows smudgeless, and the carpets in the rooms lintless, but the very potent scent of teenage-boy body odor was something nobody could get rid of, no matter how hard they scrubbed. Naturally, the girls' dorms had a smell too, but it was more flowery perfumes and body lotions, which, under the right circumstances, could be just as upsetting to my shifter nose.

Still, the sense of smell was the fastest of all the senses to adjust to a new status quo, and I forgot all about the deadly combination of B.O. and liberal cologne usage as I made my rounds. Footsteps thundered on the floors above me, students scampering as word spread that a teacher was in the building, and I was pleased that I didn't need to order anyone off to their room. Only two *lights out, guys* on the sophomores' floor.

Just because their lights were out, however, didn't mean they were in bed, dead to the world. These days, students had laptops, cellphones, and a plethora of other tech to entertain themselves well into the morning. While it was in our policy manual that we enforced strict curfews, it wasn't like we could stick our heads into each room for the duration of our night patrol just to make sure everyone was asleep. At some point, personal responsibility fell on the kids. If they stayed up too late, they'd suffer the next morning. No one could teach them that like themselves.

I could hear most of them, their conversations, through the walls. While muffled to humans, if I stopped and concentrated, I could make out distinct words through the wood and concrete. However, I had learned years ago that listening to private, personal teen conversations could only get you in trouble. Most of the time, the subject matter was something you did *not* want to hear.

Not if you ever wanted to look said teen in the eye again.

Just before starting my third sweep of the building, I paused in the stairwell to check my phone. Nothing from Calder. My brows knitted as I tucked my phone back into the top of my tights, wishing designers built these things with pockets. It shouldn't surprise me that I hadn't heard from him; night patrol wasn't exactly difficult—more tedious and boring, honestly. Friday and Saturday nights offered a higher likelihood for shenanigans, but so far, it had all been quiet.

By the time I reached the fourth floor, the after-midnight dimmed lighting had kicked in, and I paused in the stairwell doorway, frowning at the nondescript blob on the floor down the hall—a blob that hadn't been there on my last walkthrough. Eyes narrowed, I breathed in deeply. While I didn't detect a person—hardwood varnish, musky body spray, and pine-fresh toothpaste taking precedence in that moment—it certainly merited investigating.

I huffed a sigh, approaching the blob slowly, cautiously

beneath the low lighting. It looked like... a pile of clothes? Who the fuck—? And *why*? Was it a prank? The SIA males had a penchant for pranks, and last year a number of staff had been on the receiving end, either accidentally or not. This would be a first time for me.

I stopped in front of it, at a loss. As I'd suspected, it was a pile of clean, dryer-sheet-smelling gym clothes.

"What are you doing here?" I murmured, bending over to rifle through it, my knit sweater falling up my back.

The second I was down, a trio of lights flashed behind me, accompanied by the soft *click, click, click* of multiple camera phones. I shot up and whirled around, eyes wide, and caught three gangly freshmen bolting for the stairs.

Damn it. I shot off in hot pursuit, a blend of rage and embarrassment burning through me. Normally, I was so careful not to give them the chance to sexualize me. No bending over from the waist, which I'd just done. No stretching in a way that would thrust my chest out, which was tucked under a rigid sports bra on weekdays, but of course not now. My gym clothes were polo tees and track pants, hiding my figure, and I tried to keep my casual clothes somewhere in the same realm. And then here I'd gone and walked right into their trap, bending over in *tights*, my scrunched sweater exposing my lower back, wearing a bra that didn't squish my boobs down.

Seriously, Emma—get your head in the game.

With teenage boys on the loose, there was no room for error.

Red-faced and indignant, I tracked the sounds of *oh my god, go, go, go, go!* and *dude, run!* down the next two floors. The trio seemed desperate to lose me, voices cracking, laughter echoing, as they darted from the stairwell at one end of the corridor all the way across to the other. I picked up the pace, wearing my runners for a reason, and refrained from shouting at them like I wanted. No point in drawing any additional attention to all this—I'd catch them eventually, and I already had a pretty good idea of who was involved.

I plowed through the door to the second-floor south stairwell as it slowly closed, but inside their footfalls had gone silent. Heart beating only a touch harder than it would at rest, I marched down the stairs—only to pause when a velvety smooth Englishman's voice drifted through the corridor.

"Now, now, now, boys—what's all this?"

My blush intensified, and I rubbed my cheeks as I stomped the rest of the way down, hoping to diffuse the flush of color by the time I rounded on my panting trio of delinquents—and Calder. Ice blue darted up to my scowl, to my red cheeks, then back down to the three cowering freshmen in front of him. Matt Davies. Elijah Hough. Adil Agarwal. My jaw clenched: precisely who I *thought* I'd seen, their pimply, shiny faces made obvious in the much brighter light of the stairwell.

"Phones," Calder ordered, holding out his hands when I finally stopped two steps above them, blocking their escape route should they get the insane idea to run again. "*Now.*"

"But sir—"

"You can retrieve them from me tomorrow morning at breakfast," the vampire remarked coolly. He then snapped his fingers, the sound crisp and sharp enough to make *me* flinch, and the trio forked over their devices.

"And you'll be running laps tomorrow afternoon," I added, Matt and Adil jumping like they hadn't even realized I was there. Did they think I was still combing the upper floors searching for them, like their little plan had been *so* clever? I folded my arms, glare intensifying when all three burst into protests about tomorrow being Saturday. I arched an eyebrow. They fell silent a moment later, cheeks flushed, and I cleared my throat. "Three o'clock sharp—at the gym. You'll run until I tell you to stop."

The trio nodded glumly.

"All right, off to bed," Calder insisted, stepping aside and motioning for them to pass. "If I see a light on when I come by your rooms in the next two minutes, you'll go from detention with Miss Kingsley straight to detention with *me* for the rest of the day. Do I make myself clear?"

"Yup."

"Yes, sir."

"Understood, sir."

They were off like a shot, scrambling down the remaining stairs and bolting through the doorway. Their pounding footsteps echoed as the door slowly swung closed, followed by the frantic sounds of locks opening and suite doors shutting. I ran a hand over my hair with a sigh, and Calder swiped his thumb across one of the phone screens.

Then smirked.

"*Oh*, Miss Kingsley—"

"Give me that!" I snatched the phone and hastily deleted the photo with trembling fingers. While it wasn't a great shot of me, it was obvious where the camera had focused. Right on my ass. Presented on a platter for a trio of gawky teens who had *set me up*. Not exactly my proudest professional moment.

Nor my proudest *shifter* moment, either.

Unfortunately, the other two phones were password protected when Calder pressed the unlock button. He glanced up at me, but his smirk fell away the moment our eyes met.

"I'll have a talk with them tomorrow," the vampire said brusquely as he slipped the two phones in his back pockets, then took the third from me. "And ensure they delete any additional photos."

"Right." I leaned against the dark wooden railing, arms crossed, adrenaline fading. "Thanks."

Calder scratched at the back of his neck, lips briefly parted. We stood there for a moment, more awkward than necessary, until he cleared his throat. "So, are you... all right?"

"What? Yes." I pushed off the bannister and shrugged, somehow both annoyed and pleased that he had asked. "Teenage boys have been gross little pervs since the dawn of time. I'm fine."

The corners of his mouth lifted. "Right."

"What are you even doing here?"

"I'm afraid I missed the pleasure of your company."

"Well, we should really try to have one of us in each building," I insisted as I slowly made my way around the smirking vampire, taking a wide berth. "That's kind of the reason there are two people assigned every night. Two buildings. Two people. The math behind it will blow your mind—"

"Shall I stay here, then?"

I paused and glanced back at him. "Why?"

"Well..." Calder gestured from me to the bottom of the staircase, as if that explained everything. When my eyes narrowed, he let out a weak chuckle. "You know..."

"I can handle the boys' dorm."

"Can you?"

And just like that, any ounce of pleasure I might have felt about Calder asking after me was gone. Lips pursed, I faced him and hoisted my middle finger. He crossed his arms, biceps on display, and sighed.

"Very mature."

I carried on down the stairs backwards, hoping I didn't fall flat on my ass, still flipping him off.

"Really, Miss Kingsley, you're an *educator*—a role model."

Without breaking my stride, I raised my other hand, both middle fingers flying high, before disappearing around the last staircase curve.

Though I could have sworn, before I lost sight of him, that Calder had actually smiled.

Not a smirk.

Not a thin grin.

A *smile*.

Tummy in knots, I marched off to confirm that the trio of miscreants were back in bed, and by the time I checked that stairwell again, the vampire was gone.

What on earth was that godawful *racket*?

Crouched in front of my office minifridge, I grabbed the first blood cooler in the row, then nudged the door shut and stood. As I cracked open the thin, narrow canister, mouth watering at the familiar *hiss*, the din just outside my window grew louder.

Dogs. Yapping, yipping, barking, howling—*dogs*.

With one hand in my pocket, I strolled toward the large bay window overlooking the academy's main entry point, slurping down a gulp of chilled AB-negative on the way. Just as I'd suspected: dogs. A whole crew of them, tugging at their leashes, a number of familiar senior faces at the ends. They appeared to be making their way over to the roundabout in front of this building's front doors, Emma bringing up the rear.

I homed in on the shifter, dressed in a pair of jeans and one of her thousands of knit sweaters. Once, I had walked in on her knitting in the staffroom, surrounded by our coworkers, chatting, smiling—until she saw me. I'd kept my distance, especially when the wolf was armed with steel knitting needles, but I couldn't help wondering if she had *made* all those shapeless, slouchy garments she seemed so fond of wearing in her free time.

And if she made them slouchy and shapeless on purpose to hide what I knew to be a rather fetching little body underneath. My mind flashed back to our first night patrol—those black tights clinging to her shapely legs had been enough to make me want to act on a few of my more suggestive, intentionally incendiary comments.

Scowling, I swallowed another mouthful of AB-negative as a dab of self-loathing twisted my insides. Honestly. Being physically *attracted* to a shifter, of all things; she was a novelty. In time, I'd be accustomed to her looks, to her gorgeous smile and intriguing eyes, to her bouncy ponytails and lilting laughter. Then, finally, this unnatural hold she as a *woman* had over me would diminish—and her blunt personality would quash whatever sentiment remained.

Whistle around her neck, she called something to the group, then motioned them toward the roundabout. Arctic dogs of varying shapes, sizes, and colors skipped along next to their handler, barking, mouthing at their hands, at each other, their paws splashing across puddles. The rain had held off, offering us the only sunny day all week. Naturally, I much preferred the rain and the misery; while vampires didn't melt under sunlight, it wasn't exactly comfortable either. The great orb was too bright for us, our skin sensitive to its rays. Any burns we sustained healed instantly, but I found it a rather taxing ordeal overall. The weather, no matter how dreary, was certainly a factor in my accepting the academy's job offer. By the end of October, there would be more dark than light, and it would last for months. Bliss.

For now, I could put up with the odd day of sunlight, its glow usually broken up by clouds ushering in the next rainfall. Three weeks into September, the temperatures had dropped markedly. Most of the students down there were out in layers, only a few still in uniform, many wearing hats or gloves—designer labels, of course, the offspring of the global elite.

And then there was Emma in her jeans and baggy dark green knit, sleeves smooshed up to her elbows, her hair swept back in a braid with wisps of blonde catching the light of the setting sun. With classes done for the day and only about twenty minutes left until supper, the street lamps outlining the roundabout had already flickered to life, bathing the odd, rather noisy group in a soft yellow sheen.

I took another sip of my blood cooler, watching her direct the organized chaos. She appeared nonplussed by all the noise, calling out commands to the group, which the students responded to immediately. This must be that rescue dog program I'd heard so much about but had yet to see with my own eyes. In fact, in the month I had been living on campus, I'd only heard a bark here and there, and hadn't once seen any of the dogs. A part of me had thought it didn't exist, despite knowing there was a large building, a kennel, next to the gymnasium on the west side of campus.

Perhaps I ought to pay it a visit one of these days.

The gymnasium too. I had yet to step foot in Emma's domain; she had been rather testy about my being here in general, and the thought of encroaching further on her territory, as ridiculous as the notion was, had been too bothersome to consider these last few weeks. After all, outside of my lingering tension with Emma Kingsley, I'd still needed to settle into a new school, acclimatize myself to a new breed of student, and adjust to SIA's somewhat rigid, long-ingrained rotating schedule.

The dogs, all sixteen of them, finally started to settle

once the students walked them to their designated places around the paved ring. Emma called something out again, arms swinging at her side as she sauntered between the human-dog pairings, her smile effortless, warm, pleasant— a look unlikely to ever be directed at me, even if we *were* a good night-patrol team. Seconds later, the students got their dogs to sit, some taking longer than others, and then looked back to Emma expectantly.

Curious, I set my cooler on my now too-full desk, papers and texts and assignments neatly piled everywhere, and grabbed my jacket off the back of my chair. Seeing the shifter in her element, doing something that put her so visibly at ease, was worth a closer look.

Can of blood in hand, the label nondescript to onlookers, I marched out of my second-floor office and made my way downstairs.

Only to stumble into Robert Howard, a great hulking bear of a man, as he was leaving his empty English classroom just outside the stairwell.

"Calder."

"Robert." I mirrored his smile, barely feeling a thing when he clapped an enormous hand on my shoulder. "Just came down to see what all the noise was about."

The man frowned. "Noise?"

"All that barking—"

"Ah, yes, the dogs," he mused as we strolled along the corridor, headed toward the pinnacle of the V-shaped building. "We *love* having them around. Emma introduced the program last year, and it was a huge hit. She thinks it sold her interview, but I've always told her it was just the cherry on top. Nearly seventy percent of the senior class applied to be part of it, since it counts toward their community service hours."

"I can see the appeal. I suspect the dogs are quite therapeutic during a stressful final year."

"It's a symbiotic relationship," Robert insisted with a nod. We paused at the main doors, peering through the glass at the group. "See, the students get service hours, something new and interesting to add to their university applications, and then, of course, the fun of working with dogs." The man's grin returned, and he chuckled when the giant fuzzball nearest to the door nosed at its handler's knees. "But they're all rescues, you see. We adopted out nine of the sixteen last year, so a good percentage of them are new. Emma has the kids train them, socialize them, and promote them on their personal social media. The administration loves it."

I could see why; it was great PR given the way animal sob stories trended virally these days.

"I haven't seen them yet." I moved in closer, watching as the group went through a sit, down, stay routine. "Haven't really heard them either."

"They're well-fed and exercised. Last term the dogs will have the option to sleep in the dorms, given their students collectively maintain a certain grade point average."

"Hmm."

"Well, come on." Robert shoved open one of the main doors, nodding for me to go through. "Why not get better acquainted? Are you a dog person?"

"I, er..." Not really, but that didn't seem to matter. Robert bustled on ahead of me, and I had no choice but to follow or look like a complete twat. Or, worse, appear *frightened* of the creatures, something I didn't need either. So, with another slurp of my blood drink, I sauntered out after him, remaining at the top of the stone stairs as I watched the group work. No one paid either of us any mind, even with

Robert chuckling and waving whenever a panting dog glanced his way.

Well—until the breeze changed course. Suddenly, Robert and I were upwind of the dogs, and in an instant, the scene devolved into chaos. As if sensing a predator in their midst, all sixteen dogs erupted into barks and howls of varying pitches, some deep-chested and fierce, others high-pitched and panicked.

Damn it.

Besides humans, most creatures reacted as Emma had to a vampire's presence. They knew, innately, that we were a threat. It was just the way the food chain worked. However, I had hoped, maybe, with all the students around, and a wolf shifter leading the motley pack, I might get a different response this time.

"Oh, what's happened?" Robert stepped up the stairs, standing one down from me yet still almost half a head taller, as the students tried to wrangle their dogs back under control. Emma stalked across the roundabout, arms up, baying for the teens to calm them down, distract them, give them a command. She paused in the middle, surveying the breakdown of her carefully cultivated order, not moving—until her gaze landed on me.

Then she was off like a shot, boots clomping from pavement to cobblestone. She stopped at the bottom of the stairs, a hand on the railing, her smile warm for Robert and, well, all things considered, polite for me.

"Didn't mean to upset the dogs, Emma," Robert insisted. "Sorry about that."

She waved him off. "It's fine. They need to learn how to deal with distractions, and this is a good challenge. It..."

The shifter trailed off with a slight frown, her nostrils flaring ever so slightly. With Robert distracted by the still-howling hounds, her gaze slid up to me, lingering on my face, then down to my drink.

The blood.

Visibly uncomfortable, she must have caught the sweet, metallic fragrance of my AB-negative. I gripped the can tighter, flicking a brow as I lifted it and sloshed the liquid around inside.

This is how I feed, you suspicious little—

"I'm not sure what happened," Robert said, his deep baritone, that impressive gravitas, startling both Emma and me out of the moment. He then reached back and smacked at my arm. "Probably just need a bit of warming up to new people. Don't take it personally, Calder."

"Oh, I don't know." Emma crossed her arms, slowly backing away toward the roundabout. By now, most of the students had pulled their dogs to the other side, and the added distance seemed to settle them. The wolf shifter shrugged, then offered a smile that didn't quite reach her eyes. "My dogs are usually a pretty good judge of character..."

Did she just—?

My *character* was not—

Would she rather I drink from students? Wasn't it preferable that I *paid* for my blood, from reputable sources? That I didn't attack the locals? Feed from the custodian? Fuck, slurping down the ice-cold stuff from a can—I was practically *vegan*.

Scowling, I held her gaze as I took another stiff sip of blood, making sure to lick my lips and smirk after. Emma rolled her eyes in turn, equally obvious, before strolling back to her flock and their baying hounds.

"Well." Robert clapped his hands together, the sound like thunder, and cast a quick look between Emma and me.

Perhaps we had been a touch too noticeable; both of us tried to keep our little *thing* subdued around the rest of the staff. Mercifully, whether the giant Canadian saw something or not, he kept it to himself. "Never mind, then. Come on. They're serving veal chops tonight—and if we ask real nice, they might even break out the good wine."

"Yes, sounds delightful," I muttered. My fingertips dug into the can, its metal exterior creaking in protest, and I stepped aside to let Robert pass. Before I followed him through the door, probably to cut through the building and carry on to the dining hall together, I cast one last look over my shoulder. Emma stood in the middle of her students, holding them in her thrall as she spoke. Even the dogs appeared to be completely focused, each one staring at her, ears up, mouths closed—alert.

And as I trailed after a chattering Robert, it suddenly occurred to me that I didn't mind Emma's bark, her bite, her blatant impertinence, as much as I should have.

In fact, I found it rather exhilarating.

Horrified, I paused halfway down the corridor. First the physical attraction, and now *this*? Something sharp and visceral twisted in my gut. Brow furrowed, I hastily downed the rest of my drink, crushed the can, and slammed it in the nearest rubbish bin.

6

EMMA

"Miss Kingsley, I appreciate your effort, but this drink menu *really* doesn't scream A Night in Paris to me."

I offered the head of the student council a blank look, then, with a deep breath, the kind that reminded me not to rip a teenager's eyebrows off even when they deserved it, accepted the sheet of paper thrust upon me with a thin smile.

"Karen, you're not getting champagne or wine, so this is your best bet to stay on theme," I told her for the thousandth time today. "If you can come up with more exciting names, then we'll change the menu signs before we print them tomorrow, but Principal Foster already approved what we have."

The seventeen-year-old flipped her frizzy auburn locks over her shoulder with a huff. "Well, can we at least eliminate *mocktails* from the menu title? This is supposed to be a classy event."

Do not hit a child. Do not hit a child.

"It's your homecoming, Karen. We can do whatever you want." I folded the sheet of paper with the list of drinks we'd be serving at the dance tomorrow night, aptly titled Sidecar Sundays, Mimosa Mondays, and White Lady Wednesdays— three mocktails inspired by drinks *literally* invented in Paris. "But if you have a problem with something this late in the game, I suggest you come up with a solution too."

"No offense, Miss Kingsley, but I'm pretty sure that's *your* job for the next, like, forty-eight hours."

We flashed each other a pair of equally strained smiles before Karen O'Connor, student body president, shoo-in for homecoming queen, and royal pain in my ass, marched off with her clipboard and walkie-talkie.

I used to *love* homecoming as a teen. The parties, the spirit days, the big dance at the end of the week. However, back when *I* was in high school, the dances weren't this elaborate, we were all content with canned sodas and whatever alcohol we could sneak in, and our teachers wouldn't be caught dead taking orders from any of us. Things had changed, and from the tense atmosphere hanging over my commandeered gymnasium this Friday evening, I wasn't sure if it was for the better.

Still, despite the stress in the air, my gym looked completely transformed. Black fabric hung from the walls, laden with little white lights that would give the illusion of a starry night. The shop class had constructed a ten-foot-tall Eiffel Tower replica out of metal, which sat in the middle of what would be the dance floor; Phyllis and her art students were in the process of painting it *and* handmaking roses to weave through the grates.

About sixty tables had been dug up from storage, which would be covered in short white linens and scattered around the space. Karen had demanded we order custom chairs for the event, but, unsurprisingly, Foster had nixed the idea. The academy had a sizeable budget for all the yearly functions, as they considered an active life outside of the classroom essential for fostering a strong sense of school community, but there just wasn't room for the kind of chairs Karen had been lusting over. This wasn't one of her mother's insane charity galas. This was a high school dance.

Across the enormous space, a space that no longer looked anything like my usual kingdom, the double doors leading directly outside opened, and I watched, teeth gritted, as a group of junior boys carried in the long buffet table that would serve Parisian treats all night. Outside, the storm that had been hammering campus all day raged on, lightning streaking across the grey veil of rain, maybe even a little sleet. The area was forecasted for snow this weekend, but I hoped it held off; students wanted to take pictures in their dresses and suits outside amongst the greenery, not underground in our concrete tunnel system.

The wind blew both doors shut as soon as the boys were in, and I resisted the urge to snarl about my once pristine vinyl floors. Not only were people traipsing all over them in regular, everyday shoes, but the floor was going to be covered in glitter for *weeks* after this thing.

The only reason I hadn't completely lost my cool, beyond that fact that I was a professional, even in my jeans and schlubby SIA tee, was because the entire faculty had been roped into helping. Same as last year, every one of us needed to take charge of a certain element. Some found their roles easily, like Phyllis and her art, whereas others, like me, were shoved into whatever was left—like catering. I'd be in charge of the food and drinks table tomorrow night, along with Gwendolyn Bishop, who taught IB chemistry, and needed to ensure there was smooth communication between the student council and the kitchen staff. So far, things had been going fine—until this drink menu snafu.

My least favorite staff member had been assigned as a floater, helping wherever he could. Calder had shown up this afternoon the most dressed down I had ever seen him, sporting a pair of dark jeans and a plain white T-shirt, just fitted enough to contour the muscular outline of his figure. I blamed Casual Friday, the last day of our homecoming spirit week, which had also included Crazy Hair Day, Crazy Hat Day—the works.

Predictably, there had been a squabble over where the vampire would be placed, groups of teenaged girls bickering with one another until Calder graciously offered to share his time between everyone. I'd just rolled my eyes and done my best to ignore him, but he was kind of difficult to ignore with all that muscle on display, normally hidden beneath a three-piece tweed suit.

I couldn't blame the girls for fighting over him either. The guy was gorgeous. They just didn't know he was a vampiric *ass* beneath that shiny, hunky veneer.

After giving my precious gymnasium a once-over, the transformation making my inner wolf grumble, I folded the sheet of paper in half again and made my way to the far back corner, toward the door that would open to a hallway, my hallway, at the end of which sat my office. Hopefully the internet would have a suggestion or two for "cooler", more "authentic" on-theme drink names.

Never mind that the student council had come up with these ones in the first place.

One of the major items out of place during homecoming dance prep were the chairs. Stacked some fifteen high, they sat bunched together in the back corner between the door to my hall and the doors to a small corridor housing the change rooms and underground tunnel entrance. A crew of seniors had been moving them in all afternoon, lugging the large black and gold chairs up from the storage room one or two at a time. As I neared the towers, my first thought was that they were stacked too high, that it wasn't safe.

A suspicion proven correct when someone on the other side of the chair wall tripped, their shoes squeaking out a familiar cry, followed by the *clunk* of chairs colliding with chairs. The row on my immediate left teetered, stacked too precariously tall, and I staggered back, tensed, waiting to catch the damn things, then pretend it had hurt me to do so.

Only the stack never fell.

Because some gorgeous vampire dick stopped it.

Calder appeared out of nowhere, his back to the stack, catching and righting it again in the span of about five seconds. It was a risk, using his speed around all these people, but the music faintly whumping from the AV club's speakers carried on, as did the chatter, the clatter of furniture, like nothing had ever happened.

"You okay?" I called, Calder and I no more than a foot apart, my heart in my throat as he stared me down, neither smarmy nor smirking.

"Yeah, I'm good," the culprit on the other side called back, and I caught his shadow moving beneath the chair legs, marching back and forth, walking it off. "Tripped over my own feet."

"These are stacked too high," I said, still holding Calder's gaze, unable to tear myself away, my stomach flip-flopping. "Cut them down by half so they don't fall on someone."

"Yes, Miss Kingsley."

Calder smelled earthy today. Sandalwood. Oakmoss. *Musk.* My cheeks peppered with heat the longer I breathed him in, and when he eased away from the tower of chairs, I took a sizeable step back, crinkling the paper in my hand.

"I could have caught that," I muttered, then ducked my head down and made a beeline for the door. The metal handle squeaked when I gripped it, but the brightly lit corridor on the other side was mercifully silent. As soon as the door closed, the chaos outside disappeared. His scent vanished. Smoothing a hand over my loose waves, I dragged in a deep breath, then exhaled it slowly, making my way by the trio of closed and locked grey doors, behind which was all my equipment. Balls. Netting. Rackets. The final door, way at the end of the hall, offered me guaranteed sanctuary, a private place to quiet my hammering heart.

The handle squeaked again, and I whirled around at the sound. Calder stalked in, letting it slam shut behind him, and I turned away, unable to withstand that dark, brooding look for a second longer than necessary. If he wanted a proper thank-you for doing something I honestly could have done myself, he'd be waiting a long time.

I hadn't made it more than two steps closer to my office when his hand snapped around my elbow, and my inner wolf snarled when he yanked me back and shoved me against the wall. Hackles up, my lips peeled back as the folded-over menu fluttered to the ground, forgotten at our feet. Calder caged me in with a hand on either side of my shoulders, his face ducking down to meet my eyeline.

Swallowing hard, I stood straighter, elongating my spine, lifting my neck, refusing to shrink despite the way his scent flooded over me. Hours from now, it would linger on my clothes, my T-shirt, fused to the cotton, even if he never touched me.

"We're going to have a *chat*, you and I," Calder hissed, his expression stony, his voice low and rumbly. I felt the heft of it dancing across my skin, his breath warming my lips. Before I could stop myself, my gaze dropped to his mouth, to the tightness along his jaw, the tremble of its muscles.

Color warmed my cheeks again. My eyes flashed back up, and I hoped, for my sake, that they read indignant yet unfazed by this display.

"Do we need to be standing this close together to do it?" I growled back. My voice had lowered too, dangerous, a whispering hint of the beast inside. I couldn't be sure, but from the somewhat intense way he stared into my eyes, they might have changed too. Only a shade—I was nowhere near shifting, but occasionally a flicker of my wolf's eyes, yellow like the harvest moon, reared during heightened emotions. Anger. Desperation. Joy.

Arousal.

"We do," Calder murmured, inching closer, "because apparently this is the only way I can get your fucking *attention.*"

I fought back a grin, tilting my head to one side. "Swear jar, Mr. Holloway."

The nearer he drew, purposefully crowding me, the sharper the flames licking up my body burned. Slowly, the fire that had started in my cheeks spread, unchecked, unhindered, threatening to consume me. The hum of his aura tingled, danced across my skin, buzzed in my lips; I licked them, concentrating on slow, even breaths to quiet my heart—a heart that shouldn't be racing, yet Calder Holloway had a knack for spurring it on. I had called him a dead man the first time we met, but even without touching him, he didn't *feel* dead now. Not this close.

Not when he was on top of me either.

Heat flashed, this time in my belly, flaring and twisting.

"You've had your fun." That *growl*—it could put a wolf to

shame. Not bad, for a vampire. My eyes dipped down again, catching a hint of fang beneath his top lip as he spoke. "You've given me the *business*, but enough is enough. Emma, I'm here to teach, and I'm not going anywhere. If you don't like me, *fine*, but keep it professional. I'm sick of your snarky little attitude, especially when I haven't done anything to deserve it beyond the fact that I exist."

If either of us drew a deep breath, the kind that filled your lungs to bursting, we'd touch—the tips of our noses, my breasts to his chest. Dark lashes caught my eye, midnight black and too lush for a man like Calder. They flickered down, and my lips parted as I sucked in a shallow breath.

"Get out of my face, Calder."

"No."

This was too much.

I couldn't—

I couldn't breathe.

So, I pushed him—hard, slamming my palms against his chest, against the marble statue of a man standing in front of me. The blow caught him off guard, forcing him back a few paces, and I pitched forward for the follow-through. Calder righted himself quick, and before I knew it, he had me shoved back up against the wall, his hand at the base of my throat, bearing down on me with a snarl.

The heat flared again, scorching my core, pooling between my thighs.

It had been a *long* time since anyone physically overpowered me. As the alpha's daughter, his heir, my strength surpassed most of my pack members, even seasoned wolves greying around the ears. It was instinctual, natural, innate.

Calder handled me like it was nothing.

And I didn't hate it—not like I should.

It made me want to fight.

It made me want to—

The back of my head ached; a human skull would have cracked against the concrete. I grabbed his wrist with both hands, tugging, yanking, *fighting*, but Calder held firm at the hollow of my throat.

Though the twitch of his right eye suggested this wasn't a cakewalk for him either.

"Tell me we have an understanding, wolf."

I sucked in my cheeks with displeasure. This sanctimonious, pretentious, arrogant, uppity vampire jerk— had a point.

After digging into his background and finding nothing, my behavior made me no better than them, those fanged assholes who judged an entire species on mostly outdated, albeit occasionally warranted stereotypes. Calder hadn't tried to kidnap me. None of our students had bite marks— beyond the garden-variety hickeys, of course. He could always have an ulterior motive, be playing the long con. I'd be an idiot to let my guard down completely, but all this passive-aggressiveness, and sometimes full-on aggression, only made my work life, my home, more stressful than it needed to be.

Still. He was an ass. An ass with his hand digging into my throat, pinning me to the wall, making my breathing labored and my heart thunder.

A hot, grumpy *ass*.

Made even hotter when he was all flustered, his dark brows furrowed, lips in a snarl, eyes flashing with *emotion*— not the calm, cool, collected guy who smirked down at me all the time.

I liked seeing him unravel. I enjoyed it way more than I should, way more than was good for me.

So, against my better judgement, I held his stare and craned my head forward, mouth a breath away from his, the rest of me still thrust up against the concrete, then offered my best Calder-esque smirk.

"Get bent, vampire."

His hand shot up my throat, eyes flashing dangerously as they bore into mine, then dropped to my lips. They parted with a breath, torn between lifting into a snarl of my own, snapping at his lower lip, or just seizing his mouth in a searing, fiery-hot—

Down the hall, the metal door handle squeaked. We sprang apart, Calder flush against the opposite wall, mouth set in a rigid line, expression unreadable. I straightened as Karen stomped in, clipboard in one hand, walkie-talkie in the other, her cheeks splotchy.

"Miss Kingsley," she whined, voice wobbling, "the kitchen says they have no idea about our appetizer menu. Like *no* idea. Like they don't even have the ingredients, and apps set the tone for *everything!*"

I stabbed a trembling hand through my hair. "They know about the appetizers, Karen. I talked to Felipe yesterday."

"Well, then someone isn't telling the truth, because they literally just told me—"

"Okay, okay, let me go sort it out." I crossed my arms as I hurried stiffly down the hall toward her, something unwelcome tingling between my thighs, churning, burning in my core. Karen seemed totally oblivious to what she had walked in on, scratching at her head with the walkie antenna as she panic-read her spreadsheet.

"And Mr. Holloway, they're having trouble with the

photo booth setup, and no one can find Mr. Renard. I think he went to get snacks, and the tech stuff just isn't working without him—"

"I'm really the last person to help with tech, Karen, but I'll give it a go."

"Breathe," I said, my smile forced as I swept her under my arm and led her back through the doors. "It's going to be fine."

Advice I really ought to follow.

Calder's clipped footsteps followed us, and while I didn't look back, I could feel his gaze scorching across my body, branding me with a mark no one else could see.

Even after the door swung shut between us.

Even after I left the building, off to sort out the kitchen mess.

Even hours later, curled up in bed alone, the storm battering my window, one hand clasped around my throat—and the other between my thighs.

OCTOBER

7

EMMA

"Okay, so Teams Awesomesauce and Red-Five will be playing the first round, and then—"

"Hi, Mr. Holloway!"

I looked up from the list of this afternoon's dodgeball plays on my clipboard. While I hadn't worked with the junior teams yet, they'd been really intense about my dodgeball league last year as sophomores, and I had no doubt that would carry over into this year as well. A little less unclear, however, was why Calder fucking Holloway was strolling into my gymnasium, a dusting of fat snowflakes on his shoulders, wearing a long black coat and dark jeans so crisp he must have ironed them.

Someone was in his casuals today.

He flashed the thirty-two students present a beaming smile, my four teams of eight immediately enraptured. I also wasn't sure *why* the vampire was such a big hit with the academy's students. Even if they weren't in his higher- or standard-level history classes, they all clamored for his attention everywhere he went, no longer giving him the cautious space that I'd seen during the first few days of the term. I had caught a glimpse of him in teaching mode a few times, and Calder at the front of a classroom with his archaic chalkboard was basically the same creature he was the rest of the time: grumpy, pretentious, and patronizing.

But here they were, greeting him now like the prodigal son returning, guys and girls alike. I'd seen it before— teachers playing hard to get. *Not* being the warm, bubbly, chatty one who the kids considered a friend. It made them work harder for his time and attention.

I, on the other hand, had been working very hard to *not* get his time and attention. Ever since our heated exchange in the corridor outside my office, I'd steered clear. Something had come over me that day—something I had to fight, ignore, swallow. Because I'd liked his hand on my throat. I'd liked his fire, his wrath. Our bodies gravitated toward one another, and when I should have been shoving him away, scoring his cheek with my nails, I yearned to drag him closer and mark his back instead.

Dangerous territory.

Giving him space, leaving the teachers' lounge whenever he strolled in, had been my best plan of defense so far. Yet now, he had broken the unspoken accord between us: besides helping with the homecoming dance setup—a dance that had been a roaring success, Karen crowned queen by her peers—Calder never set foot in my gym. I might not have been able to claim Solskinn as a whole, neither the academy nor the nearby village it was named after, but the gymnasium belonged to me. Situated next to the rescue dog kennel, my scent drowned it, seeped into the walls. This big square building, ugliest on campus, was *mine*.

Well, mine and Walter's, but he had already expressed

his preference for the weight studio—so *technically*, all mine.

And it was supposed to be a vamp-free zone.

I swallowed hard, biting the insides of my cheeks when they tingled with heat, and then forced a smile as Calder unbuttoned his coat and greeted most of this afternoon's players by name.

"Mr. Holloway," I said, fighting to keep the sharpness out of my voice, to keep it as light and breezy as I normally did, like his presence meant nothing to me. "Is everything okay?"

Because why the fuck else would he be here unless Foster had issued a state of emergency?

The vampire's bright blues darted my way, his smile unflinching. "Oh, fine, Miss Kingsley. I've just been hearing such wonderful things all week about the dodgeball league from my students, and I wanted to see what the fuss was about."

"Oh." Death-gripping my clipboard, I stood a little straighter, held my head a little higher. Of all the faculty-run clubs, my dodgeball league had the highest number of participants. It had been a raging success last year, and I attributed that to the fact that we spent the first semester practicing and having fun.

Second semester was when we kept score, and each team was allowed to debut their own uniform in January— so long as they met the academy's decency requirements— and jazz it up with war paint and bandanas. Unlike many of the other organized sports clubs, I tried to keep the league as entertaining as possible, opening it up to all skill levels. Even students who opted out of physical education in the IB program came back to play. Dodgeball wasn't about athleticism—at least my league wasn't. It was about comradery and sportsmanship and hilarious uniforms.

Last year, roughly half the students at the academy signed up to play. This year, the number rose to about 75 percent, with nearly the entire junior class standing in front of me right now.

"I've never played before," Calder admitted, speaking more to the players than me. "And since some of you won't stop haranguing me about it, I thought I could maybe join one of the teams—just for today."

Before I could get a word in—no, preferably *fuck* no—the four teams erupted in a chorus of competing voices. Their overall message, however, was clear: they wanted Calder to play. I let out a long sigh, hugging my beloved league clipboard to my chest. Of course they did.

And they were already bickering over which team he would play on.

"Okay, okay, guys, settle down." I waved my clipboard to bring the focus back to me, only to be met with thirty-two pleading sets of eyes. I let out another little sigh. "It's just... it doesn't seem *fair* that Mr. Holloway join a team."

Given he was stronger and faster than everyone in this room, myself included, the playing field was hardly even if we stacked one team with a vampire.

"You can play too, Miss Kingsley. Then each team has an extra player."

Thank you, Kenneth. "I don't know—"

An onslaught of *please, come on, Miss* and *just for today* amongst the rest of the garbled teen chatter erupted in front of me. When I glanced at Calder, he just stood there, hands in his pockets—a vision of innocence, except for the smirk. Usually, I wasn't a pushover in the gym, although I could be a little laxer with rules and formalities for the league. Still, my gut instinct told me to put my foot down and just kick Calder out.

My brain, however, flashed back to that moment, pinned up against the wall, trapped between concrete and vampire —that one fleeting moment where Calder had actually made some sense.

"Okay," I conceded softly, my smile ballooning at the surge of excited energy from the teams. "Okay, fine. Mr. Holloway and I will play for opposing teams, just to keep things"—I caught his eye—"*even*. But don't think I won't still be reffing, even for the team I'm on."

I split us up, consulting the clipboard, penciling Calder onto the two teams that historically played least aggressively of the four. The other two didn't need the extra muscle. With Team Awesomesauce getting set up on the far right wall of the gymnasium, strategizing, I sent Red-Five and Calder to the left, then arranged all the red rubber balls— four blockers, two stingers, differing slightly in size—along the center court line. Fortunately, the preset divisions across the vinyl created the boundaries for us: two sides, plus a neutral zone in the middle.

I played strictly elimination rounds during the first semester; a simple elimination session made the matches go by quicker, which allowed everyone to get as much practice as needed. For now, all eight players were permitted on the court at one time. Come next semester, there would only be six in play per team, with two subs on the bench, and the gameplays would become more complicated.

When I spotted Calder standing just outside his team's huddle, I waved him over. My hands settled naturally on my hips as he approached, and I hastily crossed my arms instead, going from offensive posturing to defensive, to show I'd been listening to his stupid, sexy rant.

"Did they give you a rundown on the rules?" I asked, leaning back when he stopped about a foot and a half away, both of us standing inside the center circle, a bright red ball between our feet. He'd ditched the coat at some point, the sleeves of his black cardigan tugged up to his elbows, his obsidian locks slicked back—hauntingly blue eyes trained squarely on me.

"A jumbled version," Calder mused, nodding. "I suppose I'll learn the nuances once you blow that whistle of yours."

I resisted the urge to tuck the whistle hanging around my neck into my shirt. "Well, you get hit, you're out. Hit other players, eliminate the opposite team. You can block an incoming ball with these larger balls. You can't throw in the neutral zone." I motioned to the lines. "And you can get a player out by catching their ball. No head shots."

The vampire flashed a somewhat unsettling predatory grin. "Like I said—nuances."

"Okay, well." I kept my gaze moving around the gym, purposefully avoiding eye contact, because the few moments of it had already made my cheeks warmer. "When I blow the whistle, *they* will run for the balls in the middle. We won't. And no..." I cleared my throat, voice dropping. "No supernatural abilities. Make it fair."

Calder's grin faltered, and he shot me a narrowed look. "Emma. Really. Did that need to be said?"

"Well—"

"Do you think my ego so insatiable that I'd come down here just to outplay a bunch of human teenagers at something that's *barely* a sport?"

"Okay." I held up my hands and stepped back, clipboard shield sitting next to the ball bin, forgotten. "Fine. Whatever. Just play at like two percent of your actual ability."

"Same goes for you, Miss Kingsley."

I clamped down on the insides of my cheeks again when a handsome smile creased the corners of his mouth—

another flashback to that moment, the tips of his fangs poking out beneath his top lip. Heat flashed in my belly, my inner wolf rumbling to life, and I turned away, distracting myself by calling for spectators to be seated on the benches on either side of the court and for players to place one hand and one foot against their back wall.

"On my whistle!" Each word echoed, a hush settling over the chatty teens. "Three, two—"

At the shrill screech of my whistle, footsteps thundered across the vinyl, both teams launching themselves toward the balls in the middle. Calder and I hung back, and I nodded, pleased that he was at least listening to me while he was in here, even if he didn't take dodgeball all that seriously.

Balls started flying, bouncing off the floor, off students. Players called out to one another. I ducked, dodged, and weaved, avoiding a few well-aimed projectiles as I kept an eye on the proceedings. Any ball that came near me I passed off to my team, preferring to monitor. These guys were good at adhering to the rules; this year's freshmen class, who I'd worked with on Monday, must have thought I was *blind* given all the bullshit they tried to sneak by me. Little did they know just yet, but I missed nothing.

Except for the ball that slammed into the side of my hip, appearing out of nowhere and ricocheting off toward the back corner. Stunned, I looked down at the offending area, then back up—and found Calder grinning impishly at me from the other side of the court. The teams seated on the benches giggled and cheered.

"Ooooh, you're out, Miss Kingsley!"

"Yes, thank you, peanut gallery," I called back, holding Calder's gaze as I stalked to the side of the court. He shrugged, still grinning, as I shook my head. "Right. I see how it is. I'm coming for you in the next round."

Bring it, wolf, he mouthed back, and more giggles erupted from our spectators when I pointed two fingers up to my eyes, then across the court to his. Back and forth.

I'm watching you.

Predictably, the students loved my rivalry with Calder, and it kept the next several rounds light and fun—to the point where no one argued with me when I made a ref call, nor was there much of the usual trash talk between opposing players. While I still continued to scan the court for rule breaking, I actually *played* in the matches that followed—and Calder was my only target.

The vampire seemed to have shed his grumpy exterior this afternoon; I'd never seen him smile or laugh this much, dodging balls, occasionally catching them, and hurling them back at me with way less power than I knew he was capable of. I held back too, aware that a student getting in the way of a ball thrown full force by either of us could result in a broken... everything.

Unfortunately, with Calder and I focused exclusively on each other, neither of us got the other out. We were both too quick, too light on our feet, to make any of the balls land. We were also both high-value targets from members of the opposing teams, which meant occasionally we were distracted. In one such moment of distraction, I finally managed to get Calder out on a fumble, although I had a feeling he'd dropped the ball on purpose.

While we didn't talk about it, both Calder and I allowed ourselves to be tagged out by students toward the end of each match. If we didn't, we'd be the final two standing every time—and that wasn't fair either.

An hour and twenty into this afternoon's practice, and

forty-five minutes out from dinner, I called everyone in to discuss the final two games. Sweaty, panting, red-faced teens surged around me, gym shirts stained and wet, the poignant smell something I had long since adjusted to. From the look on Calder's face, he hadn't. At all.

Unanimously, the teams voted to play against Calder and me for our last match of the day—all thirty-two of them against us. I met his eye across the huddle, and his shrug and barely discernible nod had me giving the okay. Before that, however, I had the four teams split into two for one massive elimination round and added twelve more balls to the center line, just to keep everyone busy.

"This is... very enjoyable," Calder said in passing, headed toward the left side of the gym, hands in his pockets. He turned, not breaking stride as he strolled backward, navigating around our students with ease. "I can see why they all speak so highly of it."

My mouth stretched into a smile, something warm blooming in my chest, but I quickly looked away and bit my lower lip, smothering it. He didn't need to think his praise *meant* something to me. I knew my dodgeball league was kick-ass. I wasn't looking for his validation.

Even if it was kind of nice to hear.

Once we had everyone lined up against their respective back walls, I raised a hand, silencing the room. "On my whistle. Three, two—"

Thirty-two pairs of feet charged the center line, their drumbeats far more overwhelming and chaotic than when there was only half on the court at one time. Still, the chaos of double the balls in play made it more exciting. I hung back behind my cluster of teens, knowing I'd need to keep a more cautious eye out; with so many people running around, the risk of an accident had skyrocketed. On the flip side, with so many available targets, players were also being knocked out faster. At one point, I noticed Calder tracking my movements, mirroring me on the other side of the neutral zone, one of the smaller stinger balls in hand. I caught his eye, then shuffled back, using my team as human shields. He shook his head, chest deflating sharply in a huff, then mouthed, *Come on.*

I shrugged, on the verge of playfully poking my tongue out at him. No one said we couldn't use our kids as bodyguards. In fact, there was a game that involved bodyguards protecting a lone player as the other team tried to get them out. I seldom ran it, as I didn't like the idea of one person being the opposition's main target, but maybe with Calder here, we could—

Screech. Over the din of bouncing balls and laughing teens, I heard it: the telltale sound of shoes catching on the floor, the very sound I had come to recognize as someone about to fall flat on their face. Eyes wide, I scanned the room, searching for the source, only to spy Grace Flynn tripping over her shoe's untied laces. I was off like a shot, but my speed didn't matter: she went down hard before I'd even reached the center line, plummeting face-first into the floor with her hands above her head, just about to catch a lobbed rubber ball.

My whistle screamed over the roar of the game, calling a timeout, and already her teammates had her surrounded.

"Move, move please," I muttered, pushing through the clump as Grace's wails turned shrill. Grace Flynn, sixteen years old and the daughter of a US military officer stationed in Germany, had been one of my less coordinated pupils last year, and it hadn't surprised me in the slightest that she opted out of PE once she finished her sophomore year.

"Oh my god! Oh my god! My teeth! Did I chip them? Oh

my *god*!" She pushed up on her elbow, still sprawled across the floor, surrounded by fawning friends. As I dropped to my knees in front of her, I heard Calder barking for everyone to get back, to give us some room.

"Okay, Grace, can you sit up for me?" My stomach looped when she lifted her head. That—was *so* much blood. Trembling, Grace shuffled into a seated position, bright red blood smeared across her mouth, her chin, dribbling down onto her white gym shirt. Her nose appeared to have taken the brunt of the fall, a sizeable bump protruding halfway up her bridge. Around us, the crowd slowly peeled back, yielding to Calder's whip-sharp orders to *move*. Before they could all go, I tapped Grace's best friend, Siobhan, on the arm, then motioned in the direction of my office. "Go get the first aid kit from my desk—it'll be in the top drawer. Then grab the cold compress out of the little fridge."

"Yes, Miss Kingsley."

"Why is no one *answering* me?" Grace snapped, her hazel eyes wild and panicked as Calder crouched down beside us. "Are my teeth chipped or not?!"

She peeled her lips back, thrusting her face into mine, and I planted a firm hand on her shoulder. "No, I don't think anything's chipped. It'll be hard to see until you wash your mouth out. I think you split your lip—do *not* spit on the floor." My eyes narrowed, catching that train of thought before it flew off the tracks. "But I think your nose, uh..."

I hesitated. I'd gotten in trouble for differentiating between a fracture and a sprain last year and had been on the receiving end of a nasty lecture from the head nurse; if I didn't have a medical degree, I couldn't "diagnose" an injury. At the time, I'd wanted to remind *her* that she wasn't a doctor either, but that hadn't seemed productive. Still, I'd been teaching gym class long enough to familiarize myself with all the common injuries. Grace's nose looked broken as fuck.

But then again, telling her that might only cause her more panic.

"No, don't tilt your head back," Calder admonished lightly. His hand smoothed up Grace's back, fingers brushing mine before he scruffed the back of her neck. "It doesn't matter if it dribbles on the floor. Lean forward or you'll swallow the blood and make yourself sick."

Blood. A bolt of panic sliced through me. All that blood —in front of a *vampire.* It was practically a marinade. Protectiveness flared, my inner wolf grumbling as I shuffled in closer and wrapped an arm around both of Grace's shoulders. I pinned Calder with a glare, a narrowed look that dared him to so much as *sniff* in her direction, but the vampire seemed not to notice as Siobhan returned and dumped the first aid box in front of Grace, then handed me the cold compress.

"Is she going to be all right, Miss Kingsley?"

Calder glanced up as he undid the first aid kit's clasp, brow furrowing at my silence, only to glare right back when our eyes met.

"*Emma.*" His lips barely moved, the sound almost inaudible over the chatter of the other students. Heat prickled through me, a familiar sensation—the kind that consumed my body before a shift.

I blinked hard. My eyes—had they started to change?

Fuck.

"She's fine, Siobhan, thank you," I said quickly, face flushed as I passed the cold compress to Grace. She gripped it tight, tears slicing down her cheeks, her shoulders starting to shudder, and I gently lifted her arm up, a wordless command to hold the cloth to her nose—

may as well get the swelling under control as soon as possible.

Calder quickly found some sanitizing wipes inside the first aid kit and began cleaning Grace's face in silence, wiping away blood and tears alike. My nostrils flared, the blend of metallic iron and rubbing alcohol more potent than I cared to admit. With Siobhan still looming over us, I motioned to her classmates. "We're done for the day. Tell everybody to change and get to dinner."

With a nod, Siobhan disappeared in a whirl of blonde ringlets, and within moments I heard the telltale sounds of exhausted, sweaty students filing out to the change rooms. As soon as an echoey silence descended on us, punctuated by the metal door slamming shut, Grace released a strangled sob, both hands flying to her nose.

"Ow."

Broken. Definitely broken.

"Okay, let's get you to the infirmary. You might need a splint."

"I can take her," Calder muttered as we both helped Grace up, each of us taking one arm. My inner wolf snapped, growling low as I frowned at him.

Without an audience, there was no need to be subtle, and I looked pointedly at the blood on Grace's face, then up to Calder. "Are you sure?"

It took a few seconds for the message to sink in, but once it did, Calder rolled his eyes and shot me a very poignant *are you fucking kidding me?* look before steering us toward the emergency exit doors at the far side of the gym.

"Of course I'm sure," he said, low and deep, offering a growl of his own as he marched along stiffly next to Grace. He kept his strides short, as did I, Grace shuffling at a glacial pace between us with the compress on her face and blood on her shirt. Just before we reached the large metal doorway, Calder veered off and made a beeline for one of the benches, on which sat a bundle of black.

"How are you feeling, Grace?" I murmured, eyes darting between her and Calder over her shoulder, who was shaking out his thick wool coat. Grace shrugged.

"Like shit?"

"Maybe be a bit more descriptive when you talk to the nurse," I said with a grin. From behind the once white cloth, now stained red, Grace smiled back—which split her busted lower lip wider, and I hastily stuck the end of the cloth to it. "Hold this there for a second, and—just give us a minute."

I didn't want to make her wait any longer than necessary, but I had to be completely sure that a bloodthirsty *vampire* could handle escorting one of my Solskinn kids anywhere by himself. Clearing my throat, I power walked over and held up a hand. He huffed at me, eyes flashing with annoyance, and roughly folded his coat over his arm.

"*What*, Emma?"

"Look, I'm really not trying to be rude," I told him. This afternoon, having him join the teams—it had been a lot of fun. And given the terse nature of our professional relationship, what I was about to say could be like shoving a pin in a balloon. "And I'm genuinely not trying to be a dick to you right now, but I just thought—"

"Emma." He spared a quick look to Grace, then leaned forward, dropping to my eyeline, his voice a sharp whisper. "I am *far* from newly turned. I can handle a bit of blood, I promise. You really don't need to worry about her."

"Of course I'm going to worry—"

"I know you don't want to trust me," Calder continued, suddenly clutching my forearm. I looked at his large porcelain hand with a frown, and he dropped it back to his side, jaw briefly clenched. "But when it comes to the well-being of my students, you can trust that I have their best interests in mind. Or... you're just going to have to *try*."

He darted around me, not bothering to wait for a rebuttal, and I watched him cross back to Grace with a hand pressed to my forehead. Instinct demanded I argue, shove him aside, whisk Grace off to the third-floor hospital wing in the main building by myself. Wolves were protective—obnoxiously so when it came to our pups. These kids were my pups, the people on this campus my pack. They might have been human, but they were all I had.

Well, them and the dogs. Even if I spent my weekends talking to no one, full lone-wolf style, I always had the rescue dogs.

Yet as Calder wrapped his much-too-big jacket around Grace's shoulders, then gently fed her arms through the sleeves and bent down to button it up, I finally found a way to keep that innate protective streak in check. How would I feel if someone questioned *my* integrity with these kids? What if someone came at me, insisting I couldn't be around them *ever* because there was the slight risk that I might wolf out during a state of heightened emotion? It was rare for an adult shifter to lose their cool, to unwittingly let the beast free—but it *could* happen. Crazier things happened every day.

Like a vampire waltzing into my territory—because he wanted to *teach*.

What if that vampire outed me, questioned me, doubted my ability to look after my students?

I'd hate it. It would be a personal attack, a strike to the foundations of my being.

So, without a word, I hurried over and opened the thick metal door for them, immediately assaulted by the elements. What had started off as a gentle smattering of snow had morphed into a full-blown gale as the day went on, blustery gusts of freezing air kicking up the few inches of white powder that had stuck, the sky grey. It would melt by the weekend, but that didn't help Grace right now. Calder tucked her under his arm, shielding her from the screaming winds.

Propping the door open on my hip, I watched them go, squinting against the storm. They puttered along, taking the most direct route to the main building rather than the winding underground tunnels. The wind erased Calder and Grace's footprints, a sea of shifting white shrouding the ground. At the halfway point, he glanced back over his shoulder at me. Our eyes met through the pelting snowflakes, his bright blues clear as anything, even in the storm. I clutched the end of my fat, frizzy fishtail braid, nibbling my lower lip, and then nodded. He nodded back.

Swallowing hard, I stepped inside, dragging the door with me against the wind. Once it clicked in place, a thick, palpable silence settled around me, my ears ringing.

Just like that—a spark of trust. It flickered to life in my chest, burning bright as melted snowflakes trickled down my skin.

I took a deep breath, heart pounding for no reason, then brushed the streaks of ice water away and went to check on the rest of my pups.

8

CALDER

Another human missing—a father of four this time, the first disappearance since the summer. The newspaper crinkled as I folded it over and scanned the rest of the article for any pertinent information. While nothing more than a local tabloid, a somewhat gossipy comings and goings of Solskinn proper, it had broken the story before the academy's administration, before the larger national papers.

Heidrick Thompson, forty-eight, missing since last Sunday. Lived one town over. Took the dogs for a walk—and while the dogs eventually found their way home, unfazed by the frequent dumpings of snowfall, the same couldn't be said for Heidrick. His wife suspected foul play, but the police had yet to issue a statement. My brow furrowed. That made seven, if I wasn't mistaken, since the start of the summer.

As I read the personal testimony from Heidrick's family, his friends, I considered finally taking this matter into my own hands. If these people really *were* dying, if it was all connected, then the sleepy village of Solskinn, nestled between forest-covered hills and a smattering of streams, lakes, and waterfalls, was about to get a whole lot of media attention.

And I had chosen this region for its isolation, for its distinct middle-of-nowhere-ness that would have had others in my professional position scoffing. Media, police, private investigators—I wanted none of it anywhere near my new home.

Perhaps I ought to look into—

"Would you like me to translate that?"

I looked up sharply, startled, so deep in my own head that I hadn't even registered Marte's return. Mercifully, my days of blushing had long since passed, and I set the newspaper atop the nearby stack, right next to a bin of used books and a cooler of local-brewed beer.

"I understood a few of the words," I told Marte, the youngest of the academy's nursing staff, flashing what I knew to be a handsome smile—dazzling, the kind that made human hearts pitter-patter. "Another man's gone missing, I think."

The svelte woman, beautiful with her white-blonde pixie cut and angular features, moved closer and ran her fingers across the front page, lips moving as she read the news in silence. A native Norwegian and notorious flirt, she had been offering to teach me her mother tongue since I arrived in August. Little did she know, I spoke it fluently already.

Norwegian, Swedish, Finnish.

German. Icelandic. Spanish. French. Italian. Chinese. Latin. Greek. Arabic.

With nothing but eternity ahead, immortal in the truest sense, I had embraced my affinity for languages long ago, taking time here and there the last century to familiarize myself with whatever caught my interest.

Naturally, I told no one, not even the locals. I stammered my way through basic sentences, which always made them smile and immediately take pity on me. Ah, look at the foreigner trying *so* hard. All my disarming tactics had become habits, remnants of the past, of a crueler time in my very long life. While I had shirked most other tricks, it worked in my favor to appear likeable, to subtly encourage humans to accept me, underestimate me, as a newcomer *and* a supernatural predator.

Charming.

Attentive.

Perhaps even a bit bumbling.

Women like Marte lapped it up. My colleagues thought me worldly yet eager to learn, both seeking out my advice and always trying to teach me something new, something I usually already knew. The only one I hadn't been able to fool had been the woman who saw me for what I was from the beginning. Though now, three weeks into October, I had *finally* started to chip away at that icy wolf exterior.

Marte, meanwhile, needed no chipping whatsoever. Once she finished reading the paper, she touched my arm and peered up at me like some lost lamb, then nodded. "Yes, you're right. Another gone, just like the last."

"I'm sorry. Did you know him?" All these northern communities, the ones within walking or driving distance of each other, had so much crossover, so much cross-pollination; everyone seemed to know everyone, and if not personally, then they had some connection to the family name.

Marte shook her head sadly. "No, but it's a shame. He was a father to four girls. I can only imagine how distraught they are."

I hummed in agreement, noting that her hand lingered

on my arm, gripping softly through the leather. For the school's first trip to the village since term started, I had dug out the old vintage leather jacket, recently tailored for a better fit. I'd received compliments the entire ride out, situated in the middle of the small grey academy bus, monitoring a bunch of *very* loud seniors, and the garment proved once again that it was catnip to women of all ages.

All things considered, I hadn't actually needed to unearth the jacket, as I had no reason to join the others on the village trip. I paid a great deal of money to have my blood coolers shipped directly to campus, disguised as energy drinks that I refused to share whenever asked. Beyond that, I was a collector of *expensive* personal items— objects of great cultural and historical significance. Not a thing in any of the little Solskinn shops, save perhaps some of the art in its gallery, fit the criteria.

But when Emma had volunteered to chaperone the seniors' trip to the village, I jumped on the bandwagon after her. Foster had passed around a sign-up sheet at the last meeting, and even though just about every other faculty member also volunteered, thus quashing the need for me, I had scribbled my name under Emma's anyway.

To this day, a week later, I still wasn't sure *why*.

Perhaps it stemmed from some warped desire to earn her approval. My vampiric companions of old would have scoffed at the idea, but this was *now*, and the wolf shifter was the last of the dominoes to fall at SIA, despite us getting along better lately. If asked outright, I would call it a tactic, another method to integrate myself seamlessly into the campus community, to win the approval that mattered the most.

Deeper down, beneath the sinew, the bone, the essence of my being, I suspected ulterior motives forced my hand.

Something darker aligned with this bizarre need to please her.

Her—Emma Kingsley, a brash, breathtaking American with an appetite of a man thrice her size, fond of shapeless knitwear and thick braids that trailed down her back, just begging me to wrap my fist around while I—

Well. Never mind.

We hadn't even been assigned to the same bus. It wasn't like she could watch me tell students to stop switching seats while we were in motion or fend off requests from the quartet of girls seated around me when they tried to stroke my jacket's smooth, soft exterior. After the last senior stepped off the bus, permitted to wander the shops and cafés of Solskinn's paltry high streets, I couldn't find the shifter anywhere—so, really, what had been the point of all this?

I'd politely declined Robert and his wife Phyllis's invitation to the market, and without a shopping list, I had drifted about aimlessly until Marte found me. Once she had her arm looped around mine, the morning was no longer my own. She dragged me from the bookstore to the post office, and we had at last arrived in a little hobby shop, a general store that had a random assortment of craft supplies and pointless knick-knacks.

Still, the front page of the paper had been illuminating, and Marte was rather pleasant to look at, her laugh like a high, tinkling bell. What had I to complain about? At least she wasn't a beautiful idiot, even if she was a shameless flirt.

"Let's talk about something less depressing," Marte whispered, the corners of her plump mouth quirking as she reached up and tugged some wool *thing* on my head. She retreated with a giggle, flashing a gap-toothed smile as I ducked down to appraise my reflection in the beer fridge's glass door. A thick cap sat atop my head, reaching all the way down to my eyebrows, made to look like the Norwegian flag, its price tag stabbing at the back of my neck.

"Marte, now I look like a tourist," I said with a chuckle, resisting the urge to yank the itchy thing off. "I want to blend in."

"Then you shouldn't have worn that jacket." She batted her lashes at me, then held up a hand. "Oh, wait—one more thing to make the outfit perfect."

Her unzipped sunset-orange jacket, complete with a fur-lined hood, fluttered as she darted into a nearby aisle, off to find some other horrendously kitsch trinket to add to my body. I waited obligingly, because that was the sort of man I had decided to be here, arms crossed and sporting a dopey grin.

As if her antics amused me.

As if I was the luckiest man in the village to be fawned over by a twenty-one-year-old nurse.

We had been at the back of the shop for quite some time now, finding ways to amuse ourselves, to pass the time before we had to escort students back to campus. The associate behind the front counter must have had all sorts of ideas, made more salacious by the way Marte giggled at the drop of a hat. Four narrow aisles overladen with junk separated us from the front door, and while I'd heard the little bell jingle a few times since we'd arrived, I had yet to see another shopper.

Perhaps Marte's constant titters made them think twice about perusing the rear of the shop.

I let out a bristly exhale, scratching at the thick wool cap currently boiling my head and debating just how much longer I wanted to indulge Marte's girlish shenanigans. As she rustled about down the other aisle, out of sight, I tugged at the neckline of my grey cardigan. While a touch too thick to wear under my leather jacket, I chose my outfits to suit the weather—to dress as a human might in this climate. The jacket had been too light, so I'd layered up, even if the cold hadn't bothered me since I turned. In fact, I barely felt any of it, easily enduring the cycle of intense snowfall, then a warmish day where it all melted, followed by more snow. We were due for another dusting tonight, and I could have gone streaking across campus, stark naked and perfectly comfortable. Cold didn't bother me.

Heat, on the other hand—I had become much more sensitive to heat after turning.

Emma's skin was like wildfire, yet, loath as I was to admit, I had come to crave its burn. Shifters had never affected me so physically before, and I had had my fair share of experience with them. Emma Kingsley was an ever-present flame amidst all this frost; I usually sensed her before I saw her, warmth whispering across my skin, reminding me, briefly, what it felt like to be alive.

In fact, I felt it now—her presence, her aura, wild and untouchable, a mere tease of the beast within.

I paused, frowning down at my sweater, finger still tucked under the neckline, as heat rolled over me, billowing like a creeping fog. Slowly, I looked up, and there she was, standing at the far end of the empty aisle in front of me, arms overflowing with spools of lush maroon yarn, the color pleasing to the eye.

Her entire *being* was pleasing to the eye, if one could overlook her rather untamed, uncouth personality. She stared back at me wearing a black fall coat with enormous gold buttons, still done up to her neck; she must have been sweltering under there. A quick perusal of her figure showed a pair of deliciously fitted jeans. Red-and-yellow striped socks climbed halfway up her calves, poking out from the top of her brown ankle boots. Her dirty-blonde mane was tossed up in a carefree bun, golden wisps sticking out every which way. No makeup, but that was the norm for this feisty little shifter.

She appeared to be giving me a once-over too, readjusting the six large spools in her arms, too heavy a weight for an ordinary human. Her lower lip dipped between her teeth briefly, though it soon stretched into a gorgeous, albeit incredulous smile when she—

Oh. She'd spotted the fucking ridiculous hat on top of my head. Wonderful. Heat stung my cheeks, and I couldn't help but wonder if I was, in fact, blushing—something I'd always thought impossible for my kind, but in Emma's presence, apparently not.

Her supple pink lips parted, as if drawing a breath, and I could have sworn my cold, dead heart *lurched* in anticipation of the trademark Kingsley snark. However, before she got a word out, before I could rip the damn cap off, Marte burst back onto the scene, bouncing to a halt in front of me, all fluttering lashes and beaming smiles.

"To complete the ensemble," she gushed before thrusting a pair of pink aviators on my face. I blinked in shock, my world suddenly neon, and found myself leaning back when she skimmed her hands down my chest in a way that suggested a deeper intimacy between us than I wanted.

Over the top of Marte's head, I spied Emma's smile drop, her cheeks flush, and in an instant, she was gone, scampering off like the hounds of Hell bayed at her heels. I opened and closed my mouth, swallowing the urge to call out to her, and then offered Marte a thin smile.

No matter how hard I tried, I couldn't shake Emma from my mind—but what else was new? Ever since the first dodgeball practice I forced myself to attend, another attempt to get the wolf off my back—an attempt that had actually been very enjoyable—a tentative civility reigned between us.

Dormitory patrols had been more amicable, the odd bit of pleasant conversation to be had before we went our separate ways, one in each building. We had even stood next to each other at a recent assembly, in the dark, off to the side, our backs to the padded wall as Foster rambled on in front of the sleepy student body.

Once, she'd let me refill her tea in the staffroom, the two of us at the round table working on our respective lesson plans, alone, burning the midnight oil yet both wide awake. My plans had been completed for months, but there was always fine-tuning to be done; meanwhile, Emma tackled hers week by week, an approach that would have given me hives had my body been capable of such distress.

Things had been *much* easier, and not because I had lost my cool and cornered her during homecoming dance preparations, something I wished I could take back, but because I had proven myself trustworthy when I didn't devour a blood-soaked Grace Flynn.

I knew for a fact Emma had checked on the girl several times after the mishap on the dodgeball court, but true to my word, I hadn't *touched* her. Sniffed her, sure. Fresh blood was far preferable to the cold canned shit I guzzled daily. Still, I was a vampire in control and had been for some time now—since I shirked the shackles of my past and *forced* myself to tame my baser instincts. I knew that once Emma saw I wasn't a threat to her people, the tide would finally shift between us.

And now this—this odd moment. Brief. Fleeting. Something I ought to shrug off, something I should probably just forget. But the way her smile vanished, eyes flitting between Marte and me. The color in her cheeks different, distinct, even beneath the neon, from the flush of anger I'd become accustomed to from her. It made my stomach drop and twist, tighten and knot to the point of discomfort.

"I don't think *pink* is my color," I muttered when I realized Marte was still staring up at me expectantly. She smirked, long, thin fingers coiling around my wrist.

"No, you're all man, aren't you?" The nurse tugged me toward the aisle from which she had dug up this neon nightmare. "Come on—I found a few other things for you to try on."

"I can hardly contain my excitement."

Marte giggled, dragging me around the corner and into the aisle as the bell over the shop's main door tolled again.

And just like that, the heat vanished. Emma was gone, and so was my patience. Forcing my thin smile in place, I tugged off the cap and removed the sunglasses, set them on the nearest overstocked shelf, and then politely excused myself.

Outside, beneath a hazy grey sky, students bustled about between the shops, their breath fogging, laughter echoing, feet stomping across a slushy cobblestone street. I looked left, then right, frowning. Emma was nowhere to be found.

But the knot in my stomach remained perfectly intact, tightening further, gutting me, with every step I took.

9

CALDER

"Well, isn't this festive."

I had no idea where on earth SIA found the budget for so many school dances in a single year, but just one short month after the homecoming gala, here we all were, back in the gymnasium for a Halloween dance.

Attendance was mandatory for *all* staff and students. The kitchen had prepared a holiday-appropriate feast for dinner, each dish named something ghoulish, and afterwards the students schlepped to their dorms to change into their costumes, then off to the gym courtesy of the underground tunnels. Given the sun had set shortly before three this afternoon and the entire campus was coated in ice, no one dared set foot outside until the walkways had been thoroughly salted.

Mercifully, faculty had not become indentured servants to the student council this time around. Those involved in the event preparations had been given a half day today, while come nightfall the staff were assigned chaperone duties until things petered off around eleven. I checked my watch as music whumped from the nearby speaker. A tight four and a half hours of crowd patrol to go. Thrilling.

Once more the gymnasium walls were covered in black, twinkling lights attached to the fabric, along with glow-in-the-dark skeleton decorations. Two fog machines kept the ground decidedly atmospheric, and homemade tombstones courtesy of Phyllis Howard's art students littered the seating area. At nine o'clock tonight, the Ghoul King and Queen would be announced, along with the winner of the best pumpkin carving, an activity currently underway in the far-left corner, supervised by Mason Ji, higher-level mathematics. Staff members also manned the dessert and drinks tables and patrolled the underground tunnels to ensure no hijinks took place. Costumed students filled the dance floor, and I'd already had *nine* inquiries as to the story behind my Armani suit.

Frankly, it looked good on me, and I had just accepted the most creative guess when asked. So far, Slenderman, whatever the fuck *that* was, had a sizeable lead.

"Calder?" James Foster waved me over from behind the drinks table, his punch ladle shaped like an inverted skull. Hands in my pockets, I obliged, strolling over with a curious smile, and then leaned in like I could barely hear him over the top-forties racket.

"Sir?"

"Have you seen Emma anywhere? I put her on crowd control with you."

"Uh, no." I accepted a plastic cup of green liquid, which smelled far too sweet for anyone over the age of ten to consume. "I'm afraid not, but I'm sure she's somewhere."

Just as I'd been sure the wolf shifter had been on campus all week, but I couldn't find her for the life of me. It seemed she had gone back to avoiding me at all costs, our three weeks of pleasantness for naught. While I tried not to dwell on it, I couldn't help my exasperation. For fuck's sake —it wasn't like I had *done* anything to offend her at the Solskinn hobby shop. Her sensibilities couldn't be so delicate that seeing me with another woman had sent her into a tizzy.

The idea that she was jealous of Marte's flirtations, of the way the nurse touched me, was cliché and, frankly, insulting to Emma. So, I ignored the option entirely, wondering if I had done something to inadvertently scare her off.

"Well, if you see her, send her my way," Foster remarked, dressed as a gaunt Frankenstein's monster. He scratched at the back of his neck, wearing a nervous grin. "We talked about the punch options for tonight at breakfast, and I just —I thought she might like to see what I eventually came up with. Witches' Brew—clever, no?"

At our first staff meeting, I'd noticed eye rolls whenever the principal deferred to Emma, and over time it had become clear that he had a mild infatuation with the shifter. I had no idea if Emma returned his obvious affections, but the idea always made my chest tight.

And hot.

Burning, searing, scalding hot.

I flashed a quick smile, then toasted him with my purple plastic cup. "Ingenious, sir. I tip my hat to your creativity."

Fuckwit.

As a cluster of students arrived, their faces painted and hair stuck out in all directions, I slipped away and ditched my cup of sugary brew in one of the many rubbish bins around the exterior of the space. Hands back in my pockets, I navigated the perimeter, falling on my natural gifts to blend into the shadows, to slip by unnoticed. If the homecoming dance suggested anything, the risqué moves wouldn't debut until a few hours in, when the sea of bouncing teens turned sweaty and bold, hands wandering, mouths touching—as if the rest of us hadn't a pair of eyes in our heads.

I could only imagine what the poor buggers patrolling the tunnels would stumble upon tonight; in shadowy corners and empty corridors, hormonal teens would play. And we were here to stop them, ever the wet blanket, the cold shower, the iron-fisted authority. Foster had once told me that SIA had a record of zero teen pregnancies since its opening almost twelve years ago, and he intended to maintain that so long as he was running things.

So, here I was, on the lookout for groping, grinding teens in a mass of jumping, laughing, screaming costumed creatures.

It was on my third loop around the gymnasium's outskirts that a familiar voice carried over the din.

"Don't you get it? I'm Mr. Holloway."

I staggered to a halt, gaze snapping in the direction of that distinctly feminine yet oddly commanding timbre, her tone both jovial and baiting. Emma stood near a cluster of empty tables, a squadron of tiny freshmen around her, dressed in a tweed jacket, a somewhat ill-fitting white dress shirt, particularly around the chest area, and a black tie. Her blonde mane had been dragged back, yet she had somehow managed to mimic my hair's volume across the top of her head. Suddenly, her gaze flitted to mine—and she smiled.

A smile that made my heart lurch again, then plummet straight into the pit of my stomach.

"Actually—" She peeled her lips back further, flashing a pair of noticeably sharp canines. "—I'm *vampire* Mr. Holloway."

My jaw tightened. My nostrils flared. And her audience giggled, moving in closer to inspect the fakes.

"Oh my god, he *totally* looks like a vampire sometimes," one of them quipped, the rest nodding along and beaming up at the too-smug shifter.

"Seriously—get a tan. I know we're in the arctic, but *seriously*."

What the fuck was this woman doing? Did she think she was being clever?

Was *this* why I hadn't seen her all week?

Fuming, I stalked over and cleared my throat behind Emma's little gathering. The few who glanced back paled and shuffled out of the way. Emma merely folded her arms, cocked her head to one side, and continued to sneer that fanged smile—a smile I wanted to forcibly wipe off her face.

Kiss off her face.

Just to taste her outrage.

"Miss Kingsley," I said tersely. "A word?"

She kicked up one shoulder and shook her head. "Uhh, no, I don't think that's—"

"*Now.*"

The remaining freshmen girls scattered, exchanging uncomfortable glances with one another as they slunk off. With the seas parted, I strode right up to the shifter, snatched her elbow, and then hauled her unceremoniously to the far-right corner of the gym, to the door that opened into the corridor we'd had our last little chat in. Emma put up a fight—I'd expect nothing less—but not with her full strength, not so much as to cause a scene as we skirted the edge of what was otherwise a successful secondary school dance. Instead, she stomped along beside me, failing to wrench her arm free when she tried, and stumbled briefly when I pushed her through the metal door with two glowing skeletal faces on it.

Inside, a pair of lip-locked seniors sprang apart—Madison and Abdullah, two of my higher history idiots—but they too scampered off when I barked at them to return to the gym. Heads down, they scuttled by, not daring to cast an eye to either Emma or myself in passing.

"Calder, get your fucking hand off—"

"Shut up, wolf," I snarled as I dragged her down the hall, headed straight for her office, for the privacy it offered. Emma's shoes skidded along, her feet planted but useless, and when I found her office unlocked, I thrust open the door, threw her inside, and slammed it shut behind us.

I even locked it, just for good measure.

This was my first experience in her private quarters, and its bookshelves cluttered with nets and deflated balls, her desk lined with empty water bottles and crumpled paper, clothing strewn over the two chairs tucked into the corner on either side of the door—none of it surprised me. Her mess didn't surprise me, but the return of that fucking smile had me seeing red.

"Have you *lost* your mind?" I hissed, hands in fists, exceedingly short nails slicing into my palms. Emma rolled her eyes, and it took every ounce of restraint in the goddamn *universe* not to grab her and pin her up against the door, and then—

"Can you tone it down a thousand notches? It's not like they know vampires are real. To them, vampires are just sexy bad boys on TV—"

"Have you been drinking?" I wrinkled my face at her. While I didn't smell liquor on her breath, no other explanation made sense for her absurd choice of costume.

"By drinking at a work function, I assume you're

referring to Foster's terrible witches' brew? Nope—avoided that like the plague." She crossed her arms and huffed at me. "Hard liquor, also a no, though I could do with a few shots so I could actually stomach being around you."

Oh my *god*. I threw my hands up and stormed the width of her small rectangular office space, stopping again in front of the door, still at a loss. All this hostility had to come from somewhere. The woman was ridiculous on a good day, but this was something else entirely. Maybe in September I would have let this attitude fly, but not after the last few weeks. Not after she let me fetch her fucking *tea*.

Emma's gaze followed me, jaw set until her little pink tongue wet her lips, the motion revealing her recent dental work.

"What the hell is in your mouth?" I demanded, fighting to keep my voice even—to not shout at her, to not storm over and *shake* her as I pried the truth from those lush lips.

"Oh, you like 'em?" Emma smiled, framing her face with her hands, going so far as to flutter her dark lashes. "I had them custom made and shipped here this week. Picked them up yesterday. Cost me like a grand to do it, but I wanted my costume to be *authentic*."

"I'm so flattered," I said tightly. She stroked a reverent finger down her left canine, that leering smile no longer reaching her eyes.

"Yeah, I can tell. Real touched, I'm sure, by my attention to detail."

"It's quite the improvement from your usual approach to things."

Her eyes widened a fraction, as if taken aback by my honesty, by the sting of each word, only to narrow to near slits when I grinned. We had very different styles when it came to organization and preparedness—and clearly she recognized mine as superior.

"You know," she started, less teasing, her tone sharper, "I got these off this website for vamp groupies—something I'm sure you're *very* familiar with."

"What?" My brows knitted. Groupies? When the fuck did I ever have groupies? Unless she was counting the handful of senior girls who liked to sit in my empty classroom during their study hall and chat with me about nonsense, but that was a stretch.

"Groupies," Emma remarked flatly, as if saying it again explained everything. "You know—*groupies*. It's your thing. I see it now. Your shtick."

I scoffed. "Don't be ridiculous."

"No, you manipulate everyone around you into seeing what you want. You *trick* them into liking you. *Oh*"—she pressed a delicate hand to her chest, a chest that was practically bursting out of her white button-down—"I'm just a bumbling little *Englishman*"—Holy *god* what was that accent? Was that supposed to be me?—"who likes to espouse Kant and Hobbes in everyday conversation because I'm so *cultured*, but what is *technology*? Someone show me how to use the Wi-Fi even though I'm perfectly capable and am just *pretending* to be a charming, inept moron."

I blinked back at her, torn between laughing at that atrocious English accent and parroting the exact same thing to her. Mind you, my American accent always sounded forced. Best take the high road. "*Really*, Emma."

She pointed an accusatory finger at me, her other hand in a tight fist. "You make them believe you're unassuming with this *shtick*."

"We all do it!" I shook my head, incredulous that she felt the need to lecture me about supernatural assimilation. "We all do it to survive in a human's world. I'm no different than you."

"We are *not* the same." Her lips parted as she sucked in a heated breath, her eyes screaming for me to go screw myself. Or maybe screw her, under the right circumstances. I swallowed hard, hating that even now, mid-fight, I noticed how perfectly fuckable Emma Kingsley was. Her personality was a nightmare, of course, but that mouth would look beautiful encircling my cock.

And the sheer smug satisfaction I'd get from making this obnoxious little shifter scream my name as she—

Well, never mind.

"Emma," I managed, forcing myself to speak and not just stare—not just stand there like a halfwit imagining what excellent hate sex we could have, "what the *fuck* is your problem with me? Beyond the obvious—I had started to think you weren't that petty a creature."

"I don't have a problem with you, Calder." Her jaw clenched briefly when I snorted. "I know exactly what you are, who you are. I'm the only person here who does—a sanctimonious, stuck-up, manipulative *dick*."

Rage darted through me, and I tore my gaze away from her face, from her flushed cheeks and her hateful eyes, only to notice something about the tweed jacket, with its sleeves rolled up around her wrists, like it was too long. How it sat funny on her, ill-fitted and too large, while her dress shirt was clearly too small, her tie looped in a poorly executed Windsor knot. But that jacket, the pattern, the leather patch on each elbow—

"Is that my *fucking* jacket?" It had gone missing from the staffroom a few days ago, but I thought I'd just misplaced it. Emma gestured down to herself with both hands.

"Authenticity."

"You're batshit crazy. Do you know that?" I seethed, ticking off each statement with my fingers. "Messy, loud, rude, paranoid—and *clinically insane.*"

And now that jacket was going to smell of her, no matter how many times I washed it. *Stink* of the lavender, of the woodsy yet floral sweetness of her natural scent.

"Cleary, I am insane, because I fell for your shit, Calder." Her voice caught when she said my name. "I don't have a problem with you. I have a problem with *me*. I was starting to think, you and me..."

The rose blush of her cheeks brightened, a sudden rush of blood blooming beneath her skin. Emma looked down and clapped her hands over her cheeks, whispering a barely audible *fuck* as she massaged them. Had this been any other day, any other situation, I might have been smirking when she straightened. I might have offered something suggestive, just to see the blush sharpen. Tonight, I merely glowered back, because this woman had well overstepped her bounds, and I was starting to think all this *was* because she had made assumptions when she walked in on Marte and me.

And that was just so painfully *boring*.

"But now I see," she said with a nod, words softer but no less venomous. "You want us all to think you're this stand-up guy, but I've *seen* you. Before the homecoming dance, slamming my head against the wall. Grabbing me tonight. I see you for what you are, and I don't know why I ignored it. The dodgeball match—jumping in, using how much the kids like you to lower my guard... To disarm me."

My jaw tightened, aching as I ground my teeth together —hating that she had hit the nail on the head. Hating that my ploy had been so obvious. I *had* done it to get on her good side, but it was as simple as that. I wasn't the malicious bastard she was making me out to be.

Not anymore, at least.

"You're delusional, Emma Kingsley," I muttered, arms crossed stiffly as I leaned back against the door. "Fucking delusional."

"Am I?" She took a step forward. "Did you make Grace fall too? Use your supersonic vamp speed to break her nose, tip her over, make my heart hurt so you could play the hero—"

"*That*"—I shot up, stalking toward her, not missing the way her body retreated but her feet stayed planted—"is too far. Using a student of mine against me is—"

"Well, it worked." Under the intense white light, I could have sworn her eyes glistened, but one blink and it was gone. "You got me, made me think—our conversations, walking with me for patrol duty, working on schedules together in the teachers' lounge, bonding with me over Foster's micromanaging. Congratulations. You fooled me."

"Shockingly, my world here, as small as it is, does not revolve around you, nor would I ever want it to."

Emma stepped back, nodding, briefly exposing her fanged tips as she smiled. "Yeah, don't worry. I see that now. I see where I fit in your grand scheme. You had to get me on your side so nobody's watching you anymore, right? If I'm just like all the rest of them, sucked into your crap, then you have *zero* accountability."

I pointed a rigid finger at her again. "*Delusional*."

Enough of this. I hated that she read me so well—but what I hated more was that she extrapolated, went on to see the absolute worst, the base desires of a con man. A vampire must have done irrevocable harm to her in the past, because I couldn't understand where all this hatred came from.

Unless it really was about her, about disappointment and frustration with herself.

Emma had seen a piece of the puzzle, but she had acted on her own prejudices and run right off the rails. What happened to the benefit of the doubt? In the vampire community, shifters were mindless animals—thick-headed and hot-tempered. Simpletons. I hadn't assumed that about *her* the moment I sensed her.

Not entirely, anyway.

I lifted my gaze back to her. Faintly, the distant pounding music broke through the terse silence hanging between us. There were a thousand things I could say, but why bother? The stubborn creature was likely set in her opinion of me. Any attempt to change that—reason, logic, a gentle tone and a kind smile—would read as further manipulation.

So, I settled for anger instead. I sunk into my own frustrations—with her, with the way our relationship had spiraled, with the fact that despite everything I still wanted to bend her over the desk—and then nodded to her lips.

"Take—those fucking *things*—out of your mouth."

She flicked her tongue over the sharpened tip of her right fang. "No."

"Take them out *right now*, Emma."

"*No.*"

"You did it," I snapped, arms out in surrender. "You ruffled my feathers. Got a rise out of me. Showed me how clever you think you are." Another few steps forward had her retreating, toned thighs nudging against her desk. "Maybe you want to make me lose my temper again by being a *petulant child*. Make the big bad vampire show you what *you* think are his true colors, so you can lot me in with all the rest of them. Prove your ridiculous theories true. Well done." I gave her three sarcastic claps. "You've pissed me right off. Take out—those—fangs."

She swallowed hard, her throat rippling. Over the dull roar of Halloween festivities a whole world away, her heart thundered. Just for a moment, I allowed myself to listen, to relish the steady thrum between my ears. Emma's pulse seldom raced, not even when she ran during dodgeball. I thought it intrusive to listen in on something so intimate, but I couldn't help it with her. Hearing it race, like she was gearing up for an attack—it brought me more satisfaction than I cared to admit.

Satisfaction that shot straight to hell when she motioned to the door, jutting her chin out, and met my eye. "Get the fuck out of my office."

Fine. She wanted to be like that—*fine*. Clearly a bit of manhandling was the only way to get through that thick skull of hers.

I crossed the space between us in an instant, relying on supernatural speed to take her by surprise. She cried out when I clamped down on her forearms, then thrust her back onto the desk, easily slipping between her thighs.

"Let *go*," Emma growled, teeth bared as she fought me, shoved me, ripped at my suit. The fabric might tear, but I wasn't going anywhere. In this form, the little wolf shifter was no match for my strength, and when her eyes flicked to mine, the edges of my mouth lifted, *daring* her to do something about that. Shift. Right here. Expose herself just as she sought to expose me.

Emma lifted her knees instead, attempting to push back across her desk, perhaps squirm out of reach. I bore down, threading a hand into her rat's nest of a bun at the crown of her head, her hair thick and unyielding when I wrenched back. Throat exposed, Emma exhaled sharply, eyes wide, lips parted. One hand shot to my wrist, trying in vain to rip it free, while the other beat ineffectually at my chest, barely a foot of space between us.

As I reached for her mouth with my free hand, my concentration fumbled, my cock swelling to life as it pressed against her, snug between her thighs.

Against her heat.

I blinked. What was I— Fangs. Right.

The left canine came off without a hitch, snapping free from her actual tooth and clattering noisily when I tossed it on the floor. I then curled my fingers around her throat, thumb over her racing pulse, the long, slender column still wrenched back in a lovely arch. Emma snarled, the sound lifting in pitch when I tore my hand from her hair and went for the right canine. It surrendered as easily as the left, held in place by some gum-like substance that clung to the fake fang, even as I crushed it between my thumb and forefinger and scattered the remains across the linoleum.

Emma pressed her trembling lips together, glaring up at me with gold-flecked eyes, cheeks flushed, chest heaving with every panting gasp. Slowly, I settled one hand on her desk, palm to the wood, fingers splayed as I took a few barely controlled breaths of my own. Fingernails, sharp as claws, sunk into my wrist, both her hands attempting to rip mine off her throat. I held firm, tighter even, her windpipe compressing beneath my fingertips. My jaw set, my gaze like flint—yet she refused to cower.

She fought, not physically, but with an inner strength that just wouldn't back down. I could see it in her eyes, in the wolf staring back.

This *woman* was so infuriating—and probably the only creature on the whole damn planet who could look this breathtaking under fluorescent light.

Fuck it.

No more arguing. No more sniping back and forth. No more thinly veiled threats.

No more imagining what magnificent hate sex we'd have.

No more.

With a snarl, I slammed my mouth to hers.

10

EMMA

I wasn't sure what had happened. Not really. Not in any way that made sense.

One moment we were fighting, literally clawing at each other, and then the next we were tussling with our mouths, a battle of wills, of tongue and teeth and lips, each of us desperate to come out on top.

Each of us desperate to *win*.

But how did you win this?

The second his mouth found mine, harsh and unforgiving, we had both lost this fight.

And, honestly, as he nipped at my lower lip, as I ripped the top three buttons of his shirt clean off, I'd thought we would have killed each other before it came to *this*.

My inner wolf was howling, keening some agonized, desperate cry—but not in anger. I'd never heard the sound before, pumping through my veins, slicing across every limb, boiling up my throat as my lips parted for him, as Calder's tongue flicked at mine. You'd think a vampire would taste of blood, of metal, of filthy iron, but Calder was like an arctic breeze, cold and crisp. Minty, the kind that scorched down your throat and burned with every breath. Like his hands, his kiss was the frozen wastes of the north, the bitter chill of winter.

And as I yanked at his wrist, to pull him off, to drag him closer, the vampire's frostbite made me feel *alive*.

When his hand finally left my throat, I knew it wasn't because of anything I'd done. Stronger than me. Taller than me. Broader, firmer, *harder*, in this form I couldn't *make* Calder do anything; heat flashed in my core, settling between my thighs. It wasn't the thought of helplessness that aroused me—it *couldn't* be—but perhaps the idea of a worthy adversary.

The alpha's line burned brighter, ran faster, fought harder than the rest of their pack.

No one had ever been able to outshine me, no one outside my immediate family.

Yet now, as our mouths clashed, two titans pounding against one another in a great eternal battle, Calder's hands had their way with me. Long, slender fingers smoothed under the jacket I'd stolen from him, then shoved it off my shoulders, ripped it down my arms. I let him, because I knew I couldn't stop him—and bit his tongue the next time it dipped into my mouth. The vampire snarled, returning the favor with a sharp snap at my lower lip. *Now* I tasted metal. Calder kissed me harder, sucking my lip as my pulse raced, as pain stung and pleasure teased. My heart stuttered. My stomach turned over and over, but not in that tight, awful way—not in the way it had when I spotted Calder and Marte in the village.

It somersaulted, churning the heat, spreading the flame.

He shredded my only *good* dress shirt, those deceptively delicate fingers raking down the front. Buttons rained between us, then peeled off, gently clattering on my desk. I rolled my shoulders back when he tore the rest of the starchy white cotton away, then heaved a gasp the moment his mouth finally left mine. His teeth scored my skin, dragging over my chin, down my throat to the well at its base.

Bright blues flickered up as he slowed and settled atop my cleavage. My nude bra offered great support, but it was probably the least sexy in my arsenal. The sneer I expected never came; Calder's tongue dipped between my breasts, his gaze never leaving mine, his hands questing lower.

I realized then—I was shaking.

But shaking with what?

Desire?

Fury?

Indignation? Frustration? *Need?*

I gritted my teeth, and the inner wolf whined when those slender fingers undid the button of my black slacks. I'd ironed them because Calder's trousers always had a very crisp, very prominent crease down the front. Authenticity. I really had tried.

Dressed like this, I had wanted to send a message— wanted him to know that I saw him. When I'd strolled around the corner of my favorite Solskinn hobby shop and spotted him wearing that fucking *ridiculous* hat, followed swiftly by neon-pink sunglasses courtesy of Nurse Marte—I *saw* him. It was all an act, his pleasantness, his inquisitiveness, his indulgent smiles with all the faculty.

Myself included.

Calder Holloway had been fooling all of us like a pro, and I'd started to fall for the charade.

Realizing that as I stood there with spools of wool in hand, looking like a total schlub while he was meticulously groomed as ever—it had been like a silver dagger straight to the heart. A splash of ice water.

He had played me.

He had been playing me for weeks.

So I chose to dress like him for the annual Halloween dance to show him that I knew—and that, to me, Calder was still the scariest predator in Solskinn.

Scarier than me, than the beast within, and scarier than whatever the hell was kidnapping villagers.

Calder the vampire—Calder the liar, the actor, the manipulator extraordinaire.

I saw him.

And now I was letting him *kiss* me.

Lick me.

Undress me.

How the fuck did we get here? When had I stopped fighting him, his hands skirting down my thighs, his mouth over my pebbled nipple, my bra cup wrenched aside?

And why didn't I want him to stop?

Clenching the stretchy fabric of my black slacks, Calder *yanked* it all away—his mouth, my pants, his ice-cold hands and their wanton caresses. An embarrassing little squeak slipped out when the movement dragged me to the edge of my desk, and I clutched at the brim, bracing as he wrenched my pants down. He hit a road bump with my faux-leather oxfords, something I'd bought when they came back into women's fashion a few years ago and hadn't worn since, perfect now for my costume, but they soon found a place on the floor alongside the rest of my tattered clothing.

Leaving me in nothing but my nude bra, black cotton panties, and white ankle socks.

And my tie. Black. Loosely knotted, because I hadn't put much effort into the Windsor knot—just to piss him off, an affront to his prim sensibilities. Now, it trailed down my skin, silky and smooth, and I couldn't help but wonder why he'd left it.

Calder straightened, expression neither warm nor inviting as his gaze swept over me. In fact, he still looked *pissed*, two seconds away from tearing my throat out, but even that couldn't dampen the wildfire blazing under my skin. We studied each other for a beat, logic screaming for me to kick him out—and my inner wolf whining low again, the kind she uttered when she wanted to *play*, to engage in something mischievous.

Had he done something? Drugged me?

Where were my hackles, and why weren't they up?

Why, when his hands jumped to his belt, did my stomach loop and my sex tighten, pleasurable tingles radiating out?

Maybe we needed this. Maybe... this would solve everything.

I bit the insides of my cheeks, swallowing a snort as he unbuckled his belt and ripped down his fly. *Yeah, right.* Like sex ever fixed anything.

Yet there I stayed, clinging to the edge of my desk, legs still splayed open from when he'd forced himself between them. While I tensed when he stalked back to me, my breath hitching when he cupped me through my panties, I didn't retreat. I didn't push him away.

Most of all, I didn't run.

I'd just stopped fighting.

For now.

My eyes threatened to flutter closed as he massaged me, palming my clit, working my slickness through the cotton. Calder hissed, gripping me harder suddenly, his eyes hooded, obscured beneath obsidian lashes.

"You are fire," he growled, "you *infuriating* creature."

I prided myself for seldom being at a loss for words around Calder Holloway, but when those bright blues darted back to mine, I had nothing. Heat flashed in my cheeks at the thought of whispering something back, but I couldn't play that game. I couldn't talk dirty to save my life, not without dissolving into a puddle of giggles, so I went for the next best thing: snark.

"So, what," I muttered, breath quickening when his need brushed up against my thigh, barely contained, straining against his black briefs, "you're telling me a dead man can actually get it up?"

Calder stilled, a finger hooked under the soaked fabric of my panties. In an instant, his anger dissipated, replaced by something smug, something dark and dangerous— something that told me I had poked the bear one too many times. My inner wolf had fallen silent, as if holding her breath right alongside me.

"Oh, *Emma*, of course," Calder rumbled, his voice gravelly and deep, its timbre vibrating in my marrow. In a flash, too quick for me to track, his hand snapped from my swollen sex to my barely intact bun. I grabbed at his jacket, twisting the expensive material when he wrenched my head back again, neck exposed. Smirking, the vampire trailed his nose along the arc, lips faintly parted as he breathed me in. A shudder rippled down my spine as I *made* myself watch, made myself remember the gleam in his eye when he cocked his head to the side, then flashed two sharp, very real fangs up at me. "A dead man can *always* get it up—with the right persuasion."

I exhaled a breathy cry when those fangs sunk into me, breaking my toughened shifter skin, piercing my neck. My first thought was the pain, the agony of a predator ripping into my throat, but there was only *euphoria*. Sweet heat flooded my veins. Lips parted, breath ragged, my vision shifted in and out of focus as the most intense climax of my life ricocheted off every part of me. Tingling in my toes. Looping in my core. Burning in my chest. Watering in my mouth. It left me light-headed, startled —elated.

Trembling hands reached up for him, but I couldn't find my grip, fingers splayed across his still-clothed frame. Warmth trickled down my throat, pooled between my breasts, soaked through my bra. Logically, I knew what he was doing. *Physically*, I couldn't grasp it. Couldn't comprehend. Couldn't fathom the sheer *pleasure* of his bite—

Just as swiftly as it had started, the onslaught of pure ecstasy vanished when Calder pulled away. A faint prick of pain, like the first prick of a needle, and it was all over. Gasping, I skimmed my chest, my neck, and my hands came back bloody. But the euphoria still tingled between my thighs, faintly, a distant memory of what had just happened. Wide-eyed and gawking, shaken to my very core and aroused as fuck, I met Calder's eye. He smirked, icy fingertips pressed to my bare thighs, his body like marble situated between them.

"Why do you think we have groupies, darling?"

A rush of anger brought me back to, well, *me*.

His bite—the fucker *had* drugged me.

My features twisted in contempt, allowing him a split second to prepare for when I shoved at his chest. Calder caught my wrists as he stumbled back, dragging me with him, hauling me off the desk. My legs wobbled, and I swayed, unsteady on my own two feet as my inner wolf emitted another long, low whine. Less desperate this time, less eager for a romp, she too must have felt the effects of Calder's... attentions.

I rotated my wrists to break his hold, only to have him surge forward and toss me hard to the right. The concrete wall broke my fall, and I pushed myself up it, hating how hard my breath fell, like I'd just jogged a ten-mile loop in my wolf form. Calder peered down at me, hands loose at his sides, expression unreadable. A quick wipe of my neck told me the bite marks had already disappeared, healed in the blink of an eye.

Thank goodness. Rumor had it that a vampire's bite slowed a shifter's healing process; it was one of the reasons they were so dangerous.

But my body had taken his bite, his venom, and molded it into something so exquisite that I still didn't understand it.

That I still ached for it.

And he knew it too. The smirk resurfaced, my blood on his mouth, his chin, his cheeks, and he strolled toward me, nudging down the elastic band of his black boxer briefs. I tried to hold his stare, chin lifted defiantly, heart pounding, but I couldn't help sneaking a peek.

Sneaking a peek at what was a very hard, very full, very impressive cock.

Another rumor disproven. Vampires could, in fact, get it up—in all its thick glory, a smattering of black hairs at its base, a pair of veins curving around it, a glistening drop on its smooth head.

He wants this just as bad as I do.

I pressed further against the wall, fully aware that it made no difference, then offered a smirk of my own. And Calder *knew*—he knew that I knew, that I still saw him. The sharp line of his jaw, the irritation, the frustration, didn't reach his eyes anymore, and it certainly didn't reach his dick.

My smirk, however, reached something. Touched a nerve—a raw, frayed nerve, a live wire that triggered him just as his smirks always did me. Because the way he stormed over, expression stony, cock out like a sword leading the charge, and then hoisted me up, this wasn't a seduction. This wasn't a dance between lovers. As I wrapped my arms around his neck, speared my fingers into his hair, I recognized that it wasn't sweet, indulgent, or tentative like so many first-time dalliances.

And thank fuck for that. Calder's mask was indulgent, his public persona sweet. I wanted neither. I wanted his tongue dragging up the nape of my neck, sweeping the blood away. I wanted his groan as he did it, the hushed, gravelly hum of his vocal cords as he delighted in the taste of me.

And, while it stung, while it startled, I *needed* the way he ripped my panties to the side and thrust unceremoniously into me. No real foreplay—just a bite disguised as an orgasm, and a kiss that had me wet. Our noises rose in unison, in time with his body lifting into mine, hips colliding, bucking, rolling together. I fisted both hands in his hair, twisting as my sex tightened around the thick intrusion.

Curiously, my inner wolf had fallen silent.

And I had the sudden and undesirable urge to bite him back—to peel aside his fancy black suit and sink my teeth into the meat of Calder's muscular shoulder.

To mark him.

Which was insane.

If I was going to *mark* anyone, it would be my mate—my

fated mate, preferably, and I had skipped right out of Maine to avoid all of that nonsense.

So, I arched my back when he laved his tongue over the blood smeared across my cleavage. I relished the feeling of fullness, the sensation of having proper sex for the first time in years.

The weight of a man who could handle me.

Maybe even overpower me.

Still lapping at the spilled blood, a notion that ought to make my stomach roil, Calder bucked his hips hard against me. While he had given me a few precious moments to adjust to him, to accommodate his girth, there would be no more wasted seconds. No slow burn. No easy ascent into frenzied chaos. He took me hard and fast, pounding into me, hissing, groaning against my skin, his growls mirroring mine as I dragged my teeth along that rugged jawline, that razor-sharp cheekbone.

He kissed me like he wanted to hurt me, and quickly learned that I gave as good as I got. Calder might have set a brutal pace, slamming me into the wall like he was desperate to plow straight through it, but I was still a wolf. My kiss could bite. It could dominate.

I could be wild.

And I tasted my savagery when his lip split, when my teeth nicked his tongue.

When I finally twisted so viciously in those midnight-black locks that Calder's hands stopped bruising my thighs and started bruising my wrists, yanking them out of his hair and pinning them against the wall. As if sensing I couldn't be broken, emboldened by my soft moans, my muffled cries, he bucked harder, burying himself inside me, right down to the hilt with every brutal thrust.

All the while, my first true climax of the night clawed ever closer.

But I didn't want to come like this.

I wanted to do it on top of him, with Calder splayed out on my desk, my hands on his chest. Naked—or, just as naked as me—while I rode him, while my experienced fingers danced over my clit until I *howled*.

"S-so, is this how you vamps did it?" I whispered, snapping at his earlobe, sinking my teeth into his flesh. He wrenched his head out of reach with a snarl, and I bit my lip to keep from smiling too brightly. The look in his eye, the adjustment of his angle to plunge deeper, told me it really, truly *bothered* him that I could hurt him, potentially mar his moon-kissed skin.

"Did what?" he hissed, grinding my wrists against the wall, his thrusts becoming shallower, faster, barely pulling out as the symphony of slapping skin, of moaning, groaning supernatural creatures intensified. I sucked in a quick breath, my limbs clenching, the fire spreading.

"How you got your sex-god status in pop culture," I clarified, forcing myself to sound alert yet unfazed, like I had gloriously rough sex on the daily, like Calder Holloway was old news. "By some luck of the draw chemical r-reaction in your—*ah*—bite?"

That was a close one; pleasure surged, threatening to spill over and drown me. Fortunately, I *sometimes* had a hint of self-control. Sometimes.

Calder wore a concerning sort of grin as he nipped at my neck, my chin, my lips, the tip of my nose. "You think I can't make you come, Emma?"

I lifted a challenging eyebrow. "Fuck you."

He chuckled softly, slowing everything to a grinding halt.

Pleasure roiled up from my core, my nipples painfully tight pearls in need of some attention, the blood-soaked bra suddenly too constricting. As he started to rock his hips, rolling them rather than pumping frantically, the pleasure became languid, like lava oozing down a volcano's face rather than a white-hot blaze charring a grassy plain. I swallowed hard, fighting to keep my eyes open, to not succumb to the delicious burn—to not come undone in his arms.

Not while he was wearing that stupid grin.

"Ah, ah, ah," he murmured, his hand drifting down my raised arm, slowly, lazily, not stopping until it clutched my chin hard enough to make me gasp. His fingers slipped between my parted lips, toying with them, stroking my tongue, pumping in and out. I let him do it, half enjoying the salaciousness of it, half waiting for the right moment. Calder added a third finger, openly testing me. "The correct terminology is fuck *me*, Mr. Holloway, preferably with a *please* somewhere in there—*fuck*!"

I seized the moment when it presented itself and clamped down on those bold fingers as hard as I could, until I tasted blood. Calder inhaled sharply, features contorted with rage, and ripped his hand away. Dark crimson-red blood spilled across his fingers, and I tipped my head back, wearing a feral grin of my own.

"Oh, *please*," I cooed. "Fuck *me*, Mr. Holloway." I clenched around him, not missing the way his eye twitched when I did it again, harder this time, pleasure blooming, and then twirled a loose blonde lock around my finger. "There. Did I do it right?"

Calder responded by pushing off the wall and dumping me back on my desk, all the while wearing a dark, determined smile that made my stomach loop. He then pulled out and flipped me over, moving so fast, so sure, that the best I could do was plant my socked feet on the floor for stability—all the while bent over my own fucking desk, a vampire's rigid shaft against my ass, my cheek pressed to the cool wood.

But only just long enough for me to catch my breath. Moments later, the tie I'd all but forgotten about came back into play, with Calder wrapping it around his fist and wrenching it up. Smooth, silky fabric dug into my throat, and I shot upright with it to keep from choking, forced flush against him, my back fitting snugly to his still-clothed chest. I arched, needing to break the physical contact, teeth gritted as I lifted my chin up and away.

His lips danced along my throat, the threat of another bite ever present with each brush of fang. Calder dragged an open-mouthed kiss across my jaw, up to my ear. My skin prickled in response, to the frost of his touch, a sharp, wonderful contrast to the fire burning in my belly.

My hands—I had no idea what to do with them. Fight. Grab. Push, pull. I knew what I *should* do with them: gouge his eyes with my thumbs. Instead, my fingers twisted into his jacket, my head thrown back against his shoulder, my breath falling harder now with the tie tight around my windpipe.

Calder's hands, meanwhile, had purpose. The one kept me restrained, leashed.

And the other ghosted down my body, sliding a finger between the valley of my breasts, plucking at the bloodstained bra, then down, down, down, until—

"*No.*" I bucked when he yanked my panties down my thighs—when his fingers found my clit, latching onto the little bundle of nerves with unsettling precision. A moan slipped out, forced out, as he massaged me, breathing life back into the pleasurable embers in my core, working me like he had done it a thousand times before. Skilled fingers pinched and plucked and swept across, his thumb adding variety to the routine, making me twitch in his arms. He pulled back on the tie when I squirmed, when I protested, attacking his immovable forearm uselessly.

I fought because I knew I should. Because he had me on a leash. Because he was a vampire proving he could have me, use me—that he could play me all over again.

But my *god*, if he stopped, I might die.

"Tell me again," he murmured in my ear. "Tell me it's just the bite."

"Fuck you—" My eyes widened, then clenched shut as he nudged back into me, filling my slick channel inch by agonizing inch. The fullness nearly sent me over the edge, but no more than his dark little chuckle, the way he licked and nibbled the shell of my ear.

The way his fingers never stopped, never faltered, playing me like I was his instrument—tuning me, drawing the strings tighter, tighter, *tighter*...

Until I snapped.

I clapped a hand over my mouth to keep from crying out, because fuck him if he thought he deserved that kind of praise. The wildfire went rogue, scorching a path through every limb, my body trembling, my mind blissfully empty. No more thoughts, no more worries—just relentless pleasure that threatened to drown me, that consumed every fiber of my being.

My knees gave out, and Calder pressed me up against the desk, the fingers drenched in my arousal now working their way under my bra to toy with my nipple. He offered no reprieve around my neck, tie taut as ever, his mouth on my throat as he started to rock again. Every pump of his hips prolonged my climax, dragged it out as I moaned behind tightly sealed lips, as my eyes prickled with unshed tears. My body clung to him, to the way he hit that little sweet spot inside the harder his thrusts became, bucking up against me, our collision jolting, making my teeth chatter if I let it.

And I couldn't let it.

I couldn't let *any* of it—but I already had. We were a runaway freight train, and the only way to finally stop was to crash.

"Now remember, Miss Kingsley," Calder growled. His hand snapped around my chin, wrenching my head sharper to the right, my neck twisting in protest as his thrusts quickened. "No *howling*."

I blinked. No howling?

Wait.

I sucked in a few ragged gasps, the realization striking with startling ferocity. "Wait, no, don't do it again—"

The rest of the world fell away when he sunk those canines in, diving home with a snarl, his arm locking around my waist like a vise. Distantly, I was aware that we'd toppled forward, that my hands had caught us, braced on the desk—but it wasn't a conscious decision on my part, not when pleasure so fucking *intense* flooded my system. It drowned out my racing heart, silenced my inner wolf. Calder's savage thrusts faded to the background; I barely felt his hand clamp over my mouth, muffling what *sounded* like me, but couldn't possibly *be* me. I didn't make those noises. I didn't whine and cry and moan with wild abandon.

And I certainly would never, ever, *ever* whimper his name.

Eyes shut, open, I couldn't tell anymore. My first true climax of the night had created a blissful black behind my lids, and now the darkness had lifted to screaming color.

Flashes of *everything*, so long as he kept those fangs buried in my neck.

Nirvana. Pure bliss.

A high I never wanted to come down from, one long orgasm that struck every molecule in my body. I felt it in my individual strands of hair. My eyelashes. Reality faltered, splintered, peeled away the longer it went on, to the point where I wasn't sure if I was alive or dead.

And I didn't care.

Until he stopped. Until the vampire ripped his mouth away, blood splattering across my desk, pouring down my chest. Then, it all came crashing back, slamming into me as vicious as Calder's final thrust. He doubled over with a groan, forcing me down with him, trembling. His cock pulsed once, twice, and he hissed as he raked his teeth across my shoulder.

I shoved at his wrist, and he peeled his hand from my mouth. My first true breath in who knows how long was glorious—the pleasant ache in my body, too, the soreness between my thighs. Pulse still racing, I pillowed my forehead on both arms and just breathed.

Wondering when the fuck he'd ripped my bra strap.

And why he was still buried deep inside of me, one hand planted on the desk, the other loosely grasping the back of my neck.

Slowly, the gravity of the situation struck. As I lay there, chasing my breath, I wanted to hate myself. I wanted to say that I'd fallen for his bullshit again.

But I had done this, *let* it all happen, when Calder was just being himself—so what did that say about me?

"Get out," I muttered, pushing back at him weakly. For the first time since he had walked into my office, Calder did as he was told, easing out of me, his footfalls heavy as he stepped back. I melted over my desk, every muscle relaxing, and waited for the guilt—for the anger, for the regret, for the self-loathing.

Not one made an appearance.

Mostly, I just wanted to shower, then crawl into bed and sleep until sunrise tomorrow.

Behind me, Calder righted himself, zipper hissing and buckle clinking. I didn't bother to look back, eyes closed, breath deep and even, not until he opened the door and left without a word. It was then the outside world trickled in, a rush of muffled music sounding from down the hallway. I shot up, panicked, and launched myself at the door just as it started to drift shut on its own. It slammed in place, and I bolted it with shaky fingers, then slid down to the floor.

The Halloween dance. Nearly the entire school, all its faculty and students, was a mere thirty feet away.

And I'd just had *sex* in my office.

I brushed at my neck, nose wrinkled at the still-warm blood. The puncture marks had healed over, but I looked like a gunshot victim. Red droplets peppered my desk, atop which sat Calder's jacket. After all that fuss, he had left it behind.

"Oh my *god*." I closed my eyes tight, then thumped my head back against the door. Distantly, students screamed at the song change, something peppy and upbeat. I could imagine them jumping, hands in the air, smiling and laughing. Would Calder stay, chaperone extraordinaire, and pretend nothing had happened? Would he slip out the side door and into the night? Take to the tunnels?

With a weary sigh, I looked at my discarded clothing, my shredded dress shirt and crumpled slacks. Fortunately, I kept a change of clothes in my office at all times. While nothing more than my usual SIA polo and track pants, it would have to do. I couldn't go out there looking like this—bloody, ravaged.

High from a vampire's bite.

"Fuck."

Never in my entire career, in my entire *life*, had I behaved so unprofessionally.

Sex in my office. With a vampire. Thirty feet away from my friends, colleagues, *boss*, and pupils.

I clenched my eyes shut again, groaning. What the hell had I just done?

NOVEMBER

11

EMMA

At the heavy *thunk* of the tunnel door falling shut, followed by the *click, click, click* of a slow, familiar stride, I huffed and finished tying off the last of the badminton nets, longing for the days when Calder Holloway only waltzed into my gymnasium because he *had* to.

I should have expected this. After spending the week avoiding eye contact and leaving conversations whenever he joined them, it shouldn't surprise me that he had finally sought me out on my own turf, if only to give me another lecture about making our professional existence on the SIA campus difficult.

Or something equally annoying.

What had happened at the Halloween dance... It couldn't happen again, and I couldn't face the vampire without experiencing the unpleasant burn of shame, embarrassment, and self-loathing, so my tactic had been to avoid him. Hard. I stopped eating my meals in the dining hall, taking them in my office or my suite instead. I spent more time in the dog kennel, visiting the dogs after hours, working more intensely with the seniors involved in the program, even if, two months in, they no longer needed my guidance. I'd already knitted two sweaters, finished my lesson plans from now until March, and had read four paperbacks.

In a week. Five measly days. Calder had now come to find me on the sixth, and as he crossed from the tile to the vinyl, entering the gym unannounced, I knew I couldn't avoid him any longer.

Well. I *could*. I could beeline to my office. Lock myself in one of the storage rooms. Go outside and lose him in the blizzard. You know—things totally sane shifters do when approached by a vampire they'd fucked.

Instead, I finished securing the badminton net. I had a class of freshmen first period of the day, and we were starting our badminton unit in about—I checked my watch, back still to Calder as he continued his leisurely approach— nine and a half minutes. Because even if I ran, Calder could find me; the academy's campus was a finite space, and all its dark, shadowy corners did nothing to hide me from a vampire.

Besides, I couldn't help but feel a *little* curious about what he wanted. The hairs on the back of my neck stood; he couldn't have been more than five feet out, silent save for his shoes, which I knew he did on purpose. What could he possibly want to say to me now, when we hadn't had more than two seconds of eye contact in five days?

Had he come to threaten me? Order me to keep quiet about our romp in my office?

I rolled my eyes and stepped back from the post, excess white cord trailing down its side, the knot holding. Like I would ever tell a soul that I had slept with a vampire. Seriously.

When the footsteps finally stopped, I glanced over my

shoulder nonchalantly, features schooled as I took in the three-piece suit—navy tie, jacket and slacks; white dress shirt with a crisp collar; a grey vest with little darker grey buttons. Impeccably tailored, as always. I faced forward again, hoping that some sense of common decency stopped him from tuning in to my racing heart.

"What?"

"A very good morning to you too, Miss Kingsley," he crooned. "Less than six hours of sunlight today—or, there would be without the, uh, blizzard."

I crossed my arms and half turned back, figuring it would seem petty if I didn't at least *glance* at his gorgeous, smug face. "Cool. What do you want?"

Calder slipped his hands in his pockets. "I have a free block right now. Thought we could chat."

"Why?"

"Because you've been avoiding me—quite adeptly, I might add."

"So?"

His cheeks dimpled, even though he seemed to be fighting back a smile. "*So?*"

"So, you know, awkward silence and outright avoidance." I shrugged, forcing my gaze up—because if I didn't, I would look down, down to where his hands were, and I'd remember what was resting between them, how it had stretched me, filled me, pleasured me. "Isn't that better?"

Calder's dark brows lifted. "I'm sorry... Are we thirteen years old?"

My cheeks flushed. "Look, just—"

"I want to do it again."

I gawked at him, mouth hanging open, heat flashing in my belly. The vampire remained annoyingly unreadable, and I hastily closed my gaping mouth, then cleared my throat.

"You want to..." I cleared my throat a second time when my voice snagged, heart going a mile a minute and brain totally blank. "Again. You want to—again. What? *Why*?"

"Because," Calder smirked, his eyes practically glittering, "I think we have *exceptional* hate sex."

Hate sex. I wrinkled my nose at the term, even if it was, well, accurate. At no point since the encounter had I been harboring any sense of desperate longing for the vampire; the sex hadn't changed much between us, though I *was* inexplicably less angry with him.

And just a hint more physically attracted to him.

Those fingers, that mouth, that *body*—

I shook my head and made my way over to the row of sixteen rackets I'd already set out. "You clearly don't like me."

But you want to have sex with me.

"We don't have to like each other to—*enjoy* ourselves." His whisper warmed my ear, breath tickling my skin, and I lifted a shoulder to push him back. Having materialized out of nowhere by my side, Calder fiddled with the end of my braid, towering over me, smelling of sandalwood and risk. He exhaled softly, then gave my plait a sharp tug. "Everything's on the table now, isn't it? I'm an ass, and you're a waking nightmare I can't escape—"

I whirled around, snapping my hair out of reach, and held up a hand. "Okay, easy."

Calder grinned, and I found myself itching to do the same. I pressed my lips together instead, arms crossed.

"We both know the truth," he murmured. "You said it yourself. You see me—whatever. Isn't this preferable to how it was before?"

We barely knew each other. The truth—right now, it was all surface level, and what little I could glean from his files. Still, I knew he was playing everyone else. Maybe that was enough.

As we faced off, I kept waiting for my inner wolf to growl. While usually *very* responsive to people who drove me crazy, she went strangely mute around Calder.

Unless we were hate sexing. Then she wouldn't shut up.

My heart leapt into my throat when he reached for me, and I batted his hand away as the heat started to rise under my collar. "Calder, I have a class in like five minutes."

"Plenty of time..." His grin sharpened just before he slammed his mouth to mine, catching me off guard again with another one of those breathtaking, toe-curling, hard-as-nails kisses. One cold hand cupping my face, the other smoothing around my hip, Calder marched us backward, over a pair of rackets that clattered noisily underfoot, and into the wall. My stomach looped, and what I could only assume now was *hell*fire flickered to life as I kissed him back, lips parted, teeth bared.

At first, I shoved at his shoulders, moaning in protest, but then his scent, his mouth, his firm body and rough hands—well, they were more persuasive than I cared to admit. More thrilling. More intoxicating. Slowly, I molded to him, conforming to the hard lines, arching up, hands buried in his hair.

Calder was right. I didn't have to *like* him as a person to do this. I could use him for pleasure, for a little bit of fun during the long dark days of winter—or until it wasn't fun anymore.

With a soft growl that reverberated in his broad chest, Calder hoisted me up and settled between my thighs, grinding his hips. I opened wider, moaning when his hand slipped between us to rub me through my track pants. As the base of his palm did its good work, stoking the hellfire, Calder tore his mouth from mine, nostrils flared as he seemed to fight his own private battle for self-control.

"This really is the most godawful outfit," he rasped, porcelain cheeks speckled pink, his bright blues stormy as they flicked down to my polo. "Do they *make* you wear it, or...?"

Panting, I glared. "You know, you're a thousand percent more tolerable when you don't speak."

"You sure?" He eased his hand under my track pants. "I seem to recall you *like* being spoken to when—"

I dragged his mouth back to mine, kissing him with just enough bite that he snarled and snapped my underwear's waistband. *Good. Be annoyed.* The vampire was definitely more fun when irritated.

Actually, he was the most fun when he was doing—*that.* My eyes fluttered closed as he smoothed his hand between my thighs, cupping my sex, massaging the sudden slickness, then nudged one long finger inside me. My fingers twisted in his hair at the slight twinge of pain, one that bloomed into something hot and heady as he stroked my inner walls. Ankles locked on the small of his back, I dug my heels in and moaned, clenching around him. Keeping me pinned in place with his solid frame, like a rugged marble statue, Calder brought his free hand up to my face, cupping my cheek, the tip of his thumb edging around the corner of my mouth—

He froze suddenly, hands stilling, mouth retreating.

"W-what?" My hands settle on his shoulders, heart hammering, breath racing. "What's wrong?"

With an ear toward the closed doors across the gym, the ones that opened into the corridor with the tunnel entryway, the weights studio, and the change rooms, Calder fell silent for a few moments before disengaging completely. He set me back on the ground, none too gently, and retreated a good ten feet, jaw set, hands clasped behind his back.

Students. I heard them a moment later, the very faint clamor of echoey chatter in the concrete tunnels leading up to the building. My first-period freshmen. Sure, I had to strain to hear them, but even if they'd been closer, I would have missed the warning completely.

Kissing Calder made me reckless, made me forget all the boundaries I put up around myself in a *school*, an institution with underaged kids, minors. If we were going to do this, whatever the hell *this* even was, then we couldn't do it out in the open. I pressed my palms to my flushed cheeks, trying to rub out the color.

A near impossible task when Calder adjusted his tented pants with a scowl.

"Why?" I asked, my voice catching. He looked up sharply, and I expected a smirk, a sneer, a suggestive comment that would make my blushes worse. Instead, he slid his hands into his pockets and shook his head, expression grim.

"Because pretending is exhausting," he remarked tightly, "even for me. When I'm fucking you, I don't have to pretend."

Well then. That was refreshingly honest. I stared at him for a moment, swallowing hard, and nodded. "Okay."

Calder offered a barely discernible nod of his own. "Okay."

And then, in the blink of an eye, he vanished. I flinched, then inhaled sharply at the sudden gust of frozen air screaming in through the emergency exit door. When it wouldn't swing closed, I started toward it, only to pause when the vampire forced it shut from the other side.

"Oh my god." I smoothed both hands over my hair, down my fat, frizzy braid. Just outside the main gymnasium, noisy freshmen moved from the tunnel to the small entry corridor, the crowd splitting between the two change rooms like always. Their presence was thunderous now, even with metal and concrete separating us, their conversations and laughter a chilling reminder of how close we had come to getting caught.

Of how unprofessionally I'd acted—*again*.

"Okay," I whispered, headed off to triple-check the badminton nets before the start of class. Palms clammy. Throat tight. Panties damp.

And my inner wolf whining suddenly, loudly, in Calder's absence.

12

EMMA

Dear Bean,

Happy Thanksgiving! The gang's all here—wishing you were too. It's so ridiculous that that school of yours wouldn't give you the time off to fly home and be with your family.

Love you!

Mom

Seated at the end of my bed, pantyhose-clad legs crossed at the ankles, laptop on my knees, I stared at photos of the pack's Thanksgiving celebrations. It was the same as always: they had rented a local rec hall and filled it with wolves and food and harvest decorations and general obnoxious merriment.

Mom would have made her pumpkin pie, a recipe she swore had been passed down through the women in her family but really came from a cookbook we got her for Christmas as kids. My brothers would have gotten drunk and arm-wrestled. They'd have played with the pups, maybe made a scene—all in good fun, of course. And my dad—my dad would have stood up at the end of the night and made the annual alpha Thanksgiving toast. Tears would have been shed. Glasses would have been raised.

I used to play the piano on Thanksgiving, accompanying the pack's choir as they belted out tunes that got raunchier and more incoherent with every drink. The food was *everything*, a pack legend, with every family unit contributing something to the feast. It was the best day of the year for the pack as a whole, one without gossip and bickering and, most of the time, matchmaking.

I loved Thanksgiving with the pack.

But as I studied the photos Mom had sent me, probably from the rec hall mid-celebration, too tipsy to write one of her usual mammoth emails, I just felt... hollow. *Gang's all here*. It screamed subtext.

Look at what you're missing.

Another attempt to lure me back to Maine with the promise of a wholesome family experience.

I pressed my lips together tightly, my inner wolf whimpering somewhere deep inside, her cries soft and desolate, as I continued to scroll through the images. My pack dancing, singing, toasting. My brothers and cousins, laughing. My parents holding each other, the alpha pair, fated mates idolized by all members of the pack. My dad's kickoff toast, the whole clan watching, utterly transfixed. Beyond his deep, booming voice, the recreation hall would have been silent enough to hear a pin drop.

She must not know. There was no way my mom could have known about the fight dad and I had—about the horrible things he said to me just before I left for Norway.

Don't come back.

You aren't my daughter if you walk out that door.

You're *selfish*, Emma.

The pack is *your* responsibility.

I hate you. He hadn't come right out and said it, but the look in his eye that day was unlike anything I had ever seen. As the alpha's heir, walking away to pursue my own goals, my own dreams, had been the ultimate betrayal to a wolf as traditional as my dad. At this point in my life, I was supposed to be married with one heir popped out, a spare on the way.

I hadn't wanted that. I still didn't.

But looking at photos of my family, my *real* family, made my heart ache. It stole the breath right out of me, made me unable to speak, to move. Everything felt so heavy, my body weighed down with guilt, with grief. Most of the time I could suppress it. I could do my job, enjoy my students, *live* in this spectacular environment as a real wolf should.

It was always harder during the holidays.

It was harder to remember why I had thrown my whole life away, when I could have been there, in that rec hall, surrounded by my pack.

Blinking hard, I slammed my laptop shut and tossed it onto the bed. For the first time in a long time, I had actually been on track to be *early* to a school function. I'd been ready for the last hour, rocking a pair of grey stockings and the second of two formalwear dresses I owned: black with elbow-length sleeves, fitted, a sweetheart neckline and a hem that cut off just above my knees, a two-inch slit in the back. A long side braid trailed over my shoulder, tied off with a maroon bow. My lone pair of heels sat by the door of my suite, waiting.

Rather than heading out to the dining hall for the school's annual Thanksgiving feast as soon as I was ready, I had decided to quickly check my personal email. And it had been all downhill from there. Tears clung to my dark blonde lashes, and I stood with a sniffle, off to fix them in the bathroom. My movements were jerky, my limbs stiff, my stomach in knots. I tidied up my smudged mascara with a crumpled bit of toilet paper, then added a nude lip and redid my bow. Back in the bedroom, my phone's alarm went off, a reminder that I was now *just* about late for the dinner.

With another sniff, I zipped around, turning off my alarm, grabbing my unnecessary winter jacket and slipping into it, then shoving my feet into the heels. They protested as they always did, and I was even wobblier than usual as I hurried out of the suite, locked up, and power-walked into the great blustery outdoors.

While I could have taken the tunnels to the dining hall, stepping outside and breathing in a lungful of the crisp, cold air seemed preferable. Necessary, almost. Darkness blanketed the world outside the four campus walls, thousands of stars glittering across a pitch-black sky. Although less frequently used during the winter, the exterior walkways connecting all the grey stone buildings had been cleared, and my heels made muffled clicks as I strode along.

Warm yellow lamplight kept the snowy landscape bright and comforting—another tactic employed to fight the winter blues. It was a very real issue so far north, half the year shrouded in darkness; we worked hard as educators and stand-in parents to keep the students active, mentally stimulated, and happy.

It was honestly why we had a thousand mandatory dances during the year, along with countless other clubs and movie nights and board game tournaments. While only about half the SIA population was American, the academy hosted a huge Thanksgiving dinner annually, because right now, as darkness started to overtake the light, the kids needed it. Up to their eyeballs in exam prep and assignments, unable to leave campus for a breather whenever they wanted, they needed anything we could give them to boost their mood.

If only the tactic worked on homesick teachers. Arms crossed, I took in my surroundings as I followed the familiar path to the dining hall. About two feet of snow had built up around the walkways. While it had been a cold and snowy November, the wind and occasional mild days had kept the drifts from getting out of control, which meant it was more wet than white lately.

Still, seeing the pines dotted with snow, the conical rooftops steeped with sloping drifts—it was nice. Soothing.

Naturally, that faded away as soon as I neared the hall, the stained-glass windows illuminated, and a chorus of over a hundred different voices greeted me before I'd even stepped inside. They had the heat cranked high as I hurried through the building's main doors into the foyer between the hall and the auditorium. Students popped in and out of the dining hall with friends, chatting as wafts of turkey and stuffing and cranberry sauce and mashed potatoes drifted along with them.

Even though the auditorium had no place in tonight's festivities, the support staff were acting as a coat-check service before the meal began, hanging extra layers, mittens, and scarves inside so they wouldn't take up space at the long tables. Usually people cycled in and out at mealtimes; we were seldom all in there at once, filling every available seat, and as I handed my black coat over, one I hadn't bothered to zip up, I could already feel the tension headache starting behind my eyes.

"Do you know if they're letting us drink this year?" I muttered as Eve, one of five secretaries in the main admin office, hung my coat on a rack just beyond the auditorium doors. She glanced back, the skin around her thin mouth crinkling when she smiled.

"I heard Foster approved it."

"Oh, thank god."

"Term's almost over, Emma," the woman said, eyes twinkling. "Nearly there."

I forced a chuckle and stepped aside as a squad of seniors in dangerously high heels sauntered over, peeling off their coats to reveal *very* elegant gowns. I smoothed a hand down my old familiar dame, feeling a bit awkward to be so dressed up yet somehow also completely underdressed in the same breath. Resisting the urge to fiddle with my bow, I turned, ready to dive headlong into the noise and clamor, only to pause when I spotted Calder stepping through the dining hall doors and into the foyer.

Wait.

What...?

What the *hell* was on his head?

I squinted, even though he was only standing about ten feet away. Was that—? Yup. Calder Holloway, uptight vampire, was, in fact, wearing a giant turkey-shaped hat made of construction paper. A hat so insanely detailed that its enormous bird sported a dangling red wattle under its beak. When our eyes met, I clapped a hand over my mouth and doubled over, positively *dying*, struck with a case of the giggle-snorts that felt oddly cathartic.

Oh my *god*, did he ever look miserable. Even through my lashes I could see he wanted to kill—something. Me. Himself. The group of seniors sniggering at him as they swished by in their heels and gowns. I straightened up, still plagued with the giggles, and wiped under my eyes. It was difficult to admire how gorgeous he looked in that suit —another three-piece wonder, light grey with a plaid dress shirt and a deep orange tie—with that *thing* on his head.

Honestly, the guy had zero vampire street cred after he'd started working here. Zero.

As I continued to giggle, my titters setting off Eve in the auditorium doorway, Calder merely shoved his hands in his pockets and glowered, jaw clenched and cheeks sunken. I hadn't seen that expression directed at me in ages, not after we decided to engage in some mutually beneficial screwing that day in the gym. Unfortunately, the last few weeks had all been duds. Although I couldn't stop fantasizing about how *awesome* the sex could be, I had also told him I didn't want to do anything when there were students around.

And when you lived at a boarding school in the middle of nowhere, students were around all the fucking time.

So, beyond a few stolen kisses here and there, a bit of aggressive groping in dark corridors on midnight patrols, things had reached something of a stalemate between us. Calder kept asking. I kept refusing, insisting on a rain check. As fantastic as we were together physically, I also valued this job—a lot—and I wasn't about to lose it over a bit of hate sex.

Still, there was a lot of pent-up energy humming between us, and I wasn't sure when Calder would pass the point of no return and just give up. Where would that leave us then?

"I'm sorry," I said, finally forcing myself to calm down, cheeks aching, eyes wet with unshed tears. "You just look so miserable."

"And you find that amusing, do you?" he asked tightly as I closed the distance between us, the foyer finally empty. Even Eve had disappeared inside the auditorium. I stopped about two feet in front of him, unable to look away from that horrific thing on his head.

"Uh, yeah. This whole thing is pretty amusing..." As soon as I poked at the dangling wattle, I was gone again, head thrown back in full-blown cackling laughter. Calder exhaled my name softly, his annoyance hardened, and I held up my hands in surrender. "I'm sorry. I'll stop. I'll stop. But—what the fuck is on your head?"

"Swear jar," Robert Howard said, appearing out of nowhere, passing us by like some enormous ship in the night on his way to the dining hall. I rolled my eyes, waiting until he disappeared, and then lifted a prompting brow at Calder. The vampire huffed, gaze darting around the foyer.

"We all have them. It's not just me." Stiffly, he adjusted the hat, as if to make it sit better. I pursed my lips and refrained from telling him that the only way to make it sit better was to take it off completely.

And then burn it so it couldn't hurt him ever again.

"And *why* do we all have hats?"

"The freshmen art class made them for us this week," Calder said with a sniff. "Each one is personalized. Some sort of humiliating punishment for, I don't know, being teachers, I suppose."

"*Fant*astic." To be fair, Phyllis had probably given her students this assignment with the best of intentions in mind. Still, I couldn't imagine why she'd thought any of us would want to wear stupid festive hats during a formal event. Considering the monstrosity on Calder's head, maybe it *was* a punishment.

The vampire gestured toward the dining hall. "Shall we?"

I nodded, still wiping under my eyes as I headed for the doors, all the while wondering if he had come out here looking for me. Even if we weren't having all the glorious hate sex, I'd noticed Calder gravitating toward me more over the last few weeks. If we were both in the dining hall at the same time, he settled down next to me in silence, pushing food around his plate—food that I eventually ate, on top of my own sizeable portion. We sat next to each other during Sunday-night staff meetings, worked alongside each other in the library, patrolled the dorms at least once a week, and rode the same bus to the village to chaperone student trips.

It wasn't like we had been sharing our life stories. In fact, we usually didn't talk at all, unless he was in the mood to ruffle my feathers—or for sex.

But I had a suspicion that what he said in the gym, about not needing to pretend around me, influenced him more than either of us cared to admit. He didn't need to put on a show for me, because I saw right through it. Calder Holloway, vampire, could just *be*.

And I could appreciate that, now that I knew he wasn't here to sell me to some government lab.

At least, I was 99.9 percent sure of that. He could always surprise me, and it wouldn't be the first time.

Fighting a small smile, I stepped through the doors, immediately greeted by a warm and cheery dining hall bursting with happy, smiling faces, a sea of students who I was so accustomed to seeing in sweaty uniforms now dressed to impress. Hair. Makeup. Perfume and colognes all clashing with the delicious aromas rolling out of the kitchens. Most were seated at this point, the four long tables for each grade decorated with gourds and fake fall leaves, an elaborate cornucopia setup in the middle.

It was lovely, of course. Festive. Welcoming. Inclusive, whether you were from a country that celebrated Thanksgiving or not.

And it made the knots in my stomach tighter, the ache in my chest deeper.

Standing at the far end of the hall, fiddling with my fingers, I felt it again.

Guilt.

Self-doubt.

Longing—for my pack, for the familiarity of it all.

Tomorrow would be easier. So would the next day, and the next, easier each day to remember why I was here—until Christmas hit in just a few short weeks. The school allotted us time off, same as the kids. I planned to stay here and look after the dogs.

And drink. 'Tis the season, or whatever.

Tugging at my arm, Calder steered me toward an enormous table that usually made up the buffet for regular meals. Tonight, however, it was covered in decorations—and hats. Well, one hat, mine, name cards with glittery letters scattered about, showing where the rest of the faculty gifts once sat.

Thankfully, no one had made me a horrendous giant turkey. Instead, the freshmen art students had built a harvest crown, constructed of orange, red, and yellow paper leaves, along with twigs that stuck out in all directions. I grinned, pleased with the choice, and hoped I wouldn't put someone's eye out at dinner.

"Oh, I love it."

"Why does yours actually look good?" Calder grumbled as he picked it up, handling it with all the care one might give to a priceless artifact, and then set it on my head. I peered up, wincing as he adjusted it—even snapped a few of the far-reaching twigs off for good measure. He chucked the broken bits back on the table, scowling. "Why did I get *this* abomination?"

"Bitter looks bad on you," I told him, patting his chest with a patronizing smile. My gaze then drifted up again, and I let out a snort. "Yeah—it's terrible."

But somehow Calder in a hilariously awful turkey hat made this shitty day just a little bit better. I gave his chest one last pat, resisting the urge to mess up his perfectly knotted *cashmere* tie, and turned away with a sigh. Making fun of the resident vampire might have temporarily lifted my spirits, but if we were allowed to drink, I intended to get blitzed—after the students had gone to bed—so I could sleep away my day off tomorrow and forget all about those pictures.

Gang's all here.

Biting the insides of my cheeks, I dove headlong into the Thanksgiving festivities, Calder at my heels, counting the minutes until I could guzzle down a very full glass of wine and devour a whole turkey leg like a true northern wolf.

13

CALDER

Holy *fuck*, that was good.

After several hours surrounded by mountains of food I could no longer comfortably eat, inundated with smells, forced to nibble here and there while my stomach roiled, a full-bodied B-positive was *just* what I needed. Seated at the meticulously organized desk at the front of my classroom, the room dimly lit by the antique Victorian gas lamp on the corner, I nursed a mug of blood I had microwaved in the empty staffroom downstairs. While everyone else had toddled off to bed, drunk on a different sort of red delicacy, I had retreated here to grade papers.

It wasn't like I could sleep, anyway.

Since Halloween, I hadn't been able to close my eyes for one damn second without seeing Emma—her blood-stained skin, her pouty lips, her cognac-brown eyes heavy-lidded and wanting. The only cure for such fantasizing was the physical; I'd thought if I could just fuck her out of my system, my concentration would improve. However, since she had put her foot down about keeping things above board around students, the fantasizing, the reminiscing, the desperation had only gotten worse.

I could barely come to terms with it. Wanting a shifter —*this* shifter of all creatures, a wolf so palpably my opposite that it ought to make my skin crawl. Yet I craved her scent, her voice, her blood. I desired every inch of Emma fucking Kingsley, right down to the way she absent-mindedly toyed with her hair while she wrote lesson plans.

Honestly, the way she popped it between her lips, gnawing at it like a hound with a rawhide—it should have repulsed me.

Instead, all I could think about whenever I saw her was pressing her up against the nearest wall and sinking my teeth into her neck, then fucking her into oblivion.

It was a nightmare, for more reasons than one. Not only had she dangled herself in front of me by agreeing to engage in a little extracurricular sexual activity, but then she had made all these damn *rules*, and I knew that should I break them, should I push too hard, she would rescind her invitation.

And while I was all too happy to *take* what I wanted, I refused to do it when the other party explicitly said no.

So, over the last few weeks, we hadn't been at each other's throats, not once, but I had been chomping at the bit to get her alone.

Pathetic, really. A shifter with so much control over a vampire. I shook my head and took another long, luxurious slurp of my midnight meal, then reclined in my high-backed leather chair, clothes still stinking of turkey and gravy, apple pie and cinnamon. I'd only been able to conquer one essay since the feast ended, but at least it had kept me busy enough to stop obsessing about her. Mind you, if the rest of the pile was as absolute *shit* as what I'd just read, the distraction might not hold out for long.

Even though we had sat beside one another at the staff table, I had been able to ignore Emma for most of the dinner. Not only had the art students made horrendous hats for all of us faculty, but there had been plenty of other entertainment before the main course. Poems from the English students. Skits from the drama enthusiasts. Foster gave a never-ending toast to what he was thankful for this year—the academy, unsurprisingly, and all the people in it. The head chef had his moment in the sun, explaining all the dishes as his horde of underlings served them.

It had been a pleasant enough night, and had I Emma's shifter appetite, I probably would have overindulged too. As it were, my tastes had become very specific since I'd turned, and nothing could ever please me again like the lukewarm liquid in my mug.

And now, it seemed, the scalding hot blood of a wolf shifter—so sweet, so *different*.

That had to be it—why I was so infatuated with her. The sex had been excellent, but the *blood*. It was something else entirely. Something I had never tasted before, and Emma Kingsley wasn't the first shifter I had sampled in the last two hundred years.

She was an enigma. A curiosity.

Emma Kingsley was a fucking distraction.

I cleared my throat and sat forward, grabbing the next essay from the pile.

Fortunately, the following two papers proved to be more worthy of my time, written by a pair of my top five-percenters. They were spared the wrath of the red pen and had lifted my mood considerably by the time two o'clock rolled around. Just as I was about to make another blood run, I heard it—the *click, click, click* of heels along the hardwood corridor outside. I hesitated, checking the time again on my wristwatch, and straightened when the heels clicked right by my classroom door, then backtracked to it and stopped. Even without a window set in the old wood, I knew who was standing on the other side, could *feel* that wild aura. The knob creaked when it turned, and I sat back in my chair with a barely contained grin.

Finally.

Emma poked her head inside, scanning my bare-bones classroom until her gaze found me. Around us, every inch of wall space had been plastered with campaign posters from the two world wars, both of which I had lived through and were the sole course content for my upper-year classes. Between us sat a sea of unremarkable desks. Other teachers saw fit to arrange them in configurations: pairs, clumps, quads, one giant square. I preferred to keep everyone separate to limit the nonsense, but kids these days were connected to the internet twenty-four seven—plenty of opportunities for nonsense.

It was why I also made them handwrite all their notes. No laptops or cell phones beyond that door; if I saw either device outside of a backpack or book bag, it was mine for the rest of the term.

And as Emma strolled in, she adhered to that rule without realizing, wearing nothing more than the slim-fit black dress that had caught my eye at supper, a half-drunk wine bottle in hand. I could smell that it was a red from here, and from the slight teeter of her heels with every cautious step, I deduced that this wasn't the first bottle she'd worked through. Shifter bodies could metabolize alcohol faster, but that certainly didn't mean they couldn't get intoxicated.

I only hoped, as she strode toward me, skirting along the last row of the desks, that she wasn't so drunk that I would have to send her away.

After all, I was *trying* to listen to my conscience after so many decades of outright ignoring it.

Sporting a wry smile, I tossed my pen down and pushed my chair back, legs crossed at the ankles, hands threaded on my chest. Emma said nothing as she stopped at the nearest empty desk, then heavily plopped her wine bottle on top. I lifted an eyebrow, canting my head toward it, soundlessly demanding an explanation for all this. Still she said nothing, just stepped out of her heels, then slid a hand up her dress...

And tugged down her stockings. I swallowed hard, fighting the urge to sit up straighter as she rolled them down her thighs, over her knees, along her calves, dragging with them her black panties. Once she had stepped out of the nylon and cotton, she unceremoniously bundled them up— in stark contrast to my instinct to neatly *fold* the lot of them —and tossed them next to her wine.

My cock twitched, swelling eagerly as she strolled over with her bare legs, her uncovered cunt. I shifted up and settled my hands on the armrests, studying her in the quiet, in the dim lighting that wasn't a problem for either of us. While she appeared drunk, the line she walked far from straight, her eyes were less hollow now. Sure, she had laughed at the feast, chatted, but there had been an emptiness to her smile that I couldn't place—nor was it my responsibility to do so.

All the makeup from before had been removed, the skin around her eyes slightly pink and swollen, perhaps from the cleaning agent. The braid had vanished, in its place a slovenly bun with a lock of blonde coiling out the back.

Yet if my steadily hardening cock had anything to say about it, she was still beautiful.

Lower lip caught between her teeth, she hitched her dress up her thighs with one dainty hand, then climbed onto my lap, straddling me, looming over me as she settled. Each soft breath smelled of red wine, but her natural scent won out—every time, no matter the occasion, there was that damn lavender. I fought the urge to sweep the backs of my knuckles up her cheek, to smooth the flyaways, to catch her lip with my thumb. Instead, I kept one arm where it was, lazily hanging off the armrest, while the other hand curved over her ass.

Just because I could.

She arched like a cat in a sunbeam, her hands on my chest, her hips tilted, her backside filling my cupped hand. I would never admit just how well she fit to me—but I'd known that from the first day we met, when I had her pinned to my office desk, our bodies molded together like two pieces of a whole. It was more obvious now, how snug she felt against me, her curves encouraging my body to yield after a lifetime of standing rigid as a fucking mountain.

I swallowed hard, tipping my chin up when her fingertips grazed my neck to my jaw, burning my flesh with her touch.

Scorching me, right there, her body's intensity unlike anything I had ever experienced before. So fucking *hot*, Solskinn's own little blonde ray of sunlight—sunlight I had yet to seek shelter from, against my better judgement.

Eyes heavy-lidded, face cast in shadow, Emma brushed her lips against mine with a soft sigh. I watched her, even as her eyes closed, thinking it a sigh of surrender, responding to her tentative little kiss with the last of my self-restraint. When her little pecks and nibbles had gone on long enough, I surged up, catching her mouth in something fiercer, darker, something that had her soft sighs sharpening, her eyes snapping open.

She tasted of red wine and temptation. Dangerous. Seductive. Sweet, too, her tongue flicking at mine when it invaded her mouth, nothing more than a tease, beckoning me to chase. Hadn't she learned her lesson? There was no teasing a vampire—we had never had cause to hold back.

With a growl, I slipped both hands under her dress, kneading the firm, round globes of her ass. Her hips rocked, grounding down against my shaft. If I pushed her off, would I find her arousal smeared across my trousers? I gripped harder at the thought, fingers bruising the womanly flesh beneath them, marking it, albeit temporarily. Shifters couldn't scar, couldn't bruise—and while I hated the fact that Emma hadn't been forced to hide my bite from the rest of the school in the days that followed our first tryst, it certainly made the prospect of drinking from her simpler.

I nipped at her lip, hard, relishing her gasp, the trickle of blood spilling into my mouth. Planting a firm hand on my chest, Emma pushed—pushed herself back, pushed me into the chair. She fought for breath, chest heaving, and my cock responded eagerly, painfully hard between us. It took such effort to make a shifter's heart race, but Emma's danced for me whenever we were alone.

"Bite me," she whispered, her voice low and silky, and had my heart been capable of it, the damn thing would have danced too. My lips twitched up, canines elongating the few millimeters necessary to pierce her skin. *Bite me.* Had she any idea what a command like that did to me? Such an enticing invitation—how could I possibly refuse?

I shot up, one hand under her dress as the other fisted around her messy bun, and dragged her neck to meet me.

There were so many more enjoyable places to sink my teeth into, but Emma's neck was exquisite; it screamed for my attention, the skin begging to be broken with my teeth. They sunk in, hard and true, piping-hot blood spilling into my mouth, and I groaned the moment the sweetly metallic liquid flooded across my tongue.

So *good*. So... unique. I'd never tasted someone like her before, never enjoyed the way someone responded to me as I did with Emma. The second my fangs pierced her, she was off, moaning and writhing on my lap, her head thrown back in wild abandon.

We all knew what our bite did to others, the pleasure it induced. I'd once been told it was a toxin vampires released, rendering our prey useless, but I had never cared for the science before. In fact, I had never cared that it pleasured anyone before, but hurling Emma into a whirlpool of desire from which there was no escape, to make her feel like she was drowning in it, brought out the smug bastard in me. All her underhanded comments, her curses, her glares, her indignation and anger—all erased by my bite. Just for a moment, I *had* her. I *owned* her, and she fucking asked for it.

As she writhed, trembling, rocking her bare sex against my bulge, I could have sworn she whimpered my name. Thinking it a shame to ruin what was probably the one nice dress she owned, I drank carefully to avoid the mess I'd made on Halloween.

Back then, covering her in blood, even if her body's essence regenerated within minutes, had been about sending a message. It had been purposeful—and fun. We were past that, onto another chapter of this tumultuous relationship, and I didn't want this to be the last time she showed up, drunk, looking for a good, hard fuck because I had sullied her dress.

Nimble fingers found their way to my belt, plucking at the buckle, wrenching it open. Her breath quickened, body shaking in my arms as the venom of my bite worked her into a frenzy. With the zipper vanquished, Emma slipped a hand under my briefs, and I groaned against her throat when she found me and pulled me out—not exactly difficult, given all the blood I was taking from her had gone straight to my cock.

She stroked me, up and down, rocking her hips in time with her hand, and I tightened my fist around her hair as pleasure ricocheted through my body. My hips jerked in response, a puppet on the end of her string, and before I could even *entertain* the idea of her mouth around my shaft, Emma hoisted herself up—and lowered herself onto my cock. I exhaled sharply the moment my head speared her molten opening, so deliciously tight and wet that my eyes all but rolled back. She sank all the way down, her channel dancing around my length, adjusting to the size as she moaned.

Ordinarily, I preferred at least *some* foreplay. Blood wasn't the only part of a woman I loved to taste—but that wasn't what this was between us. We weren't tentative kisses and languid groping. We were speed and certainty, seeking out our own pleasure, using the other to attain it.

Emma rose up and down twice before I tore my mouth from her throat. Blood dribbled down my chin, coated my lips, and I let my head fall heavy against the leather padding behind it, mouth open, fangs exposed, utterly transfixed as she rode me. In an instant, the puncture marks on her throat healed, leaving only a faint red stain across her skin —and nowhere near her dress, I might add. The corners of my mouth twitched upward, pleased, but my lips snapped together seconds later when she purposefully clenched around me like a snare.

Now *she* wore the dark grin, bucking her hips, undulating on top of me as her fingers bit into the leather on either side of my head. Bracing herself, she rocked harder, rising up and slamming herself back down, dragging me one step closer to oblivion with every move she made. Enigma. Curiosity. Fucking *distraction*.

How was it that all I wanted to do, from now until the end of days, was watch her swirl her hips, forehead pinched with the effort, eyes half-closed as she chased her high? I could sit like this for hours, a king on his throne, enraptured by the concubine on his lap.

Why?

How had this woman ensnared me?

Something in her blood?

I swallowed thickly, still tasting her sweetness. No, the blood was different, but not tainted. Not poisoned.

Preferring not to dwell on my newfound weakness, I finally moved. Hands planted on each armrest, I stood, easily lifting her and savoring her squeak of surprise, her eyes wide, breath catching as she clung to me. With a sweep of one hand, I cleared my desk, sparing all those Hitler-Mussolini-Stalin comparison essays what was bound to be a rough, unbridled, unthinking *fuck*.

I set her at the edge of the desk, then hoisted her knees up higher, shifting the angle and plunging deep inside. Emma threw her head back with a cry, lips parted, chest heaving—an utter vision. Ordinarily, she drove me mad, but when I had her like this, so raw and exposed, so open and vulnerable, she was a fucking masterpiece.

What the *hell* was wrong with me?

Scowling, I took her by the hips and retreated, only to

pound back in moments later. If only I had no qualms about tearing that dress to pieces; I would have liked to watch her bounce in all the right places. Emma's hands scrambled for purchase, one reaching back to support her on the desk, the other skittering up my arm and curving around my neck. I gave her that, a few precious seconds to find her bearings, before brutally driving into her, over and over again. The desk creaked beneath us, its legs scratching across the hardwood with every savage thrust.

Her lips soon found mine, desperately, if only to muffle her cries, and I slanted my mouth over hers, swallowing each one with the same eagerness I did her blood. They were addicting, all the little sounds she made, all the sounds *I* tore from her. Almost as addicting as her taste, her smell—the way she kissed me. Every kiss was fire, biting, relentless *fire* that threatened to consume me from the inside out.

Yet I craved that too. I craved this shifter's burn.

I took her harder, faster, refusing to admit something so preposterous—even to myself. Her elbow buckled, and she crashed down with it, yanking me along too. Smirking, I hauled her over the edge of the desk and wrapped an arm around her waist, pistoning my hips as she scrambled to reach the far side, fingertips just catching over the ledge.

If only I'd stripped her naked. What a sight to behold.

In need of another taste, I dragged my tongue across the bloodstain on her neck, lapping up what was left with a growl. As soon as the sweet red liquid touched my tongue, I turned wild, fucking her like I hadn't been able to with any human lover in years—*decades*. Emma could take my brutality. She could withstand the creature, the predator, the *monster* I truly was, the one I was forced to hide in front of everyone else.

She took it all—and asked for more, nudging my head with her chin, steering me to the other side of her neck.

"Insatiable wretch," I hissed, brushing my fangs against her skin, dragging it over her racing pulse.

"Shut *up* and just do it—"

I complied happily, plunging into her throat just as fiercely as I did below. Her whole body lifted, molding to me, legs snapped tight around my waist. She abandoned the desk in favor of clutching at me, hands buried in my hair, hips rolling to meet my every thrust. Sweet lava oozed into my mouth, and I drank greedily, *fucked* greedily, taking all that I wanted and still hungry for more.

I was the insatiable one, not her.

Pathetic.

I blocked out the needling little voice by losing myself in her, by drowning in Emma Kingsley until I plummeted into the abyss. My climax hit hard, pleasure surging like a roaring tidal wave, and I ripped my mouth from her throat, only to slam it to her lips instead, staggering forward, pushing us back up the desk until my thighs collided with the wood.

Until my desk slammed into the row of student desks, initially a good six feet away, and sent my gas lamp tumbling. By some miracle, it didn't shatter, though the light immediately extinguished.

"Calder, *fuck*—" Emma's moans turned ragged, her body quivering beneath me, perhaps assaulted by her own climax. Combined with the thrill of the bite, it must have been quite overwhelming for a creature with such heightened senses. I, meanwhile, couldn't feel my fingers, my toes. Couldn't think clearly. Certainly couldn't *speak* clearly, so I didn't dare. As I waited for the sensations to settle, for the pleasure to ebb, I just sprawled on top of her like a lead weight. Forehead pressed to the desk, hands on her ass, her thigh, I listened to the rhythm of her strong heart, her gasping breaths.

A thick, dark silence blanketed the room around us, the same as one might find outside this time of the morning. Eerie to some. Ideal for me, perhaps for Emma, both of us trapped in a world of noisy, smelly, emotional humans just about every other second of the day. Here, in the darkness, neither of us had to pretend. When I finally forced myself up and out of her, I didn't even bother to retrieve the lamp. I could see just fine, and as I shuffled back and fell unceremoniously into my chair, I assumed she could too. After all, wolves were creatures of the night, just like me, whether the stubborn, thoroughly ravished shifter on my desk cared to admit it or not.

Emma lay there for a few moments, dress hitched up around her hips, ankles on the edge of the desk, knees together, until her breath evened out. Then, she slid off and went straight for her things, navigating the dark with ease, as I'd suspected. While she slipped back into her panties and heels, she just crumpled up the stockings in one hand and snatched the half-drunk bottle of red wine with the other.

And that was that—she was off, headed for the door on surer footing than when she had first arrived. I frowned, elbow on the armrest, chin on my fist as I watched her go.

"Emma?" She stopped just shy of the door, sighing heavily, her head down. Was this regret? Had the sex been *sobering* for her? Because I felt intoxicated for the first time in an age. "Are you all right?"

"Fine," she said without missing a beat. Gone was the croon of a seductress, replaced with something hollow again. I sat up straighter, still undressed and in no hurry to right myself, and leaned forward.

"Hmm. Right. Completely fine, eh?"

Bun destroyed, her hair tumbled down her back in utter disarray. The sudden urge to pick through the knots, to trail my fingers through the chaos, struck hard, and I curled my hands to fists, chest suddenly tight. Mercifully, the desire passed when Emma finally peered back at me through the darkness, wearing an expression that just screamed *fuck off, Calder*.

I could practically hear the words in my head.

The knob creaked, and the room flooded with dim light from the hall as she opened the door and disappeared through it. Heels clicked quickly down the corridor. In her absence, the door only fell half-closed, a streak of yellow cutting across my classroom.

Her scent lingered—in the air, on my clothes, fused up my damn nostrils.

With a huff, I pinched the bridge of my nose. Not only had I failed at fucking her out of my system, but after tonight, I was more distracted than ever. Emma Kingsley, with her sweet blood and fiery kiss and top-shelf cunt, was in far deeper now, right down to my marrow, and perhaps there was no way to ever get her out.

I closed my eyes and let my head thump back against the leather.

Fuck.

DECEMBER

14

CALDER

Another term come and gone.

The final few days before the Christmas holiday had been an absolute nightmare. Not only had I spent an eternity tackling midterm prep with my own students, but the whole faculty had been roped into transporting all one hundred and forty-two of our surrogate children—Foster's words, certainly not mine—to the airport in Bardufoss, where they would catch the shuttle to Oslo, then onto wherever home was for the two-week holiday ahead.

December 21st, the final day of classes, had been plagued with an annoying mix of endless midterm questions and a noticeably checked-out glaze from all my students.

Yesterday, December 22nd, we had loaded everyone and their mountain of luggage into the academy's buses and zipped them off to the airport. Given the number of buses, three trips were required throughout the day, back and forth from the small Bardufoss air base. Half the staff hung back in the terminal, there to help with check-in and boarding and oversized luggage complaints. I had been stuck on the buses, my head exploding with the inane chatter of teenagers—holiday plans and Christmas wish lists and will my boyfriend actually stay in touch and oh my god I forgot my mobile phone charger back at the dorms...

I was actually going to miss the little buggers.

About a third of the staff caught the final flight to Oslo, while the rest of us stayed behind for the holidays. No students were permitted to remain in residence, but if we signed some legal document promising not to sue should we slip on a patch of ice or what have you, staff could live in their academy-provided residence year-round.

Given the number of bridges I had burned back home, Solskinn seemed as good a place as any to spend Christmas. According to Robert Howard, the staff always threw a huge party on Christmas Day and celebrated the new year in Solskinn proper, so at least there was something to look forward to.

In the meantime, I had papers to grade, assignments to eviscerate, and January midterms to prepare for my juniors. My office also needed a thorough clean, layered in a full three months' worth of grime, and I had spent this morning sorting and tossing junk, dusting the antiques I outright refused to let the cleaning staff touch, and organizing my filing cabinet. It had kept me occupied well enough, two mugs of microwaved blood warming my belly and Wagner's timeless compositions blasting from my laptop.

I was nearing the end of *Götterdämmerung*'s third act when I heard the howl of a rescued sled dog. A distinct sound against a normally muted landscape, it was soon joined by a chorus of other voices; the academy mutts were on the loose, trundling across the snowy landscape, snapping at the fat, fluffy flakes beneath a light grey overcast. From my office windows, I had a perfect view of the pack's sheer *joy*—all the leaping, barking, yipping. All the burying of their faces in freshly fallen snow, sniffing around the covered fountain in the middle of the main roundabout.

Beyond them, the school's gates remained closed. Shortly after Thanksgiving, the regional police announced the disappearances over the last year were linked, with all those missing last seen around the same patch of forestry. Thus far, no bodies had surfaced, but the academy had doubled their security team to assuage any parent concerns, and trips to the village had been suspended for all of December until the local authorities could completely guarantee student safety.

So, a dozen private security officials now roamed the campus, half of them set up in the two guard stations at the main gates, the rest patrolling on foot. It seemed a bit unnecessary to me; I had yet to detect any predators sniffing around the school, and the increased presence of men in black uniforms only unnerved the students.

And, really, Emma and I were better security than those earbud-wearing apes. Our senses were sharper than any computer or camera, and we could respond in a flash when necessary. Unfortunately, with the supernatural still relatively in the closet, we were forced to defer to the human specialists—for now.

Trailing after the unleashed dogs, Emma strolled along the semi-cleared paths, her hair in a thick, high ponytail. Sporting a thin green coat, grey leggings, and a pair of sneakers, she appeared to be gearing up for a run. As soon as she came into view, the dogs went barreling back to her, barking and charging, tails wagging so hard it was a wonder none of them experienced lift-off.

She seemed to enjoy their enthusiasm, her smile the

widest and most natural I had seen in weeks. Something had been off with her lately, and it had been quite clear that she'd only visited my office after Thanksgiving dinner to deal with whatever was on her mind. Not that I cared—the sex was still fantastic, and that was the whole point of this. What did it matter if we were both using each other to achieve our own ends?

But if we were just using each other for physical release, why had I grabbed my own thin jacket and abandoned my office cleanup to meet her? I could have easily just let her go about her business with the dogs, who, without their student handlers, would be her responsibility for the next two weeks.

Yet here I was, marching through the empty, silent corridors of the main building, hoping that I hadn't missed her in the time it took me to get from my office window to the front doors. I hadn't, and as I shoved through, zipping up my jacket and shoving my hands in my pockets against the bitterly cold air, as if the cold *bothered* me, I found myself pleased to see her. Yesterday had been a bit of a blur getting the students sorted. Emma had been involved in some capacity, but this was the first time I had seen her since yesterday morning.

For all I knew, she could have hopped on a plane at the airport and left with all the rest of them.

As I stalked down the stone stairs, I was pleased that she hadn't. After all, she was the name I'd been assigned at the start of the month for the staff Secret Santa and her gift was already in the mail.

Still though. I fucking loathed myself for being excited to see her, for the way my lips yearned to curve into a grin.

It was just the sex. I was a man, after all, and the sooner I accepted that I desired her—physically and nothing more—

meant it would be easier to get through the day without ruminating on my choices. I just wanted to fuck her, that was it, and there was nothing wrong with wanting to fuck a gorgeous shifter, although many in the vampire community would strongly disagree.

But the sex was great and that had to be why, as I approached her, I wore a soft smile, my cheeks speckled with heat. And as for the excitement suddenly pounding through my veins—well, two weeks of no students meant plenty of opportunities for more great sex.

Right. Sure. Let's go with that.

As soon as the horde of mishmash rescue hounds caught my scent, the barks turned full and deep, all sixteen of them whipping around in my direction. I stopped halfway between the roundabout and Emma, who had been crouched down dealing with one of the smallest of the lot, some fluffy white thing with cropped-tipped ears, and held up my hands. Emma glanced up, looking from her dogs to me, then stood.

"*Hey*," the shifter snapped, cutting through the chaotic symphony. "That's enough."

In an instant, all sixteen fell silent. Some even sat, while most of the others turned tail and padded back to her.

I slipped my hands back in my pockets, appraising her. Emma Kingsley was clearly the alpha of this pack, asserting an effortless control that had all present submitting with no more than three words. She had barely even raised her voice.

Always so impressive, alpha bloodlines. They were still shifters, but something inside made them so much *more*. Perhaps that was why she tasted so sweet, so intoxicatingly addictive.

Emma motioned for the dogs to stay put, and they did,

all eyes on her as she crossed over to me wearing a teasing grin and shoes woefully unsuited for the weather. Without so many humans to fool, both of us could finally dress down a little, unfazed by the elements.

"Did you come out here for little old me?" She tipped her head to the side, ponytail bouncing. I shot her a measured look.

"I'm afraid it's difficult to concentrate with all this racket." My gaze jumped from dog to dog. "What are you doing?"

"Taking the dogs for a run."

"And you're doing this—" I pursed my lips for a moment. "—off-leash?"

"Off grounds, too." She crossed her arms, expression faltering, as if she had heard an accusation in my question when there wasn't one. "Anyway, they listen to me."

"Hmm." That was an understatement. Innately, each canine knew to bow to Emma. Without a lick of training, she could bring them all to heel. "Do you intend to run as one of them?"

The pink in her cheeks, courtesy of the cold and the gentle wind, suddenly brightened. "Maybe. Why?"

"Can I join you?"

"Join me—for a run?" She looked me up and down quickly, from my brown boots to my dark jeans, then the thin leather jacket. "You're not exactly dressed for it."

"I can keep up, I assure you." It wasn't that I was itching for a little extra time with Solskinn's resident wolf; I was eager to see her shift. The only way to get the full, true picture of a shifter was to experience both sides of them. Who knew what was lurking beneath the surface of that attractive exterior? Her wolf could have been her polar opposite, or, more likely, the creature would round out

Emma Kingsley. At last, I might finally understand her. This vexing woman, both mouthy and subdued, part of the group yet more often a recluse. From her looks, even a bit of her temperament, Emma ought to be the cool girl, the loud, in-your-face athletic type who always roused the troops.

Instead, I'd seen a quiet but confident woman who liked to drink and knit in equal measures. She could blend in with the group. Nearly all the faculty liked her, some— James Foster—more than others. But she frequently distanced herself from her social circle and spent far more time with a vampire than her kind would approve of. A wolf without a pack. Emma was a rarity, for more reasons than one.

Maybe her wolf would clarify things, give me the whole picture.

Stretching out her right quad, Emma studied me for a long moment, eyes slightly narrowed. "You want to come for a run with me? With us?"

"Sure. Why not?" I shrugged. "Bit sick of tidying my office, really."

False. I *loved* tidying.

After she'd stretched out the other leg, she retreated a few steps, still appraising me with a look that was starting to get under my skin, and then finally nodded. "Okay. You can come—as long as you don't speak."

My eyebrows shot up.

"I just want to run," she insisted, "with them. Just a quiet, peaceful run. So... keep your mouth shut and you can come too."

I drew a breath, ready to drawl something back that was bound to make her growl but then thought better of it. Instead, I pressed my lips together and nodded, though my smirk couldn't be helped. Emma rolled her eyes and motioned for me to follow. With a sharp whistle, all the dogs flocked to her side—and we were off.

I jogged alongside her out the main gate, waving to the security apes, and took a sharp left along the wall surrounding the grounds, then into the trees, easily keeping pace but knowing full well that we both could have pushed ourselves harder. The dogs fanned out around us, keeping their distance from me while remaining in a tight radius around Emma. Clearly this wasn't their first venture out together, running what appeared to be relatively well-kept forest paths, even with all this snow. I cast Emma a sidelong glance. How often did she go for runs in the surrounding woodland—and how often in human form?

Questions burned at the tip of my tongue. About her. About the more primal role she played with these dogs—and the one within her own wolf pack. But being out here, away from the humans who plagued my day-to-day life, felt good. The remoteness, the chill, the looming trees, the distant mountains, our brisk pace... It did wonders for my head, clearing it, silencing the thoughts, until I was just *moving* alongside Emma in the glow of her quiet confidence, one of the pack, going wherever she led me.

So, I kept my word. I didn't say a thing. Not during our run, and not when I eventually tugged her off the worn trail, the snow up to our knees, and fucked her against the exposed trunk of an old rowan. The dogs busied themselves around us, digging in the snow, chasing one another, plopping down for a nap, panting, never going very far while their leader was otherwise occupied.

I said nothing as the heat of her body scorched me, invigorated me, made me feel *alive*. Not when she came, muffling her cries against my shoulder, and not when I did the same, my teeth in her flesh. Not after either, when I kissed her, crushing her swollen lips to mine as she fumbled to right her clothing, my hand around her throat.

I said nothing. Not on the brisk jog back, Emma's cheeks stained red and her tread lighter. When we parted ways at the main gate, she headed for the kennel surrounded by her pack, me back to my office, alone, I still didn't say a word.

Silently, I swallowed my disappointment at not seeing her shift, at not meeting her wolf form, because the sex and the blood and the cold air and the solitude from all but her had been enough.

More than enough.

Emma Kingsley—being with her—was more than enough.

15

EMMA

After spending Christmas Eve drinking to forget, our faculty festivities the following day were just what I needed. Ordinarily, the thought of dragging myself out of bed, hungover as fuck, to attend brunch with my colleagues, even if I liked most of them, would have been my idea of hell. However, this morning's meal with all the staff who stayed at the academy for the holiday had been, well, wonderful.

Robert and Phyllis had showered me with gifts, even though I'd told them not to, and it almost felt like I had parents all the way out here. Parents who cared about my well-being, gifting me with socks and scarves and chocolates and spools upon spools of wool. Parents who didn't judge me for my life choices. Parents who were happy if I was happy. And maybe they'd noticed I hadn't been all that happy leading up to the holidays, bogged down with the old familiar guilt and self-doubt. Maybe they'd realized I'd needed them, even if I was too set in my lone-wolf ways to admit it.

Beyond all that, which would have been enough for me, the kitchen had served mimosas with brunch that put everyone in a good mood. Calder had been in rare form, pleasant and jovial, chatting as though he really was that sweet, bumbling Englishman. Foster streamed Christmas classics in the auditorium, with eggnog and *juleøl* circulating the aisles of tipsy, noisy staffers.

Last year, only about six of the teaching staff stayed behind, but we had fourteen this year, plus nine of the support staff, six from the kitchen, and three from janitorial—and all the security squad. Sure, the vest-wearing goons refused to partake in the celebration, or smile, but they had seemed very pleased with our delivery of leftovers from dinner—*ribbe*, *Pinekjøtt*, Cornish hen, plum pudding, mini chocolate lava cakes, the works.

All in all, it had been a surprisingly awesome Christmas Day, and as day turned into night and the holiday party officially kicked off in the teachers' lounge, I realized I'd been having so much fun, pleasantly tipsy since brunch, that I hadn't once thought about my pack or all the old familiar things *they* would have been up to today, incommunicado on their pack vacation to Cancún.

I hadn't needed to think. I'd had a family, a pack—right here, with these wonderful people.

To be fair, all the booze probably had something to do with my mood. I wasn't usually this giggly, nor was I ever keen to play Foster's stupid party games, but I'd been a good sport since eleven this morning and wasn't about to stop now.

After a round of charades, Christmas Mad Libs, and Name that Carol, Foster stood up on a chair, swaying, his gaunt cheeks bright pink, and announced that it was time for Secret Santa gifts to be exchanged. My stomach did a little loop, and I set my mug of spiced eggnog aside, joining the others as all thirty-two of us swarmed the mountain of gifts stacked up on the coffee table.

At the start of the month, all the staff, not just teachers, had signed up for the gift exchange, confirming that they would be here for the holidays. Foster and his assistant drew names from a hat, then told us our person in private. From there, we had about three weeks to find a gift.

Three weeks for me to mull over what the hell to give my vampire fuck buddy. As I picked up the squishy package, I couldn't help but second-guess *everything*. What if it was too simple? What if he didn't like the color? What if he tore me to bits over my wrapping job?

I glanced down at the gift. Actually, that last one wasn't a what-if. I'd wrapped his present yesterday, drunk, and it showed in my excessive use of tape. At least the wrapping paper was pretty: shiny silver patterned with candy canes and tree ornaments.

Well. Maybe not pretty.

Kitsch. Calder with his cashmere ties and tailored suits would probably think it was kitsch, just like my gift.

My stomach somersaulted again, and I swallowed hard, just standing there as everybody dispersed around the cramped room.

Go get it over with.

"Hey."

My head snapped up, and there he was, *right* in front of me. A rush of his musky cologne hit me hard, and I pointedly ignored the exposed muscly forearms, his white dress shirt sleeves rolled up to his elbows.

"Hey, so, I got you for Secret Santa," I blurted, then thrust the gift at him so abruptly that it smacked into his navel, right at the tip of his deep green tie. Heat flooded my cheeks, stomach looping again, and when I finally looked up, I found him frowning. Calder opened and closed his mouth a few times, staring at my shoddily wrapped gift, and then cleared his throat.

"Oh."

Oh? *Oh?* What the hell was that supposed to mean? My arm wavered between us, the booze making me paranoid. Was he disappointed that I was the gift giver? Did he expect it to be a prank or a joke or just absolute shit?

I retreated somewhat, bringing my gift back to me. Of course he'd think one, if not *all* those things.

Before I could force something clever and nonchalant out, however, Calder reached into the pocket of his dark grey slacks and pulled out—

"I got you as well," he said, offering me a slim, beautifully wrapped rectangle. We both stared at our respective gifts for a moment, then looked up to each other. I let out a little chuckle, some of my weird, drunken paranoia dissipating.

"Oh. That's a coincidence."

"A bit," Calder muttered. After a quick scan of the very full, somewhat stuffy and hot room, he motioned toward the corner nearest the door, one of the few spots that wasn't overcrowded with people. I nodded, trailing after him as he strode over and faced me. Scratching at the back of his neck, he held out my gift. "Well. Happy Christmas and all that."

"You too."

We swapped presents somewhat hesitantly, and I resisted the urge to hold the rectangle up to my ear and jostle it around like an animal. Because this felt very... grown-up. Not only was it impeccably wrapped, with no mismatched, poky corners and the appropriate amount of tape, but the paper was gorgeous. A full, lush red with gold stripes.

And mine was candy canes and tree ornaments and dollar-store silver. Kitsch. My palms felt clammy as I carefully, gently, popped open one end, trying not to obnoxiously shred the wrapping to pieces like I usually did.

"So, did you use a whole roll of tape for this, or...?"

I looked up, eyes wide, genuinely a bit embarrassed at my inability to wrap Christmas gifts like an adult—because if I'd done it sober, it would have only looked marginally better. For the first time in our entire history, Calder seemed not to notice my discomfort. In fact, he was focused on the gift and smiling one of those small, barely there smiles, the kind you hid from everyone but yourself.

My inner wolf yipped excitedly at the sight, the same noise she made when she wanted to get out and play, but I ignored her and went back to carefully unwrapping my present like I was defusing a bomb.

"Oh. Emma." Calder let my horrible wrapping paper fall to the floor, holding my gift with both hands. "This is..."

I stilled, the booze paranoia surging again. Over the last two weeks, I had knit Calder a sweater for Christmas. I'd found the loveliest maroon wool at the hobby shop in October, coincidentally the day I had finally figured out the vampire's angle in Solskinn, and for some reason I'd thought it would be a great color on him. Noting that he didn't own a single piece of SIA paraphernalia, I had even sewn the school emblem onto the breast.

I'd been really proud of it. The stitch was complicated and intricate, and the final product was cozy and soft.

But now, it seemed so, so—*trivial*.

Calder looked up at me, expression unreadable. I stared back, mouth dry, throat like sandpaper when I gulped.

"I, uhm, like to knit."

"I know," he said, his voice rumbly and deep. A shiver

shot down my spine.

"Uh, yeah. So, I kind of just guessed with the color and size and whatever."

He hated it—he had to. Calder's seemingly endless collection of perfectly fitted suits probably cost more than I earned in a year teaching back in Maine, and I had gone and *knitted* him a maroon sweater?

I'd thought he would wear something *handmade*?

He hated it. He hated it, and for the first time, he was about to be really fake and really nice about just how much he hated it. I'd fucked this right up.

And for some reason that *mattered*.

Just as I was about to word-vomit the long, rambling, embarrassing apology surging to the tip of my tongue, Calder brought my gift to his nose. His body lifted with the deep inhale, his eyes closed, thick obsidian lashes splayed across porcelain-white skin. I stilled, suddenly lost for words, and my lips parted when he finally glanced up.

"It smells like you," the vampire noted.

It *smelled* like me?

What, exactly, did I smell like to him?

I resisted the urge to ask.

"That... was unintentional," I said weakly, gripping his gift so tight in both hands that the paper crinkled noisily under my fingers. I loosened up and held it behind my back so he couldn't see my fidgeting.

Calder's mouth lifted into a strange sort of smile that made my stomach loop pleasantly. "It's lovely, Emma. Thank you."

"You—you don't have to wear it," I insisted, unable to accept the compliment as genuine. He might have *sounded* sincere, but he couldn't actually *like* this gift—could he? I cleared my throat, still dry and scratchy, in need of a shot or six of whiskey. "I'm not very good at giving gifts, and we, uhm, you and I... You don't have to..."

I pressed my lips together when he carefully pulled the sweater over his head, handling it as though it might come undone with the slightest movement.

Or maybe with reverence.

I couldn't tell.

But he got it over his head just fine. His muscular arms filled each sleeve but didn't stretch the stitchwork, and it rolled nicely over his broad chest. The hem reached just beyond his belt, neither too long nor too short, and the academy's emblem sat just where I'd hoped it would over what I knew was a rock-hard pectoral.

It worked on him, the color. Not every guy could make maroon look sexy. My fingers twitched, itching to reach out and skim my work—just to assess the feel, of course. I gripped them tighter around my gift, keeping them right where they were.

"It fits well," he mused, tugging the sleeves up so the scrunched bit of white dress shirt poked out around his elbow.

"Uh, yeah. Pretty good for not taking any actual measurements." May as well compliment my handiwork rather than his body. Calder, however, smirked down at me as if I'd done so anyway.

"I'm not surprised, really," he said, running a hand over his chest, admiring the school crest, "given all the time you've spent ogling me—"

He chuckled when I gave his arm a none-too-gentle smack. Shaking my head, I went back to opening my gift, tearing into the wrapping paper with vigor now. Inside, I found a blue velvet box. My brows furrowed. Did he buy me a *pen*? It wouldn't surprise me, given the thousands of ancient knick-knacks cluttering his office. Still, all those hours spent knitting, and this guy went and bought me—

I popped the lid open.

Not a pen. A necklace. Calder had bought me a *gold* necklace for Christmas. The slim chain looped twice, suggesting more length than the box allowed, and in the middle of it all, a delicate moon-shaped pendant made up of thin branches of swirling, knotted golden ivy.

"You got me jewelry?"

"It's, well, you know..." Calder cleared his throat, cheeks splotched a dull pink as he fidgeted with the sweater's sleeves, pulling them down to his wrists, then jerking them back up to his elbows like he just couldn't decide. "I know you don't really wear anything because of the nature of your, er, profession, but everyone could use a few good pieces— according to the internet, anyway."

Now it was *finally* my turn to smirk. "Right."

"Look, don't read too much into it," he muttered, scanning the room with more interest than a staff Secret Santa exchange warranted. "It was the simplest available. Some had diamonds and gems and the like. Naturally I avoided silver, but you know, the moon and wolves and, uh... It's nothing, really."

I swallowed a snort. And I thought *I'd* been awkward about *my* gift. "Still jewelry though, Mr. Holloway. Lots of implications there."

"About as many as gifting a man with a handmade garment positively dripping in your scent, eh? Bit territorial of you, wolf."

"Now who's reading too much into things?"

"Still you, I think."

I rolled my eyes. "Oh my god. Here."

After carefully removing the necklace from its

confinement, I shoved the box into Calder's hand. While long enough that I could slip the chain over my head if I wanted, I instinctively went for the clasp, undoing it before reaching both ends around my neck and attempting to reconnect them under my thick, messy braid. My fingers fumbled over the dainty fastener, but I managed to get it after a few tries, lower lip caught between my teeth. The moon pendant hung over the swell of my breasts, making my white knit sweater and frayed jeans combo almost look classy.

Swallowing hard, I lifted the pendant for a closer inspection. Delicate, about an inch in size, each point of the ivy leaves sharp enough to sting my curious fingertip. Not only was it beautiful, but holding it made me *feel* something —something I couldn't explain, and maybe didn't want to. But my inner wolf howled, the kind of full, pure cry we bayed into the night sky, the kind that connected us both to our pack, be it in wolf or human form. The sound rattled around my brain. It made my heart pump faster, surer, made my throat tight—made my eyes water.

I blinked back the sudden rush of wetness with a sniffle, then mustered up as genuine a smile as I could without coming across like a huge cheeseball. "Thank you. Really. It's very nice."

Calder nodded when our eyes met, his hands in his pockets, suddenly looming a step closer than he had been a minute ago. "Do you... Do you want to get out of here?"

Heat flashed in my belly, and my heart skipped a beat at the gravelly timbre behind his words, the dark look in his eyes.

"Yes," I breathed.

Wordlessly, the vampire grabbed my wrist and led me out the door.

16

CALDER

We made it down the corridor, up the stairs, and halfway to my office before Emma pounced. I had every intention of locking us away in there for the rest of the night, to make good use of my desk, my chair, hell, maybe even the bay window overlooking a black, starless night.

The wolf shifter had other plans, however, stopping me by yanking at my arm and throwing herself into a kiss that had every drop of blood in my body shooting straight to my cock. Groaning, I marched her back against the wall, crushing her there with my lips, my hips, hands cupping her face, fingers on her neck.

She tasted like eggnog and nostalgia. Kissing her, plundering her mouth with my tongue and sullying her braid with my fingers, had me feeling... sentimental. Wrapped in Emma's gift, something homespun and personal, smelling so sweetly of her, harkened my mind back to holidays as a human: snow-covered London, all the family gathered around a fully dressed tree, an enormous roast to be shared between my flat and the next. Snapping crackers, harmonizing carollers, Christmas cards arriving by

Penny Post. So many flickering candles that it was a wonder we hadn't burned the whole lot to the ground, another slum in flames.

I hadn't thought of those times in years. But today, surrounded by so much good cheer, my colleagues pleasantly drunk from morning till now, seeing Emma *smiling* after so many dour days—well, it had been very pleasant.

And what better way to top off the holiday than this, fucking her until her smiles turned sinful?

I very much liked my gift. It had been unexpected, but most of Emma Kingsley veered into unexpected territory. In my old circles, money talked, and I'd fallen back on familiar habits when I sought *her* present for this Secret Santa gift exchange. After I had torn open her shoddily wrapped package, I'd realized my mistake.

My gift had been all wrong for her. Sure, another woman may have squealed over such a fancy gold trinket, but Emma would have appreciated something more thoughtful, surely. She was a purveyor of handmade gifts that felt so lush, so luxurious, that she could sew a designer label into it and no one would know the difference. This sweater could have cost thousands it was so soft, so perfectly molded to my figure, yet all I wanted to do was smell it—sit in my office, in the dark, surrounded by the comfort of my things, and breathe her in.

Sentiment. Emma's maroon sweater, complete with a Solskinn International Academy crest, dripped with it. Oozed it. Sentiment wrought the downfall of many a man, yet tonight, I loved it. I never wanted to take it off, even as I bent her over my desk and ravished her.

And from the way Emma kissed me, so deeply, so openly, her hands tangling my hair, tugging, then falling to my tie and attacking the knot, it appeared Emma enjoyed her gift too. That momentary blip of fear, the one that made my chest tight and my throat dry, had been unfounded.

My hands slipped lower, abandoning the svelte line of her jaw for the delicate column of her throat. Her pulse thundered beneath my fingers, but it was the gold chain I sought instead. For a split second, during the ordering process, I had considered buying the necklace in silver. The metal burned shifters, and I'd thought, maybe for a laugh...

But now, as I stroked her skin, tracked the blood pounding through her veins, my thumb traced the line of gold and I *felt* something. Something possessive and dark and desperate, something I could never dare admit to. Even though I knew, logically, that tonight might very well be the only night she wore my gift, I suddenly yearned to see her in it every day. I longed to have her wearing that and only that, the full moon settling in the valley of her breasts, rosy pink nipples standing tall on either side like sentries.

We had marked each other tonight.

The thought had me growling, shifting into this primal, physical beast on par with the animal inside her. Catching her lower lip between my teeth, I hoisted her up, settling between her thighs as her ankles crossed behind me. My pine-green tie, flecked with barely visible silver stars, cascaded to the ground in a flutter of cashmere, and Emma's greedy fingers ripped open the top button of my dress shirt before skirting up my neck and back into my hair. I bit at her lips again, hard enough to make the sumptuous bottom bleed, and she bucked with a gasp as sweet, sweet fire dribbled between us, grinding her hips against my shaft, and drew me closer with her insistent heels on the small of my back.

I'd just raked my fangs across her neck, ready to plunge

in as I spirited her away to my office, when I heard it—a very faint, very nasally little voice: "Oh, uh, hi, guys."

Emma stiffened, her fingers twisting in my hair so hard it actually hurt, and I closed my eyes with a sharp sigh.

Please.

For all that was good in this world.

Tell me we hadn't just been discovered by James fucking Foster.

"Get off," Emma hissed, shoving at me. "Let go, let go, get *off*."

Fuck. How the hell hadn't I heard him coming? As we untangled, I couldn't help but marvel at the impossibility of a human sneaking up on either of us, but maybe the alcohol had dulled Emma's senses—and she had dulled mine.

Because there was James fucking Foster, our boss, standing just around the curve of the hallway with four stacks of giant red cups in hands, their color matching the hue of his sunken cheeks.

"We, uh, decided to play beer pong," he said weakly, looking between us as I tried my best to subtly right myself, tucking my cock up and out of the way so I wasn't tenting my trousers. Emma, meanwhile, appeared beautifully disheveled, her whole face as red as Foster's, her hands pressed to her cheeks like that might hide it. The academy's principal and resident micromanaging gnat held up the cups as evidence, voice extra tight as he said, "The guys suggested it. I've... I've never played, but we... the art room had... these."

Ah, yes, Mason, Kent, and Evan—the trio of young male mathematics teachers who also managed the basketball club, the AV club, and all the games nights. Students *loved* them. A few of the staff idolized them. If they could find a way to inject hard liquor into any staff function, they'd do it like their lives depended on it.

Not my type of colleague. We hadn't exactly got on since I'd started; they thought I was the bumbling boring Englishman I portrayed, and I thought they were fuckwit morons.

"Oh my god. Oh my god. Oh my *god*," Emma whispered, and when I glanced over, her eyes brimmed with tears. For fuck's sake. This wasn't the end of the world—no need to look like that. Huffing, I zeroed in on Foster, and in the time it took the man to blink I was directly in front of him, a hand on his shoulder, our gazes locked.

"James Foster," I murmured, my influence washing over him, leeching out my fingertips, wafting on my breath, in my voice. The principal straightened as his pupils dilated under my control. "You never saw us. You went to the art room, found your cups, and returned to the party. This hallway is empty."

"I never saw you," Foster parroted back to me, as all humans ensnared by vampiric influence were prone to. "This hallway is empty. I've got my cups."

"Good." I gave his shoulder a little squeeze, the pressure paired with a predatory smile. "Now—off you trot. Beer pong awaits."

He matched my smile with a dreamy one of his own before toddling along down the hall, bypassing Emma without so much as a cursory glance. I waited, watching for the stairwell door to finally swing shut, and then faced the wolf with a *Now, where were we?* on the tip of my tongue. But that fucking *look* remained, painted across her features— one of horror, embarrassment, and shame—and when she met my eye, I could practically taste the shift between us.

"We can't do this," she said, voice barely above a

whisper, strained and tight. I frowned, readjusting my ever-present erection so it was less obvious jutting out between us.

"We're fine."

"I don't want you doing *that*"—vampiric influence: *so* helpful for dealing with irritating interruptions—"to the humans here. It isn't right."

"Emma," I said with a cool chuckle, "you're not serious."

She smoothed her hands over her hair, her blush no less dampened in Foster's absence. Her heart thundered, perhaps even harder than when I'd been kissing her, and I tried not to take that as a slight.

"Of course I am—*look* at what just happened! Foster! Foster happened," she snapped as she started to right her rumpled sweater, her skewed necklace. "We can't... If we didn't live and work in the same place, then sure, maybe, but the risk is just too high here. I've been ignoring it for some reason, and I just can't anymore."

Annoyance sliced right through all that sentiment, that desire, as if this was a personal rejection of *me*, which was ridiculous. And petty. "Emma, it isn't against the rules for staff to fraternize."

I'd looked it up in the faculty rule book before I ever floated this little arrangement, although I would have proposed it either way.

"No, but it's frowned upon," she countered, crossing her arms, jostling my gold gift, "and Foster is super intense about it. Unless you're married, then he thinks stuff like *this*"—she gestured between us—"will distract us from our work."

I couldn't stop the enormous, over-the-top scoff from flying past my lips, but *really*. The way Foster looked at Emma on any given day suggested he wanted to fuck her ten ways from Sunday. "This is ridiculous. Nothing's happened. We're *fine*."

"Yet," she stressed. "Nothing's happened *yet*, but we've had more close calls than I'm comfortable with."

Where had all this come from? Had it been brewing in her little shifter mind all this time, or had Foster triggered something unnecessarily dramatic? Because that was what it felt like: unnecessary drama. I'd dealt with him. We were alone, wearing each other's gifts, Emma's scent seeping into my skin. Nothing would stop us from walking the twenty feet to my office and barricading ourselves inside for the rest of the night.

Nothing but Emma, apparently. I bristled as she turned and started off toward the stairwell, her arms still crossed.

"I'm going back to the party," she said, all that fire from a few minutes ago extinguished. "Are you coming?"

I scowled at her for a moment, then rolled my shoulders back. "No."

The sole reason I had been so keen to participate in all these pointless holiday festivities, from the mimosa brunch to the movie marathon in our pajamas to the gift exchange, was *her*. To be around her when she was smiling, laughing, joking, it was divine, almost as intoxicating as her blood. I had no desire to immerse myself back in a sea of colleagues who bored me and support staff who I never spoke to anyway if Emma and I weren't...

What the fuck had been the *point* of the last few weeks?

For her and me to warm to each other so that she could walk away?

"So, what, you're done, then?" Petulantly, I held my ground, expression cold, tone even frostier as Emma stopped just before the door to the stairwell. "That's it? One mishap and it's over?"

With a soft sigh, she faced me, clutching the golden moon in one tight fist. "I love my job. I love this school. I love my kids and my co-workers. I don't..." She wet her lips, blush intensifying again. "I don't even hate you anymore, but I shouldn't have complicated any of it with this. So, yeah. I guess I'm done."

Fucking ridiculous. My annoyance sharpened to outright anger, so visceral and raw, cutting up my chest and threatening to spill out on the floor. "Right."

"It'll be easier this way. I mean, we can still be, you know—"

"Friends?" I asked dryly. "Are we *friends*, wolf?"

We were now, to some degree. It was more than what it had once been—she had knit me a fucking sweater. But I couldn't stand to hear her say it. *We can still be friends.* I swallowed the burning desire to tell her we hadn't been friends to start with, because, wearing this damn sweater, I couldn't be that cruel. Fucking a shifter had made me soft.

She stared at me for a moment, all the color drained from her cheeks, and then let the gold pendant fell back against her chest. I heard her swallow thickly, even with this sudden and vast distance between us.

"Well, I mean, it's just sex, right?" Emma held my gaze, each word a perfectly thrown dagger, nailing the target every time. She shrugged, cloaked in a sudden and painfully forced nonchalance, and I adopted a similar air.

"Yes, I suppose it is."

"Okay, so..." She fiddled with the gold chain. "Are you coming?"

Back to the party—no. Definitely not. Because with my tight chest, my splotched cheeks, my dry throat, I knew this wasn't just sex, not anymore, and I hated myself for letting that happen. Hated myself for the sentiment, for the fact that I cared, that I craved more than her sweet blood. And I had absolutely no desire to go back downstairs and *pretend*.

"Fuck off, Emma."

With that, I stalked off to my office, locked myself inside, leaned back against the solid oak door, brought the sweater to my nose, closed my eyes—and *breathed*.

17

EMMA

"One hour to the new year!"

Solskinn's most popular pub erupted in cheers, and I lifted my drink to toast alongside tonight's patrons. *Stjernelys* was positively bursting and had only gotten more cramped with locals, SIA employees, and folks from the surrounding farmsteads as December 31st went on. Unlike the nights leading up to this, I hadn't drowned myself in whiskey or vodka or any number of the delicious beverage options offered. It had been beer from dinner to now, and I hardly felt a buzz. Still, the atmosphere was electric as we counted down to the new year, all of us warm and toasty as the temperatures outside continued to plummet.

My grin faltered, however, when Calder and I caught each other's eye across the table. His half grin dropped too, and I looked down at my nearly empty pint of lager, cheeks warm, then tucked a few wisps of dirty blonde behind my ear.

We hadn't spoken in days, not since the night of the staff party, a night that I only remembered in vague detail. I'd been festively drunk leading up to our falling out, but everything after that was a blur. Somehow I'd made it back to my bed, and I learned yesterday that I had Phyllis and Robert to thank for that. Always looking after me, those two.

But Calder and I—radio silence across the board. He barely even glanced my way, so, in turn, I tried not to look at him either, because whenever I did, this nauseating loneliness punched me square in the gut. Every. Fucking. Time. And, you know what? I got enough of that when it came to my own pack; I didn't need Calder Holloway and his bitterness, his avoidance, his steely-eyed glint, for whatever reason, making me lonely too.

It was petty on both accounts. I could have been a mature adult and just talked to him, but the unsettling effect all this had on me, paired with the look in his eye that night —*fuck off, Emma*—had been deterrent enough. I might have been drunk on eggnog and lust, but that *look* had seared itself into my brain, flaring whenever the ache inside me was bad enough. While my inner wolf whined whenever we were in the same room but refused to make eye contact, I remained steadfast, because *he* was the one who had made a big deal out of nothing.

Sure, I could have put more thought into ending our physical relationship, but things had felt good between us lately, and not just when we were having sex. We could be friends—if he hadn't been such a petulant jackass.

So, here we were, out with our colleagues, watching them all get drunker and drunker while I nursed my beer and Calder drank nothing. Foster had already fallen asleep at the head of the table, his glittery New Year's headband catching the dim light anytime he shuffled about, showing no lasting effects from Calder's vampiric mind control. Phyllis and Robert had been butchering karaoke for the last half-hour, but no one seemed to mind; the academy nurses alternated between dancing on the bar and taking shots with the locals.

And Calder and I sat at opposite ends of the table, pretending the other didn't exist.

But he was wearing the sweater I'd made him, and my new gold necklace stood out like a neon sign against my dressy black blouse—so what did that say about us?

What the hell were we even doing?

I huffed and downed the rest of my drink, forcing myself to dive back into the endless banter of the male mathematics clique, which, to be fair, was mostly sports talk —college football, NBA stats, world cup predictions—and given what I did for a living, I could get on-board with that.

Even if the person I'd rather be spending my New Year's Eve chatting with would only talk sports if I pointed a gun to his head.

Or, you know, a stake to his heart—whatever.

The night had been pleasant enough if I ignored the brooding vampire. We'd all squished into one of the school buses for the ride down to the village, a security goon offering to drive us, and watched fireworks in the early evening. The event had been full of families, and while it had gotten me thinking about what the pack was up to tonight, I could distract myself enough with the brilliant display of light and color. From there, it was off to one of the restaurants, where we had a proper Norwegian feast, and then we all marched up the street to *Stjernelys* for booze and good company and satellite TV to ring in the new year.

In about an hour, we would trudge back outside for more fireworks. I welcomed the bitterly cold air, as the night was clear and the snow had held off, but I couldn't imagine the inebriated humans around me lasting more than ten minutes before demanding we return to the bus.

And then it would be over. Another year, another semester—gone. In a few days, the kids would be back, and I could find even *more* reasons to avoid Calder if he continued being a sulky child.

I mean, *seriously*, this guy. Sitting at the far side of the table, talking over an unconscious Foster with a gaggle of our coworkers, his pleasantness so forced I could smell it from here. That furrowed brow, that tight mouth. His distant stares and aloof once-overs, all the while wearing *my* Christmas gift.

Did I want to keep having awesome sex? Uh, *duh*.

Did I enjoy the way my loneliness vanished whenever I was around Calder, around someone who just *knew* exactly what I was? Sure. I too liked that I didn't have to pretend, that I could go at him with all my strength, that I could drop shifter lingo into casual conversation without fearing I'd just outed my entire community.

But did I want to keep having close calls, potentially fall out with my boss, and risk my position at the academy? No. Not for a guy who couldn't even be friends with me after I closed my legs. Not when I felt so, so... *vulnerable* without him. Not a chance in hell.

As I nodded along, only half listening to Mason lament his fantasy football team's performance this year, I felt it— that piercing stare from the other end of the table. Sighing, I glanced down at my lager, then lifted my gaze to Calder. Sure enough, there were those bright blues, unblinking as they bored holes in my forehead. A slight flicker of my brow had his furrowing deeper, and he turned away, hand wrapped around his untouched glass of dark ale.

Oh my god. Stomach looping, I rolled my eyes and excused myself. Picking my way through the pub proved more difficult than it had a few hours ago; with all the booths and tables occupied, newcomers had been forced to stand, the crowd pushing fire code limits. Thankfully, the bar was manned by four bartenders and a bevy of waitresses, which meant putting in an order for another lager was far easier than the process of actually reaching the oak-topped counter.

Drumming my fingers on the stained wood, I scanned the rows upon rows of liquor bottles lined up along shelves, then, out of the corner of my eye, spotted a familiar head face-plant. Her forehead hit the bar top with a too-solid *thwack*, and I pushed my way around the cluster of chatting old men between us, my hand settling between her shoulders.

"Marte?" Without waiting for a response, I pulled her upright. "You okay?"

The nurse's white-blonde hair had fallen over her face, shielding her angular features, and I brushed it back with a sigh as she muttered something to me in garbled Norwegian.

"What?"

"I-I think I maybe need to go back," she mumbled, slurring her words, swaying atop the bar stool. When she twisted to look at me, she would have fallen right off had I not been propping her up. "I need... to go to bed."

From the smell of her, she probably needed her stomach pumped too. She was such a petite thing—tall but slim—and it didn't surprise me that a dozen rounds of shots might have put her down for the count.

"But no one wants to go back with me," she added, eyeing my new drink when the bartender set it in front of us. Since I had no desire to wrestle it away from her, *or* to be soaked in vomit forty minutes before midnight when she caught a whiff of the creamy, spicy, butterscotch brew, I pushed the pint glass away.

"Okay, well..." Although it was downright impossible to see much in the crowd of people, I could pick out the familiar tones of the nursing staff somewhere to the far right. Shrieking, high-pitched giggles and rapid-fire Norwegian gave the group away; with their head nurse back in the States for the holiday, they had really been able to let loose. It'd been entertaining to watch, but now Marte was the unfortunate by-product of all that letting their hair down.

I couldn't just leave her here by herself, nor did I want any of the guys eyeing her along the bar to "help" her back to campus, not with the rash of local disappearances ruled suspect by the police, possibly criminal. A quick check of my phone told me I could get her to the academy and still make it back for midnight if we left now, and given the security goon who'd driven us was six drinks deep with one of the local girls, apparently I'd be learning how to drive a bus tonight.

"I'm going to take you back to school," I half shouted, articulating as clearly as I could for her gin-addled brain. "Give me thirty seconds to grab our coats."

She nodded, her eyelids struggling more and more to open fully after every heavy blink. Yikes. Shaking my head, I paid for my drink, gave it to the gruff old guy flying solo beside Marte, then told the bartender to watch her for two minutes while I got her things. He gave me a noncommittal shrug, then toddled off to serve a rowdy group at the other end of the bar. Perfect.

"Thirty seconds," I reiterated to Marte, tapping the counter in front of her. "Stay right here, okay?"

The nurse nodded, her eyes bloodshot. "Okay. *Tusen takk*, Emma."

I gave her shoulder a squeeze, grinning. "You're welcome, but you can thank me when we figure out if I can drive the bus or not; otherwise we're walking."

She chuckled weakly, but her expression suggested she either hadn't heard what I'd said or just didn't understand the gravity of walking the half-hour trek back to campus in this weather. I pursed my lips for a moment, waiting, watching as her gaze shifted in and out of focus, then nodded. Okay. Coats.

Mine was right where I'd left it on the back of my chair, and I was sure to let the mathematics clique know where Marte and I were headed. Gallant gentlemen that they were, not one offered to accompany us; Kent even had the nerve to *laugh* at the idea of me driving the bus. Dicks.

Marte's coat, however, remained far more elusive. The nurses had moved from our staff table to their own booth shortly after we'd arrived, and by the time I came rooting around, all their stuff was one jumbled mess, and not a soul present was coherent enough to help me sort through it. So, I had to hold up every near-identical black, fur-lined coat, one at a time, and wait for some giggling drunk nurse to claim it—hats, mitts, and scarves too. Eventually, by process of elimination, I found Marte's, but when I shoved my way back to the bar, she was nowhere to be found.

"Your friend went outside," the lone female bartender told me, her frizzy, grey hair stuck out at all angles, her blue mascara heavily gooped in the corners. She spoke with a thick Norwegian accent, but like many, even all the way out here, didn't stumble once over her English. "I tried to stop her, because she was just in that little dress, but she was determined. Something about a bus."

Damn it, Marte. "Thank you."

I flashed the bartender a smile and a quick wave over my shoulder before bulldozing my way to the front door. A few clusters of plaid-clad men tried to stop me to chat, but I barrelled through without responding to either the English or the Norwegian come-ons.

As soon as the solid pub door slammed shut behind me, the intrusive buzz of conversation inside fell silent. I stood there for a moment, my jacket open, the loose bits of hair that had escaped my braid crown fluttering in the frigid but gentle breeze. Snowflakes fluttered down in the warm yellow lamplight, the sky an inky black—soon to be painted every color of the rainbow if the guys strolling by with a wagon of fireworks had anything to say about it. I nodded and smiled when one tipped his cap to me, then scanned the otherwise empty street for Marte. Over half the village was in the pub behind me, while the rest were likely at home with their families.

And I was out here, alone, searching for a drunk nurse. With her coat thrown over my arm, I jogged down the snowy lane to where the security goon had parked the bus, but no luck. Her scent carried on the next gust of wind: a mix of gin, sharply sweet floral perfume, and sweat. Just what my sensitive nose needed.

"Marte?" Chin lifted, I tracked her scent through the village, knowing this would be easier if I'd shifted but not wanting to take the time to properly undress and stash my clothes somewhere. Mind you, if Marte passed out at the sight of my enormous wolf form, it would probably be easier to get her back to campus...

No. I hugged her coat to my chest, taking another quick whiff to better zero in on her scent. I eventually picked up her tracks just outside Solskinn, the indent of her heels the only footprints visible in the veil of pure white.

Behind me, the village and all its warmth, its homey comfort, sat beckoning. Ahead, the only paved route back to the academy, a *barely* two-lane path covered in snow, plowed into the forest. A mix of leafless birch and alder trees bowed over the road, giving the illusion of a tunnel in the darkness. To my left, a mass of soaring pines—and Marte's tracks, leading directly into the trees.

My shoulders slumped, arm dropping to my side, her coat kissing the ground. "What the hell, Marte?"

Was I seriously about to go looking for her in the pitch-black forest at—a quick check of my phone—eleven thirty-seven at night on New Year's Eve?

Damn it. I was.

Tossing her coat over my shoulder, I trudged into the deeper snowbanks, my jeans instantly soaked, my aged leather boots doing a serviceable job barring the wet and my thick wool socks keeping my feet warm.

"Marte?" I slipped halfway down the ravine but managed not to lose my balance as the ground evened out. The trees answered, rustling in the wind, and darkness peered back. My eyes narrowed, calling on my inner wolf's sight to see through the black. Had anyone been around, they'd see my eyes change, lighten, suddenly burning bright as a midnight moon.

No sign of her.

"*Marte?*"

Officials had released a statement at the start of December: stay out of the forest.

This forest.

Because everyone who had gone missing since July was last seen going into *this* forest, a forest that stretched on for miles, connecting all the surrounding villages. I hesitated, one hand pressed to the trunk of a birch, its rough exterior speckled white and grey. I was a wolf, and the forest had always been my friend. Yet, the hairs on the back of my neck stood straight up. My inner wolf growled a long, low warning.

Then I heard it: the rich, dark, full-bodied wail of a violin.

I staggered forward, beyond the tree line, encased in shadow as the sound surrounded me, invaded me, whispered across my skin.

And suddenly my body was no longer mine. I moved like a puppet on a string, walking, marching further into the darkness without meaning to, searching out the source of that *music*. It drowned out my inner wolf—it drowned *me*.

Serenely, I floated around the trees as the melody *swelled*, and as it quickened, so did I.

Because in that moment, I *needed* the violin, I needed its song. I needed it like I needed air, and as I descended deeper into the dark forest, a single thought trumped all others, screaming inside my head: I would do *anything* to find that music, anything to attain it.

When I did, I would give it everything it desired.

And the creature wielding the bow—I would worship as a god.

18

CALDER

"Are you planning on drinking that, or are you just going to stare at it?"

Lost in my own thoughts, I hadn't even noticed that my colleagues at this end of the table had up and left, replaced, at some point, by Robert Howard. Fortunately for the rest of us, he had finally stopped caterwauling on stage with his wife, the karaoke king and queen dethroned by a gaggle of inebriated nurses screeching in barely discernible Norwegian. I straightened, nose wrinkled, unable to decide which was more torturous.

"I suppose it's not to my taste," I said, pushing my enormous glass of ale away. It wobbled across the uneven wood, settling in front of a passed-out James Foster, who continued to snooze away, unperturbed by the festive din around him.

"I could fetch you another one," Robert offered, his cheeks pleasantly rosy. "Bartender says they've cut all the prices in half for the next twenty minutes."

I checked my watch; that would bring us to midnight, and the thought of forcing down *more* human sustenance than I'd already done tonight made my stomach turn. What I wanted was sitting in a cooler in my office and entirely inappropriate for public consumption.

Well, no, what I wanted most of all was sitting at the far end of the table and had been fielding my withering glances all night without so much as flinching. Clearing my throat, I cast another glance down the way, only to find Emma gone. The math trio remained, growing louder by the minute as they argued about something or other, and Emma's chair was empty. I sat up straighter with a frown. Where the hell had she gone?

Not that I had the right to wonder about her whereabouts. I'd made a complete ass of myself after she'd insisted we stop whatever the fuck we had been doing since Halloween. My ridiculous ego was still bruised, and I'd thought that if I blocked her out completely, pretended she didn't exist, then I could eventually forget that I had not only actively pursued a shifter, but I felt something akin to heartache when she suggested we just be friends.

Pathetic, really. In so short a time, I'd ignored the fact that she drove me absolutely insane and started to *feel* for her.

It must have been the air this far north; it made me weak. Sentimental and weak, mooning over some foul-mouthed, disheveled, procrastination-prone, perpetually tardy wolf shifter.

Her severing ties, demanding we cease the one thing that had been driving me further into her arms, should have been a godsend. Maybe then I could finally get some perspective and rationalize why Emma Kingsley was completely and utterly wrong for me in every way, but I'd been a moody, petulant fuck ever since that night.

And here I was, searching her out in a crowded pub, more alert than I'd been in days.

"Kent told me Emma's taken Marte back to campus," Robert said, and I looked to him sharply, wondering why he felt the need to tell me specifically.

"What? Why would you—?"

Was I really so obvious?

The enormous fellow shrugged, then scooped up my discarded drink, took a quick sip, and downed the rest of it without a word.

"She... Are they driving?" I sputtered, continuing my scan of the overcrowded space. No point in maintaining the charade, not when he saw straight through it. The security oaf who had schlepped us all down to the village appeared in no condition to get behind the wheel of *any* vehicle, much less a twenty-ton bus.

"I've already gone out to check," Robert told me as he set the empty glass down in the middle of the table, then affectionately adjusted Foster's headband, *Happy New Year* scrawled across the bit of thin cardboard on top in glittering gold. When he looked up at me again, the English instructor wore a little wry smile that suggested he *knew* he had my full attention. "Bus is still there, no sign of the girls. Must have decided to walk back. Can't imagine why in this weather—"

I didn't hear his rationale, because I was already off, stalking through the herd of humans, headed straight for the main door. Slipping into my leather jacket, I grabbed the pointlessly thick scarf from its pocket and wrapped it around my neck a few times before shouldering my way into the freezing outdoors.

Honestly, was she drunk again? Emma hadn't appeared as intoxicated as the rest of our colleagues, but perhaps she was just good at hiding it. Because why the fuck else would she decide to *walk* back to the academy on a night like this? The inky-black darkness pressed in on the village, forced back by the scattered street lamps and muted light on the other side of double, perhaps triple-paned windows. It was so dark that anywhere without another source of light, like the road leading back to the school, would be impossible for humans to navigate. Beyond that, the temperatures had reached an all-time low; Marte wouldn't make it in that little outfit she'd been wearing.

Oh, and there was a fucking *killer* on the loose.

Sure, no bodies had been found. None of those missing were confirmed dead, but I had my suspicions—suspicions Emma ought to share, given her familiarity with the world's supernatural predators. Going out into the night, alone, drunk, with a human who would only slow her down, was probably the stupidest thing she'd done so far.

I shouldn't have cared. I should have stayed with the others, maybe grabbed another beer to at least *pretend* that I was enjoying myself on a night like this.

Yet as I stalked to the outskirts of the village, quickly locating and following a familiar set of tracks in the snow, I realized my problem: I cared too much. Even after she had rejected me, after she had chosen SIA over me, after she had floated that insulting *let's just be friends* line—I fucking cared about Emma Kingsley.

I mean, I was wearing the damn sweater she'd knit me. Anger roiled in my gut, concern fueling each hurried step; clearly I was more of a lost cause than I'd thought.

Weak, sentimental old fool, lusting after a shifter. Developing feelings for her—obvious enough feelings for Robert bloody Howard to notice...

Wait.

I paused, still as stone.

Was that—a violin?

Bewildered, I looked to the soaring pines, to the black emptiness between, to the blanket of untouched snowfall. That *was* a violin, its notes clear as anything, carrying on the wind from the depths of the forest. I stepped toward the nearest snowbank with a frown. No other music accompanied the instrument, and it oozed Schubert, dripped in the composer's dark drama.

In fact, this melody, this tune—it was *Der Erlkönig*.

It had to be.

A few tweaks and variants, yet my ear for classical arias wouldn't betray me.

How fitting, this piece, based on an old poem about a father and son riding through woodlands so similar to these. In the poem, the boy dies, butchered by the evil elf-king of the forest while still seated behind his father.

"Are you out tonight, *Erlkönig*?" I murmured, eyes narrowed as I scanned the tree line. No sign of Emma, but up ahead her tracks veered sharply left into the deeper snow, then down the slope, almost as if she had slipped, and into the forest. Teeth gritted, I followed in her wake, striding through snow that reached just beyond my knees. "Emma?"

Only the violin answered. I hastened my pace, easily tracking her footsteps through the forest, her faint scent of lavender clinging to the bark. No longer was this about locating her and Marte, a chastisement on the tip of my tongue about venturing into the deathly cold night alone and on foot. This was about *finding* her—period.

"Emma?"

Because something about that violin was very wrong. I seldom felt the prickle of fear anymore, the kind that creeps along the nape of your neck, then flits down your spine and knots tightly in the pit of your gut, twisting, twisting, *twisting* until you succumb.

But I felt it here. Surrounded by a silent, watchful forest, fear wormed its way into my rigid vampire heart. No one else accompanied the violin: no carollers, no musicians. At no point did I hear the hiss and crackle of a roaring bonfire, nor did I see its reassuring orange sheen amidst the darkness. Bitter, cold night was all these woods had to offer me, paired with a whisper of Emma on the path ahead.

And the relentless violin.

"*Emma!*"

My call barely echoed, swallowed by the elements, and I ran now, adopting a speed that would render me nothing but a blur to whatever dared lurk in these shadows. I kept to the path the wolf shifter had forged for me, looping around trees, cutting abruptly one way and then the other, pushing myself until the pines gave way to a clearing.

Until I finally found her.

Until I finally found *them*.

Marte and Emma, their backs to me, shuffled like zombies across the clearing. I stepped out of the trees, bewildered once more to find a perfectly round space plopped in the middle of a dense forest without a lick of snow—just dead, frozen grass. While the wind rustled through pines around us, not a hint of breeze touched my face as I strode further into the clearing. It no longer toyed with my hair, burned my cheeks. It was like I'd entered a dead zone.

A place where all things came to die.

The girls were headed straight for a pond also shaped as a perfect circle, its surface dark as the deepest ocean, yet frighteningly still too, like a great black mirror. And beyond *that*, the violin.

More specifically, its player.

I staggered to a halt, jaw dropping for the first time in an *age*. For there, seated on a boulder on the other side of the pond, was a shirtless man in tattered trousers. Muscular arms dragged the bow across his instrument, his eyes closed, his face handsome. In fact, he was rather attractive, but I couldn't imagine *that* was the lure for either Emma or Marte, who continued shuffling along, mute, arms limp at their sides.

Handsome fellow, playing a violin in the middle of the Norwegian wilderness, situated next to a body of water…

I reared back, nostrils flared, eyes wide.

Was that a bloody *fossegrim*?

I'd thought the water spirits had faded into legend. Native to our surroundings, the creatures were said to possess a gentle temperament and a proclivity for fiddles. In fact, they spent their entire lives inhabiting springs and rivers and waterfalls, playing their instruments, beguiling any who happened upon them. What they liked most, the stories said, was a willing audience.

But I had never heard of one *bewitching* their listeners like this, so literally, and at such a distance too…

My gaze flickered to the black pond again just as something rippled beneath its surface. The water settled seconds later.

"*Emma!*"

If my heart could pound, it would. The prickling fear sunk its claws in deeper, and I was off like a shot, headed straight for Marte, as the nurse was the closest to the water's edge. I reached her in the time it would have taken her to blink twice, hooked an arm around her waist, and hurled her back across the clearing. She landed in a heap beside what looked to be her big, fur-lined coat.

"Hva pokker er det du gjør?" *What the hell are you doing?* I demanded savagely, snarling out each word as I glowered up at the fossegrim—a creature I still couldn't wrap my mind around in this day and age. His eyes opened, dark blue and flecked with a strange sort of starlight; tears sliced down his flushed cheeks as he continued to play, beautifully at that. It was the most exquisite music I'd ever heard in my life, but it was doing something to Emma, to Marte, and I couldn't allow it to go on. Tensed, I gave him a moment, then pointed at the violin. "Nå er det nok." *That's enough.*

He shook his head slowly, sadly, and hastened his bow arm, quickening the tempo. While inexplicably beautiful, its tune alluring to all save vampires, for no spells, no magic, no trickery worked on us after we were turned, this wasn't a *true* fossegrim's fiddle. Those instruments were said to mirror the sounds of the forest itself: the whisper of wind through the leaves, the skitter of wildlife, the rush of a trickling stream. Amidst all that, a melody, yes, that sounded like this—but a real instrument of the fossegrim was so much more.

And as far as I knew, it didn't turn its listeners into dead-eyed zombies.

What the fuck *is this?*

With a shake of my head, I turned on the spot and sprinted for Emma, *loathing* the fact that I hadn't the faintest idea what was going on here—or why.

What I did know with increasing certainty, however, was that neither of these women was going anywhere near that damn pond.

"Emma..." Her slack expression remained fixed even as I charged her, and those glazed-over eyes stayed glued on the fossegrim. Fucking hell. When I was within reach, I clamped down on her shoulders and shook her, harder than I could ever shake a human. "*Emma*, it's a spell!"

Or—something. *Fuck*. The helplessness, the not knowing, made the situation about a thousand times more frustrating. I shook her harder, feet planted as she tried to bowl right over me. Whatever had her under its thrall might have reduced her motor functions to undead shuffling, but she was determined to reach him.

Or maybe that pond—and whatever had caused the faint ripple in the water.

"Emma!" Fuck it. Lips peeled back in a snarl, I lurched forward and sank my fangs right into the meat of her neck. As soon as I made contact, punctured her flesh, she emitted a high-pitched gasp, her whole body flailing, hands up and fighting. Good. At least the spell or curse or *whatever* could be broken.

"C-Calder?"

I stayed a few beats longer, just to be sure, sweet metallic fire scorching down my throat until I finally tore away. The shifter staggered back, her eyes wide, cheeks pale, mouth hanging open as she groped at her bleeding neck. I held up a hand to settle her as soon as she started to panic, to shake, her breath coming faster.

"Emma—"

"What the fuck, Calder?" she cried, taking in her surroundings with all the mania of someone who'd woken up in a stranger's bed, or a dingy alley, or the middle of a field with no memory of how they got there. "What the *fuck*? Where am I?"

Her voice had reached a pitch only dogs could hear. "Emma, something's happened..."

Behind me—splashing.

I whirled around to find Marte and her tiny gold New

Year's Eve dress had made their way back to the pond's edge. Her stockings were ripped, her hair mussed, her face vacant as she crawled along.

"Marte, for god's sake," I hissed, zipping over to her at top speed. While I moved fast, Emma managed to keep up, stumbling to a halt at my heels seconds after I reached the crawling, shivering nurse. Marte's teeth chattered violently, her dead stare fixed on the lake, and as soon as I touched her, she screamed.

Screamed like I was tearing her to pieces.

"Calder!"

Over my shoulder, I noted Emma standing about a foot from the pond's edge with the same dumbstruck expression I'd had only minutes earlier. Unfortunately, I couldn't get a word out over all Marte's screeching. Her shuffle had morphed into a scramble; whatever was in that pond *had* her. Either that, or the stuttering, complex pace of the fossegrim's violin had spurred her into a frenzy. Whatever the reason, it stopped—*now*.

Grasping her by the chin, I forced myself into her line of sight, and the second Marte's manic eyes met mine, I whispered, "*Sleep*."

Once again, my influence proved stronger than whatever the fuck was happening in this clearing. The nurse stilled, her eyelids falling, her body limp.

Asleep. For now.

Behind me, Emma's panting panic had quieted, but somehow it seemed louder than before.

Louder—because the fossegrim had finally stopped playing.

Gently, I lowered Marte to the ground, yanking my enormous scarf off and pillowing it under her head, setting its fat tails over her pale arms. When I stood, I found Emma and the fossegrim staring each other down, perhaps even sizing each other up. Then, those ethereal blue eyes slid to me, their starlight shimmering in the darkness.

Softly, sweetly, with a voice like a whispering meadow, a rustle of wood chimes, the fossegrim murmured, "Jeg beklager så mye."

"What?" Emma sounded harsh by comparison. "What did he say?"

I'm so sorry.

"I... He..." Like a hooked trout, I gawked at the creature seated atop that jagged boulder, arms limp at my side. Sorry. Sorry for *what*, exactly?

"Calder?"

"He—"

A second great splash silenced me. With all the speed of a striking viper, two long, black, algae-covered arms shot out of the water and snapped a pair of claw-tipped hands around Emma's left ankle, then *yanked* her into the pond. She screamed as she went down, scrambling at the dead grass along the shoreline, her body disappearing too fast, too sudden, even for me.

"*Emma!*" I dropped to my knees, racing toward the undulating black mirror. Below, faintly, I caught the sight of her hands, her outstretched fingers. I plunged my own hands in, desperately searching her out, only I couldn't reach her. Just like that. In the blink of an eye—*gone*.

Gobsmacked, horrified, I sat there for a moment in a terse silence. How could this have happened? How could that *thing* be faster than *me*?

"What have you done?" I hissed, glowering up at the fossegrim, fear giving way to raw, unbridled fury. "What have you *done*?"

The creature merely stared back, his face placid even as

tears streamed down his cheeks. Star-flecked orbs watched as I sat up on my knees and ripped off my jacket, then Emma's gift. While I could have dove straight in, she would need something warm to wear when I pulled her out, something dry and comforting to wick away the black water.

Just as I was about to plunge headfirst into the murky depths, she broke the surface with a screaming gasp, flailing in the middle of the pond, accursed water splashing everywhere.

"Calder!"

"Here," I bellowed, crawling for her, half in the water, beckoning her into my arms as she frantically paddled toward me. "Emma, here!"

As soon as she was within the most tenuous reach, I surged forward and captured her wrists, then hauled her the rest of the way out of the pond. She broke free from my grasp, only to claw up my arms and curl around my neck like a noose. Feet planted on the dead, frozen earth, I shot back, half crawling, half dragging us away from the water's edge.

With Emma's panicked breath in my ear, I watched grimly as those arms broke the surface once more. Black, thin, dripping with muddy green algae, spindly fingers groped along the shore, searching for their escaped quarry. Claws sunk into the rock-hard ground upon finding nothing, then whipped back into the water so furiously that a new prickle of fear in me surfaced.

Trembling, Emma glanced over her shoulder. Frigid water sluiced through my clothes, soaking me as we clung to each other. The pond settled in an instant, the ripples dissipating, its surface once more an unnerving black mirror. Then, seconds later, a head poked up in the middle. Curtained with black, snarled hair, the creature's slate-grey skin made its obsidian eyes sharper, more distinct in the darkness. Emma's breath hitched; even without pupils, that thing's gaze was palpable. Frightening. Emma's shifter figure radiated heat, positively burning on top of me, but she continued to shiver—not from the cold, surely.

Like a crocodile hovering at the surface, the rest of its immense body below, the creature lingered for a moment, unblinking, before submerging without a sound. Seconds later, the pond's surface stilled.

An explosion ripped across the landscape. Emma screamed. I flinched. And in the distance, fireworks erupted over Solskinn. Midnight. Another year had come to pass, and in the waning moments of the last, I had endured fear, confusion, and outright panic for the first time in a century.

And now, in the initial moments of this new year, bloody *fireworks* had set me off, my usual steel nerve nowhere to be found as Emma clutched at me and I clutched at her.

To our immediate right, pinwheels of color burst against a black midnight sky. Fizzing, whirling, screaming fireworks of all shades, crackling over the landscape. It was quite the display, one usually reserved for far larger cities, but the Norwegians seemed to take great pride in their fireworks. How long it would last, I had no idea, but I couldn't move, not with Emma curled up on top of me, shaking, soaking wet, her breath falling in uneven beats. A few feet from us, Marte remained under my thrall, asleep and likely in desperate need of a few more layers.

Amidst the chaos, bright color painting our surroundings every few seconds, the fossegrim stared at me. Tucking both arms around the shifter on my lap, I met his gaze over Emma's shoulder, my hand on the nape of her neck. The creature's dark brows flickered up, the serene expression splintered by anguish.

"Hjelp meg." *Help me.*

What the bloody hell was I supposed to make of that? My gaze hardened, turned frosty, and I refocused on Emma when she finally extracted her arms from around my neck, then sat up, hands planted on my chest.

"Okay," she growled through chattering teeth, staring me down like *I* had something to do with this. "What—the *fuck*—is happening?"

I swallowed thickly, hands settling on her lower back like they had a mind of their own. I needed a convincing lie until I discovered the truth, one that would keep her out of this mess, one that would keep her safe. But as she stared at me, I faltered. Lying my way through all kinds of situations had always come easy to me, yet in that moment, I had *nothing*. No white lie. No teasing retort. Nothing. "Uh, Happy New Year?"

Emma blinked back at me as the corners of my mouth twitched up—and then gut-punched me so hard I could finally see the stars.

JANUARY

19

EMMA

"What the hell *was* that thing?"

We moved at a good clip through the pitch-black forest, with me relying more on Calder's intense night vision than my own. I stumbled along slightly behind him, one hand hovering at his back just in case the dizziness, the light-headedness, the nausea that tagged along for the ride finally got the upper hand.

Despite everything, I would have preferred holding on to him right now, but he had his hands—and arms—full, literally, with an unconscious nurse. While I wore the maroon knit, the rest of me still soaked, Marte wore every other piece of dry clothing Calder and I could find between the two of us, except for his slacks and white undershirt. Given her lips had started to turn blue, we moved swiftly, cutting directly across the forest, following the fireworks, to take her to the village—which wasn't ideal, but it was closer than campus.

My wet jeans clung to me with every step and probably would have frozen solid if I didn't naturally radiate heat. Still, my teeth wouldn't stop chattering. My throat ached from screaming underwater, the taste of that *thing* lingering...

"I can't say what it was," Calder muttered, shifting Marte in his arms as we detoured around a rotted tree stump. "I only went to check on you two, because why the *fuck* would you walk a human anywhere far in this weather?"

Annoyance skittered through the emotional hurricane festering inside me, and I glared at the back of his head. "I *wasn't* going to walk her back to campus. Not really. It was just a joke, but then she took off while I was grabbing our coats, and I went to find her, and then—"

"The violin?"

In an instant, my irritation vanished, replaced by something darker, something colder. "Yeah. The violin."

At the time, listening to the music, I had been both aware and not, my body operating completely out of my control. My mind had been at peace in the fog, content to just follow the music and submit to the player. Calder's bite had been a harsh wake-up call, tinged with a sharp, unfamiliar pleasure that I felt in my teeth. In an instant, I'd been back in the real world, bleeding, my inner wolf baying so loudly that it had felt like a bomb had gone off inside my own head.

The idea that something could enthral a shifter like that, take complete control of me—it didn't sit well. What if the player had forced me to shift somehow? I hadn't been able to hear my inner wolf. What if he had made me *do* things?

Arms crossed, I jogged a few paces to fall in line beside Calder. "Do you... know anything?"

"I have some theories," he said with a sniff, eyes constantly on the move, prowling across the dark landscape. "But I want to confirm them first."

I huffed, breath fogging in front of me. "Calder—"

"Just let me work how I work. I don't want to say anything that might be untrue."

"It would be better if we bounced ideas off each other," I said, waiting until he glanced down at me to roll my eyes. The vampire stopped so suddenly that I carried on a few long, hurried strides without him, and when I faced him again, he shrugged, jostling a sleeping Marte.

"Well, go on. Let's hear your ideas."

"I..." In that moment, I was all physical. There was no space in my brain for the mental side of this, for flipping through my admittedly limited Rolodex of supernatural beings to find the answer. "I don't have any right this second—"

"Then let me sort it out." Calder resumed his unforgiving pace, stalking by me so quickly that I had to run to catch up. While desperate to tell him that this wasn't just *his* issue to sort out, that I was the more involved of the two of us, I bit the insides of my cheeks and carried on beside him in silence.

After all *that* had happened, the air seemed to have cleared between us. Sure, he was still a pompous ass, walking all over me, assuming I'd have nothing to contribute, but maybe he had a point. He was older and a total nerd for pointless, boring facts, for stories that most people tuned out the second he launched into another teachers' lounge monologue.

And he had kind of just saved my life.

At the very least, he had come looking for me. After a week of unpleasantness, after all the insults hurled and the feelings muddled, Calder, a vampire, had screamed a shifter's name when that thing pulled me under.

I owed him a *bit* of credit, even if I'd been the one to free myself from whatever the fuck that creature was in the pond. A chill sprinted through me at the memory; hurrying through the forest, I could still feel its clawed hands snapped tight around my ankle, dragging me into the black as my ears popped, as my lungs screamed.

The only way out had been to fight.

A wolf always fights. Always. To their last breath.

So, unable to see more than an inch in front of my face, I'd folded over underwater, grabbed onto one wiry arm—and sunk my teeth in.

"That thing," I started, my voice catching until I cleared my throat, "tasted like dirt."

Calder looked down at me, his brutal march slowing just for the moment, and I stared straight ahead, eyes prickling with tears I refused to shed.

"Like dirt and ash and dead flesh—"

"Make it a habit of eating dead flesh, do you?" he mused, mouth lifted in a half-hearted smirk—bait I couldn't handle right now.

"*Calder*—"

"I know, I know," he muttered, the road finally in sight ahead, lamplight fighting to breach the pines. "I'm not... I'm just saying things. I'm sorry. You did very well, getting away from it. I was about to, you know, dive in..."

I squared my shoulders, sensing apologetic and contrite wasn't a tone that sat well with Calder Holloway. "No sense in it getting both of us."

"Yes, but *I* wouldn't have drowned."

I stumbled, foot snagging on something rigid in the snow, heart in my throat, vision blurred. While I waved Calder off, balance regained, I couldn't stop the thundering of my insides, couldn't shirk fear's sudden death grip on every part of me. Tonight, I could have drowned. That thing could have pulled me to the bottom of the pond and just held me there. Hell, it could have held me five feet below the surface and the results would have been the same.

I could have died tonight.

As fireworks crackled and hissed, their explosion of color illuminating the forest's edge, a nagging thought settled in: What if people *had* died there?

What if all the missing villagers, the ones who had last been seen entering these very woods, met such a fate?

"What are we going to tell people?" I forced out. It wasn't like we could go to the police and expose the entire supernatural community. Calder cleared his throat, each controlled, even breath whooshing from his nostrils in a fleeting fog. The forest's density petered out as we neared the road, but before we stepped out of the shadows, we needed a story.

And I *hated* that. Calder might be familiar with pulling the wool over everyone's eyes, but I wasn't. I just wanted to do my job, go for runs with my rescue pack, and knit things in the quiet comfort of my own room. Was that so much to ask for?

"We tell them Marte wandered off, drunk," he said at last, pausing at the final clump of trees. A snow-covered slope soared ahead, the vampire's brief pause punctuated by fireworks and cheers. Calder studied the woman in his arms, the human who had started to shake in her sleep, then exhaled sharply. "You went to fetch her, and I joined when you texted for my assistance. We found her together in the woods." He levelled his gaze to mine. "And we say *nothing* of the violin, its master, or the pond creature."

"But—"

"Not until we figure out what the hell they both are."

I hesitated for a moment, lower lip caught between my teeth as I weighed the collective safety of Solskinn, the immensely stacked odds in favor of the hot guy with the magical violin against magic-less humanity, and then nodded. "Fine. Agreed."

"Okay."

"And why am I wet?"

His lips briefly pursed, as if catching a chuckle. "You're wet because... you slipped. Fell into a drift. Soaked to the bone and in need of a slow thaw."

"Maybe I fell through some ice?"

"The ice is very solid this time of year," Calder said with a shake of his head. "I've no idea why *that* pond looked as it did, or why it isn't just a block of ice, but I'll consult my books. Something foul is keeping it as is."

I snorted. Something foul was the fucking understatement of the new year.

Calder canted his head toward the slope, and I moved without a word. Out of the forest, I took the lead, clambering up the snowy little hill with my soaked, frozen coat hanging over my arm. Once at the top, I reached for Calder, helping him, perhaps unnecessarily, the rest of the way up with Marte in his arms. Heads down against a freezing rush of air, we made our way back to Solskinn, guided by the yellow glow of Gothic iron street lamps and ceaseless blasts of fizzing, whizzing fireworks.

Just as we breached the outskirts of the village's main strip, the hairs on the back of my neck stood up. One by one, they rose. Beneath the sweater, my skin prickled, even though I was still unaffected by the morning's temperatures. My steps slowed. My brows furrowed. My gaze jumped from shadow to shadow, searching out the threat. Beside me, now ahead of me, Calder carried on, haunting blue eyes fixed on the firework display erupting from the village center.

A flicker in the supernatural veil. A shift in the air around us. A new bleak aura. Did he sense it too? "Calder..."

My inner wolf snarled, and I finally stopped, wondering what else I could *possibly* have to deal with tonight on top of everything already—

"Happy New Year, Holloway."

Calder stiffened, his entire body seeming to lift and tighten as he paused, then whipped around. Nostrils flared, eyes narrowed, he glared down the source of that nasally rasp behind me. My inner wolf snarled again, and my body suddenly hummed with energy. If I didn't rein her in, I'd shift. Swallowing hard, I took a deep breath and slowly turned around, clutching my coat, a shield of nylon and cotton.

A shield against two vampires, their angular, porcelain faces illuminated by the latest batch of fireworks. Red. Orange. Blue. Flashing purple. Then back to deathly white. The pair wore gnarly leather jackets, jeans, and thin cotton tees. The only things durable enough for this climate were their worn hiking boots, tips splattered with something suspiciously dark.

Stained.

Bloodstained, maybe.

I stood taller, shoulders back, chin lifted, as Calder strolled to my side. He didn't run, I noticed. In contrast to his tight expression, the vampire *sauntered* like he hadn't a care in the world.

"Strange company you keep these days, Holloway," the bald vampire mused with a nod toward me. His dusky companion smirked, hands clasped in front of him.

"Not much to do this far north." Calder tipped his head to the side, appraising them, his whole demeanor frosty. "What are you doing here, boys?"

The vampiric pair glanced at each other, and the six-foot-four beanpole sporting a head of luscious chocolate brown hair shrugged.

"Oh, you know, the usual," he offered, his accent suggesting Spanish roots. Piping-hot kinetic energy thrummed through me, my inner wolf demanding I shift, demanding I run, demanding I howl to the moonless sky and *charge*. In the distance, more cheers—cheers from my boss, my colleagues, my friends—as a particularly intricate array of colors flashed across the black. I crossed my arms tighter, hugging my jacket and frowning when Calder stepped in front of me. The brunet vamp some ten feet from us leaned to the side, peering at me around him. "We're just... seeing the sights. Meeting the people. Sampling the local cuisine."

"Getting a bit of *hunting* in," the bald vampire added, and my blood ran cold when he too set his sights on me. His companion flashed a cruel smile.

"Surely you of all vampires know, Holloway—this time of year, wolf's in season..."

**TO BE CONTINUED IN DARK DAYS: SEMESTER 2 —
LIVE FEBRUARY 2019**

PREORDER NOW

Sign up for the exclusive mailing list to stay in the Dark Days loop!

THANK YOU FOR READING!

Thank you so much for reading! You are faaaabulous.

Also. My b about that cliffhanger. It was a rough one, I know, but Calder and Emma will be back in the totally kick-ass, sexy, nail-biting conclusion February 2019.

(Book 2 is also 25% LONGER than Book 1, so yeaaaay!)

If you enjoyed the first half of Calder and Emma's paranormal romance and want to support the duet, please consider leaving a review at the retailer of your choice, including Goodreads. Reviews help indie authors thrive, and I read all of them.

Lots of love,

Liz

ABOUT THE AUTHOR

Liz is a Canadian author who grew up in the Middle East. She has a degree in Bioarchaeology from Western University, and when she isn't writing about her own snarky characters, she is reading about other people's snarky characters, babying her herb garden, loitering on social media, or taking care of her many animals.

Liz dabbles in both paranormal and contemporary erotic romance. Her paranormals are usually dark and angsty, and her contemporaries are stress-free smutfests, but you'll find both full of feels. Most of all, she loves writing realistic characters in fantastical settings.

More from Liz Meldon:

PARANORMAL ROMANCE

The Hunt – a Demon Romance
> Predator (#1)
> Prey *(#2)*
> Stalker *(#3)*
> Killer *(#4)*
> The Hunt: Book Bundle #1
> The Hunt: Book Bundle #2
> The Hunt: The Complete Edition
> *The Uprising (Spring 2019)*

Dark Days – a Vampire/Wolf Shifter Romance
　　Semester One
　　Semester Two

Lovers and Liars: Immortal Wars – a fantasy and paranormal romance series about the old world gods going to war
　　Court of the Phantom Queen (2017) – Book #1 (fantasy romance, novella)
　　Apollo's Priestess (2017) – Book #2 (shifter paranormal romance, novella)
　　To the North (TBD) – Book #3 (fantasy romance, novella)

Contemporary Erotic Romance

All In Trilogy – Sugar Daddies, Billionaires, and Menages – oh my!
　　Finn (#1)
　　Cole (#2)
　　Skye (#3)
　　All In Trilogy: Book Bundle + Bonus Content

Unbowed – standalone erotic romances featuring kink escorts the alpha men who love them
　　Belle: Part 1
　　Belle: Part 2
　　Penny: Part 1 (2019)
　　Penny: Part 2 (2019)

Erotic Short Shorts – an Erotic Short Story Series
　　Happy Hour (2016)
　　Holiday Hell (2017)
　　Bliss (2018)